Mircea
Eliade

Time, Death, and the Unspeakable Secret

Mircea Eliade
Time, Death,
and the Unspeakable Secret

This is the first publication of this collection in
one volume

First published in 2025 by Istros Books
London, United Kingdom
www.istrosbooks.com

Edited by Bryan Rennie

Design and layout: pikavejica.com

Printed by CMP, Poole, Dorset, UK

ISBN: 978-1-912545-513

PRODAN ROMANIAN
CULTURAL FOUNDATION

The publishers wish to thank the Prodan
Romanian Cultural Foundation and the
Arts Council England for their support of
the work of Istros Books.

Supported using public funding by

ARTS COUNCIL
ENGLAND

Mircea Eliade

Time, Death, and the Unspeakable Secret

Translated from the Romanian by
MAC LINSCOTT RICKETTS

Edited by
BRYAN RENNIE

Contents

Acknowledgements

"A Fourteen-Year-Old Photograph" was translated from "O fotografie veche de 14 ani," in *Nuvele* (Madrid: Colecția Destin, 1963). It was previously published in the *Louisburg College Journal of Arts and Sciences* in 1974. "At the Gypsies'" was translated from "La țiganci" in *La țiganci și alte povestiri* (Bucharest: Editura pentru Literatura, 1969). "The Bridge" was translated from "Podul" (Prof. Ricketts expressed his gratitude to Horia Ion Groza for his advice), also in *La țiganci și alte povestiri*. This translation was first published in *Ființa românească*, 4, 1996 and reprinted, along with the translator's short article "How *The Bridge* Was Written", in *Archaevs*, XV, 2011. "The General's Uniforms" was translated from "Uniforme de General" in *În Curte la Dionis* (Caietele inorogului, 1977). "Incognito in Buchenwald" was translated from "Incognito la Buchenwald" in *În Curte la Dionis*, Paris, Caietele inorogului, 1977. "In the Shadow of a Lily" was translated from "La umbra unui crin" in *Nuvele Inedite* (Bucharest, Rum-Irina, 1991). This translation first appeared in *Waiting for the Dawn*, edited by Davíd Carrasco and Jane Law (Boulder: University of Colorado Press, 1991, pages 150–170) and appears here with thanks to the University of Colorado Press, permission conveyed through Copyright Clearance Center, Inc.

All of these translations are now copyright by Eglantyne Books Ltd. and appear with their permission and the permission of the Eliade Literary Estate.

The editor would like to thank Sorin Alexandrescu and Liviu Bordaș for their help with questions both linguistic and historical, and Susan Curtis of Istros Books for her continuous encouragement.

SORIN ALEXANDRESCU

Mircea Eliade: The Philosopher as Storyteller

Translation from Romanian
by Alistair Ian Blyth.

Prologue

These six short stories, written between 1959 and 1982, are selected from Eliade's fiction conceived in the United States where he taught History of Religions from 1957 until his death in 1986. It was a particularly fertile period for him: a total of twenty-four novellas and short stories were published as a complete edition.* The stories have an autobiographical background, although they do not refer directly to any personal event or situation. Written in Romanian, with Romanian protagonists sometimes living in the United States or western Europe, they dramatize universally human situations that transcend national or local particularities. They recall philosophical questions raised in his history of religions, although they do not aim to provide answers. Eliade's fiction can either be read independently of his philosophy or placed in relation to it. In almost every text a certain strangeness typifies the situations and the behaviour of the characters arising, not from cultural backgrounds but from the ways in which they experience the unexpected in everyday life. Often incapable of understanding, many characters do not see any reason for dread, but rather something incomprehensible and out of the ordinary, the presence of *something* immaterial and vague is felt not as dangerous, but as something impossible to ignore, lending meaning to the everyday, certainly, but a meaning that is impenetrable.

Sinuous paths interpenetrate these narratives, often continuing from one to another, as the characters move between stories although no explicit chronological or narrative connections are made: the narrator seems to be fascinated by paths leading from one story to another but not eager to

* Mircea Eliade, *Proză fantastică*, vols. 1–2, Bucharest: Tana, 2007.

clarify any destination. The frequent connections between these stories reinforces their *effect*, rather than clarifying their *meaning*.

1. A Fourteen-Year-Old Photograph (1959)

This first story introduces Dumitru, a man "from the Danube", as he calls himself (as if Romania were unheard-of in America) when he comes to the Church of Redemption seeking the faith healer who had, a few years earlier, healed his wife Thecla, by merely looking at her photograph and praying to God on her behalf. Dumitru shows him the photograph with which he was able to cure Thecla of her asthma and even to rejuvenate her, making her resemble the photograph, which had been taken ten years before. The healer finds a new lease of life, believing in himself once more, and in the power of genuine faith to change the world. He declares: "Dumitru, with his naive faith and his vain idolatry is nearer the true God than all of us. And he will be the first to see him—the true God, when he shall show his face anew. Not in the Church, nor in the University, but he will show himself suddenly, unexpectedly, here among us" (p. 28).

The story's ending is highly significant because it is as if Dumitru's innocence becomes all-pervasive, as if it imbues every character, regardless of what each might say or do. (Significantly, in Eliade's work we do find neither criminals nor disreputable schemers, nor model characters.) Henceforward, the author's discourse dissolves into that of his characters. The likes of Dumitru and the faith healer vanish and the likes of Gavrilescu, Ieronim, and so many other unforgettable characters take their place.

2. At the Gypsies' (1959):
A Torturous Path from the Real to the Unreal

'At the Gypsies" is rigorously constructed. Eight starkly separated episodes arranged in perfect symmetry constitute distinct phases of the protagonist's journey: 1) on board the tram; 2) at the Gypsy women's; 3) the three women; 4) at the Gypsy women's: the dream; 5) on board the tram and at Voitinovici's; 6) at home; 7) in the horse-drawn cab; 8) at the Gypsies': the final departure. After an introductory episode set in Gavrilescu's everyday world there follow three episodes at the Gypsies' house, then three episodes in the outside world, which has now become "abnormally" disorganized, and finally, the return to the Gypsies' and a final departure. Gavrilescu's oscillation between Real and Unreal is organized dialectically:

$$\text{Real} \rightarrow \text{"Unreal"} \rightarrow \text{"Real"} \rightarrow \text{Unreal.}$$

The Real, i.e., Gavrilescu's everyday life, drains away when he arrives at the Gypsies' mysterious garden; he "exits" the Real and "enters" the "Unreal." Differentiated from the Unreal proper, the "Unreal" represents only an intermediate exit from the earthly world, passing from the everyday into the bewitched world of the Gypsies, a necessary limbo. The third term, the "Real," denotes a return to a world that has preserved only the appearance of the everyday, but which is full of alienating surprises. All four phases are stages in a spiritual journey between Life and Death, between the Profane and the Sacred.

The narrative suggests profound differences between these worlds that are not denotatively named, but connotatively suggested, drawing attention to the strange relations between nuances that are obvious to the reader, but which the protagonist cannot see. Eliade's artistry resides in suggesting the existence of a murky area around the character, *undescribed* as such, imperceptibly changing into something else. The narrator conveys to us both what the character sees but cannot understand, and what we as readers understand even though we never see it. We only *suspect* that what we see is not what exists for Gavrilescu, and only later do we understand how he is mistaken.

Eliade's gradual construction of the reader's understanding is something found in almost all his stories. The narrator is the only one who, at the confluence of two or more narrative worlds, has knowledge of them all, but Eliade also knows that the difference between them is ontological. This ontology differs in the structure and logic of the world in question in a deeper way than the narration suggests. The first concerns the way in which the author himself, the philosopher Mircea Eliade, sees and understands the world, the second in which he narrates it in his role as writer. The obvious construction of 'At the Gypsies" as an allegory of death, or rather of the passage into death, does not require mythological arguments because, from the literary perspective, it rests on the text's *convergence of connotations.*

Eliade's art thus resides in the *systematic fissuring of the literal,* in other words, in the furtive insertion of the connotative into the fissures of the denotative, guiding the meaning towards a *different interpretation.* From Şarpele [*The Serpent*] (1937) onwards, we constantly observe in Eliade's work such an *effaced insertion* into the text of terms that are symbolic in value or which signal something other than their literal meaning: let us call it the *technique of dual narrative,* which is presented discreetly, without any fireworks.

3. The Bridge (1963)

The narrative does not initially identify the speaker who declares, "all sorts of things happen" (p. 81). Several other unidentified people join the conversation, giving the impression of a theatricalization of narrative frequently found in Eliade's work. One character talks about a cavalry lieutenant, "so handsome that one could speak about him only in terms of negative theology ... a cavalry officer represented in terms of negative theology constitutes in itself a mystery, a paradox, a *coincidentia oppositorum*" (p. 82). Eliade seems to be winking at us from the background when he also adds that the lieutenant was a passionate reader of the *Upanishads*: obviously, the narrator is the twin of the historian of religions. 'The Bridge' was written in 1963, when Eliade was fifty-six. Early in the story the narrator muses: "'Vladimir!' I said to myself, 'how old are you now?' I knew how old I was: fifty-five" (p. 96).

Later, Vladimir's conversation is interrupted by Onofrei, who tells a different story, albeit with the same theme of "all sorts of things happen," a story which adopts a typically Bucharestian tone of light banter. The storyteller quickly moves not from one item of gossip to the next, but *from the quotidian to the non-quotidian*. Ambiguous scenes, and above all language that shifts from the sphere of profane to that of the sacred, are defining for many of Eliade's stories. Here, as in 'At the Gypsies", reality gives way to another indefinite world that is *real in a non-everyday way*, or unreal in our everyday world, without explaining the transition from *the real to the unreal*.

The camouflage of ultimate reality in the everyday—and sudden access to it by a certain person, but not by others, occurs constantly in these stories without ever being explained. Is the Lieutenant the wounded Adonis of myth, and is this why he is dying? We are not given the answer. Of the ten or twelve women who appear in the Lieutenant's drawing room, "one of them incarnates—without her knowing it and without anyone else's knowing it—a great goddess," (p. 105) although the next night another might be the goddess. All the major characters of the story are, in a way, double, and the overall question is of their real identity, just as it is the question of the Lieutenant's identity.

At the end of the story, as the train on which the conversation takes place nears Cernavodă, somebody says that to reach the coast, they must cross the bridge over the Danube. This accurate statement is suddenly understood to imply danger, especially when Onofrei restates it as follows: "We *know* we must cross the bridge. I repeat, *we know*, and we also know what this could mean: to cross it and be unable to return" (p. 106). Against the general disquiet aroused by these words the narrator remarks that the bridge is solid, but Onofrei was talking not about the solidity of the bridge but about its meaning. "The bridge at Cernavodă might camouflage a mystery. I say *might*, and I add: for *some* of us … Symbolism tells you that the bridge signifies a passage to something else, to another world, another mode of being. But symbolism can't guarantee in advance what kind of *other world* you will integrate or what *other mode of being* you will attain" (p. 109).

At this point Onofrei shakes hands with them all, steps out of the compartment, walks down the corridor towards the exit from the carriage, and, as if by coincidence, when he reached the end of the corridor, the train stopped—and he got off. "I hadn't suspected a station existed so close to the Bridge. I've never been able to remember its name," the narrator concludes (p. 111). Thus, the mystery grows deeper. Did Onofrei alight in the middle of nowhere, or did he only *seem* to alight to mask his even stranger disappearance from the narrative? Those introductory words ("all sorts of things happen") had the effect of making whatever might subsequently occur sound *unrealistic* and that this works back through the whole text. Onofrei's disappearance into some unknown place has an unexpected *anti-narrative effect*, as if dissolving the meaning of everything that has been said. What now guarantees the correct ending of the story? 'At the Gypsies" operated no differently: *the believable and the unbelievable constantly intersect with each other*. In this story, as in 'At the Gypsies", what the central character experiences, at *his* level of understanding, is contradicted at *our* level: the reader understands the author of the text directly, independently of the characters, or even at odds with them.

The following quotations from the story are a concise summary of Mircea Eliade's own philosophy in general, here very simply transposed in the words of a character who might himself also be a persona of the author. The camouflaging of the ultimate reality as the everyday and the sudden accessing of it by a certain person, but not by others, constantly occurs in other stories as well as we have already seen and as we will further also see, but without it ever being further explained why and how.

"For our minds, ultimate reality, *being*, is a mystery; and I define a mystery as that which we cannot recognize, that which is unrecognizable. This, however, could mean one of two things: either that we can never know ultimate reality, or else that we can know it at *any time*, provided only that we learn to recognize it under its infinite *camouflaged appearances*, in what we call immediate reality, in what India calls *māyā*, a term I would translate as immediate *unreality*." (p. 102).

Onofrei's final disappearance into some unknown place is an unexpected *anti-narrative effect*, as if dissolving the real meaning of everything that has been said. Who and what now guarantees the correct ending of the story, namely Onofrei alighting from the train *exactly* before the bridge?

In this story, as in 'At the Gypsies", what the central character, Gavrilescu, experiences, at *his* own level of understanding, is contradicted at *our* level: the reader understands the author of the text directly, independently of the characters, or even at odds with them; which is to say, he or she also understands the complexity of the *meaning* of what happens, even if it remains *irreducible* for some of the characters. Generalisation thus operates *from the specific Romanian setting outwards to the general human meaning*.

4. The General's Uniforms (1971): Eliade and Everyday Unreality

Ieronim Thanase and his companion Vladimir Iconaru appear without any preliminary explanation. They intend to steal, or rather secretly to borrow from Ieronim's uncle, two general's uniforms to use in an experimental play. In his uncle's attic, rummaging in trunks, Ieronim imagines scenes from the past, and, to his companion's perplexity, new scenes as possible extensions of present ones. Ieronim's language is deliberately theatrical, linked to memories of childhood, but also because to him the theatrical does not mean an alternative *to* the real, but an alternative *in* the real, a *different* reality than the one expected. Thus conceived, the fantastic is not fantasy as opposed to reality, but *a different course* of events *in* the real life than the one that is expected. The *fantastic* is for Ieronim, and for Eliade, something that is *deemed* by the speaker or viewer to be *real* but ultimately is *not* so. The fantastic does not arise by itself, but is created, presented, or *staged* as such: its existence is *unnatural*, but *real*, and occurs somewhere *within* the everyday, without being *part* of the everyday.

The *theatrical*, on the contrary, is something *natural*, but *un-real*: deliberately, "created" by somebody, "seen as such", or "framed" within a context. The theatrical does not exist, nor does it ever appear, by itself as such. The fact that it is *un-real, but natural* means, in other words, that although un-real, it is not "supernatural", but rather *natural*: it is created not by occult forces, but by actors.

Bucharest is a positive presence here. The house where the story unfolds, on Strada Popa Nan, was then, and still is, close to Strada Mătăsari, where the novella *The Cape** begins. This area encapsulates the "Bucharest of old" in the author's memory—the old, pre-war Romania, which for him is "eternal", and about which he will write in almost all his subsequent stories. This world is the *unreal Bucharest*, the Bucharest of Eliade's youth, suspended in eternity outside the history that came after it: a Bucharest simultaneously *theatrical* and *fantastical*, sacred, eternal, impervious to history. His trilogy of stories about theatre and reality is set in this world: 'The General's Uniforms' (1971), 'Incognito in Buchenwald' (1974), and 'Nineteen Roses' (1978–79).**

Ieronim remembers an almost mythical relative, the *Generăleasa*, i.e. the widow of a General, who arranges for him to play a theatrical role before his family and other guests. Ieronim was six years old at the time (p. 161). At a signal during dinner, a curtain at the back of the dining room falls away to reveal a huge mirror. In the mirror is reflected the young Ieronim, emerging "out of a fold in the draperies"

---

*   "Pelerina" written in 1974 appeared in English translation in *Youth Without Youth and Other Novellas*, Columbus: Ohio State University Press, 1988.

** This latter, "Nouăsprezece trandafiri," is also in *Youth Without Youth and Other Novellas*.

(p. 162). Barefoot, wearing a tattered shirt, laughing. Ieronim recites poems and sings. Something resembling the seabed appears in the mirror, and Ieronim declares that he can return whenever he likes, together with his friends the dolphins, seahorses, and other creatures of the sea. He laughs violently, wildly, and starts "to walk back and forth in front of the mirror, constantly discovering other caves and precipices, and tropical vines with flowers of incomparable beauty. Among these forms he spied the improbable silhouettes of the guests, with glasses of champagne as tall as a boot or as wide as a bucket in their hands; and amid them, sitting like a priestess in her armchair, was *Generăleasa*" (p. 163). An extraordinary vision, where that which the child sees *from the stage* merges with what those in the dining room see *on the stage*. This dual world, normally impossible, but suddenly somehow accessible to the child, makes him take leave of his senses because it *conjoins reality and fiction*. He is applauded "as an actor", but he frightens them all because "he was speaking, talking as in a dream, with a voice … from another world, because it did not resemble any human voice. And although it was incomparably sweet, it paralysed everyone" (p. 164). All of them were afraid that he had lost his mind, or perhaps that he was a child prodigy: which expresses the dual possible explanations for such an explosive attitude: madness or divine inspiration!

Here is the ambiguous fact that the theatre can lead both to one losing one's mind and to having one's mind sharpened. Ieronim is presented to the director of the Town Theatre. He is taken care of, but also given a special education. He later says that he is afraid of nothing, "because after all that's happened to us, and to *me*, I have rediscovered the meaning and function of drama, the way I knew it as a child" (p. 170). This is a profound expression of the supremacy of art in general and of Eliade's fiction in particular: "To be unafraid of anything means to regard everything that happens in the world as 'spectacle': This means that we can intervene at any time, by using imagination, and we can modify the 'spectacle' in any way we wish" (p. 171).

5. Incognito in Buchenwald (1974)

This story is written in two different keys and some words produce a different note depending on the key in which one reads them. As elsewhere, the narrative begins *in media res*: "They were all gathered in front of the window," (p. 183) without any explanation. The text seems realistic, surprisingly when compared with Eliade's earlier stories. Its immediacy is reminiscent of Aldous Huxley's narratives of the contemporary world, although it betrays no influence in themes or types.

Ieronim Thanase receives an unexpected visit from a woman he does not know, the sculptor Marina Darvari, while he is holding a theatre rehearsal at home. The confrontation of theatre and "real" life is here extended. The rehearsal allows for improvisation and the actors suggest that Marina's arrival be incorporated. When Ieronim irritably asks what the point of this would be, the actors reply in chorus: "*The meaning we create, Ieronim. The meaning we reveal, through* spectacle. *Through* spectacle, *Ieronim, without beginning and without end!*" (p. 187).

The "spectacle" continues with a dialogue in which a "guard" shouts at a "prisoner," commanding report on another prisoner said to be a Bodhisattva. Marina immediately "remembers," without it being explained how, that this is a title of one who will become a Buddha, and that the play is set in the Buchenwald concentration camp. Ieronim explains that freedom should not be discussed only in a Judaeo-Christian or Existentialist or Marxist context, but also from new perspectives.

The story refers to a political truth by stepping outside a political framework of discussion. As in other texts by Eliade, we might rather speak here of the *fictional* expression of a *political* truth. The fact that he wrote plays* draws attention to the fact that the fiction he wrote is often *theatrical*. Eliade inserts the *theatrical* into his prose and tends to *dramatize* scenes and characters in his texts. Unusually for Eliade, this seems to be the main theme of this story, namely that *humanity is superior to the forces that try to destroy us and, even in Buchenwald, the people destroyed there were ultimately stronger than those who destroyed them.* By comparison, in 'At the Gypsies'', Gavrilescu shows himself to be inferior to the situation in which he finds himself, as the *human condition* cannot in fact be discussed in the same way as *politics*.

Ieronim and Marina seek "the connection among things, events, everything that happens around us" (p. 215), and Ieronim realizes that Marina "wanted to say to us that *anywhere* and *at any time* we can be happy, that is, free, spontaneous, and creative ... *at any time*, in any circumstance—if we know how to look, how to understand, then ..." (p. 216). Perhaps those in Buchenwald, too, saw things this way, "'But how can I show it to others?' he exclaimed suddenly, his voice abruptly rising. 'How can I show them that this same light is hidden everywhere, in all things, however ugly they may be? In any spot of dampness on any wall, in any spattering of mud?'" (p. 217). At this point thunder strikes—the same

---

*   See Mircea Eliade, *Tutto il teatro, 1939–1970*, translated and edited by Corneliu Cicortaş, Milano, Edizioni Bietti, 2016.

motif as in *Youth Without Youth**—Marina kisses Ieronim and tells him: "I knew that one day I'd find you again!"

Marina and Ieronim have known each other for a long time: he forgot her, we do not know why, she arrived as a stranger, but drew closer to him, joining in his theatrical and at the same time philosophical game. What connection exists between the two of them and Buchenwald and theatre? Nothing is said about it, nor is there any hint of it when he meets her again. On the other hand, why should we demand that we be told the ultimate truth at the end of a narrative, as we are in the classic novel?

6. In the Shadow of a Lily (1982)

'In the Shadow of a Lily' was the last short story that Eliade wrote, and it revisits many of the questions discussed above, with several fresh nuances. The words of the title were uttered by an initially unidentified Romanian who declared, in March 1939, before the war and his departure from the country, that he would be reconciled with another Romanian, with whom he had quarrelled, only "in the shadow of a lily, in paradise." The mystery of the words gradually attracted numerous Romanian émigrés in Paris, as well as French intellectuals, who tried to decipher it, and who, in the case of the former, were also fascinated by the possibility that the phrase might mean the end of their exile and a return to their native land. This mystery is also correlated with another, more immediate one: certain trucks disappear as they round

---

*   *Youth Without Youth and Other Novellas*, edited by Matei Calinescu. Columbus: Ohio State University Press, 1988. Reprinted as *Youth without Youth*, University of Chicago Press, 2007 the main story of the title was made into a movie by Francis Ford Coppola in 2007.

a bend. Mysterious military camouflage? Or else an event that quite simply cannot be explained, the same as, say, UFOs? Or perhaps a sign that a new Flood is on the way, the End of the World, and a new Noah's Ark is being readied for survivors, who gradually vanish before meeting somewhere in paradise, in the shadow of a lily?

This story might be viewed as Eliade's literary testament, as it is also the only one that is set in France, introducing Romanian characters as well as French characters who speak Romanian or are interested in the Romanians' problems. This was the setting in which Eliade spent his summer holidays: the very place where he wrote the story was Eygalières, in the Bouches de Rhône *département*, in the south of France, at the house of his good friend Ioan Cuşa, the publisher of Romanian émigré magazines. The future meeting was not to take place in either Romania or France, but in a well-known place hidden from mortal gaze: in the shadow of a lily, in paradise. Who else could this suggest, after the strange term had circulated for decades among Romanian émigrés? Who else but they themselves, those who were to vanish gradually, unobtrusively, from the worldly scene, the same as he? "It is no serious matter," they will have said to one another, "we will meet again in the perfumed shade of a lily."

The meeting was to take place sooner than imagined, in 1986. Significantly, another short story, 'Dayan,'* closes with a prophecy found in the Aztec calendar, which held that the end would come in 1987. It was not the end of the world, but of Eliade himself. Reaching that end a year earlier, Mircea

---

*   Written in 1979, "Dayan" was first published in *Nuvele Inedite*, Bucharest, Rum-Irina, 1991. Unpublished in English translation it is available in Italian (*Dayan e altri racconti*, translated and edited by Corneliu Cicortaş, Bietti, Milano 2015), French (*Le Temps d'un centenaire/Dayan*. Gallimard 1981. Folio 2007), German (*Dayan / Im Schatten einer Lilie. Zwei Erzählungen*, Suhrkamp 1988), and Spanish (*In Tiempo de un centenario*, Editorial Kairós SA, 1999).

                    THE PHILOSOPHER AS STORYTELLER

Eliade might have answered, had he been asked, "Do you know the path? I know it. And I also know the place. It is not far." It is in the shadow of a lily.

Epilogue

Eliade's literary texts do not function to reveal anything, to explain the world, or to demonstrate the sacred/profane dialectic. Their function may be the opposite: they prevent any such revelation, even if they suggest it or, paradoxically, are aimed at showing how and why such a revelation is impossible. Every story is the history of the failure to provide an unequivocal explanation of the enigma articulated at its beginning. It might likewise be argued that the sacred/profane dialectic is illustrated negatively, but such reading might seem forced. Eliade's characters often intuit that a certain word or object signifies something, but they do not always succeed in identifying what. Or if they do succeed, they "disappear" shortly afterwards; they become new absences whose words must once more be interpreted by those still present.

Eliade's stories advance four semantic positions, of which only the second, let us call it the "surplus" one, registers the sacred meaning as such, alongside three types of profane meaning. Some of the characters in the story, the *initiates*, such as Iliescu in 'In the Shadow of a Lily' perceive the sacred meaning but cannot convey it to others. Other characters, the *interpreters*, having arrived at an incomplete meaning, are unable to attain the sacred meaning despite their efforts, in which case all they can do is narrate their failure in their own stories. The third category of interpreters, the profane, understand and repeat only the profane type of meaning, while the final category are unable to understand anything much, neither the first nor the second category of reaction, nor even the failure of the third. Eliade's stories refer to present failures and past successes in deciphering mysteries. The narrator does not follow the initiate to a position of understanding; however, he remains engulfed in the interval, the world between the sacred and the profane, on the threshold of a meaning of which he has a premonition, but which is forever inaccessible and ineffable. He narrates nothing but the drama of not being able to express that which, somehow, he does know.

A Fourteen-Year-Old Photograph

FOUR YEARS BEFORE the same thing had happened. He had found the church unexpectedly when he began to be afraid he had lost his way. It was a practical sort of building, of indeterminate age, differing in no way from the surrounding buildings. There were so many people that he had stopped by the door, disoriented.

This time, however, the church was empty. He saw a custodian by the altar, and he headed in his direction on tiptoe.

"My name is Dumitru," he began, smiling. "I don't believe that you will still remember me. I was here four years ago. To tell the truth," he added after a short pause, lowering his voice, "I had come by mistake. I thought there was going to be a festival of the Baltic Associations. My wife, she is Latvian. I knew it would please her a lot to know that I had crossed half the city to attend a Baltic festival. And let me tell you, I was impressed when I came in: this whole church, full of people, and Dr. Martin speaking from the pulpit. He was speaking with fire and sincerity, like a prophet."

"A festival of the Baltic Associations," the custodian murmured, blinking his eyes. "I seem to remember ..."

"But you see, this was just the marvel of it," Dumitru added, smiling again. "The festival had taken place the week before, and I didn't know it. I was mistaken about the week. I had read the advertisement but I hadn't noticed the date carefully ... Great is the power of God!" he exclaimed gravely.

"I'd come for a festival, and instead, Dr. Martin was preaching here, in this church—preaching and performing miracles!"

"I seem to recall," the custodian said again. "A festival of the Baltic Cultural Associations—all the Baltic Associations. It was very beautiful. Speeches, choirs, dances ... I remember now."

"I'm sorry I didn't see it too," Dumitriu began after a pause. "I had the dates confused, and I arrived a week too late. But as I told you, that's how the miracle happened: through a mix-up of dates, a matter of a week."

"I remember very well," the custodian resumed. "The choirs and groups of children with bells ... No, no, I'm mistaken. Those children with bells were here on another occasion. But it was a festival ..."

"And now, because business affairs have brought me here again, I thought I'd come to see him and thank him—Dr. Martin, I mean."

The custodian shook his head decisively. "He wasn't at the festival. Perhaps you want to talk to Dr. Williams. He's the one in charge of those things—meetings and festivals ... Come with me," he added, starting toward a side door. "He may not have left yet; the council meeting's just ending."

When he reached the corridor the custodian began walking faster.

"It's not that I have anything against him," Dumitru began, tagging along behind, "but you see, I came for Dr. Martin. The great preacher and miracle-worker. I came to thank him for the miracle."

The custodian stopped and turned his head in surprise. "For the miracle?" he repeated. "Then it's not Dr. Williams. He's with social and cultural activities. It must be Dr. Taubes. But he doesn't come to the office except mornings."

"But what about Dr, Martin?" asked Dumitru shyly. "He's the one I want to see."

"I don't remember him," the custodian said, scratching his head absent-mindedly. "What sort of man is he?"

"Ah," Dumitru began with fervour, stretching his arm out full length. "He's like a prophet. Tall, handsome, with thick black eyebrows and flaming eyes. He speaks with fire and inspiration!"

"I don't know who he could be," the custodian declared. "Perhaps someone from the committee. Come with me, the session's over now. Dr. Williams will tell you who he is."

Entering the room, Dumitru became suddenly confused. He remained standing beside the door, twisting his hat in his hands. Around a long table about ten men were seated. Several turned their heads casually toward the door, then returned to their business. But since Dumitru remained silent, soon he felt all eyes focused on him. Almost without realizing it, he took a step forward and began to speak.

"I don't know if any of you gentlemen remembers me, because four years have passed since then. In this holy church God took pity on Thecla and me, and he worked a miracle. I had come for a festival, when all at once I see the miracles begin. Sick people of all sorts standing in a line, each one more ill than the one ahead of him: heart disease, asthma, rheumatism—and through prayer and concentration they are healed one after another. With my own eyes I see it!"

Someone at the table leaned toward Dr. Williams and whispered to him.

"This must have happened on February 8."

Dr. Williams appeared not to have heard him. He kept his eyes fixed on Dumitru, straining to understand him, to guess what he meant to say. He was having difficulty especially understanding certain words which Dumitru mispronounced due to his excitement.

"When it came my turn and he placed his hand on my forehead, I felt a fire burning in the region or my heart. But I wasn't there on account of myself. Nothing was wrong with me; I was there for a festival. But Thecla was suffering from asthma—she'd suffered since childhood, and no doctor in the world had been able to cure it. 'It's not for me' I said, 'but for my wife, Thecla. She suffers terribly from asthma. Can you do something for her?' 'I can do nothing,' he answered. 'But God is all-powerful. Have you anything of hers with you?' 'I have a photograph,' I told him, and I pulled out this picture."

Dumitru laid his hat on the carpet, hunted in his wallet, and produced a photograph. Then he took a few steps toward the table, holding the picture in such a way that everyone could see it.

"He held it up like this then, too, in the church. And he shouted, 'This beautiful young woman is suffering and perishing. She is far away from us.—How far is she?' he asked me. 'Over 2,000 miles,' I said. And then Dr. Martin folded his hands together …"

"Wait a minute!" Dr. Williams interrupted him. "How do you know that this man was Dr. Martin? Who told you?" He spoke irritably, almost severely. Dumitru became silent, overcome with embarrassment.

"Who told you about Martin? How do you know it was him?" asked a perfectly bald man unexpectedly who had been smoking pensively with his head resting against the back of his chair, his eyes half-closed.

"Everyone in the church knew it was Dr. Martin," Dumitru said, taking courage. "The famous preacher and wonder-worker, Dr. Martin, the one who cures by concentration and prayer, who with God's help performs miracles in many holy churches."

"It couldn't have been him," Dr. Williams interrupted. "He has no powers. He didn't stay with us very long."

"Dr. Martin," Dumitru persisted. "The one who speaks with fire, like a prophet, who applies telepathy to faith."

"It would be better if we told him the truth," someone near the window said gravely.

Dumitru turned his head toward him expectantly.

"Friend," Dr. Williams began, clasping his hands and bringing them to his face a moment, as though he were starting to pray. "The ways of the Lord are obscure, but you must find out the truth. The so-called Dr. Martin was neither a doctor of theology nor did he have any thaumaturgical powers. Moreover, he wasn't an honest man, he didn't fear God."

"I don't believe it!" Dumitru shouted suddenly. But then he was ashamed of having done it, since it shocked the whole group for a moment. He fell silent and his face reddened.

"It was a great trial for us all," said the gentleman beside the window.

"This so-called Dr. Martin disgraced our campaign of healing through prayer."

"We'd planned a large-scale campaign," added Dr. Williams with a bitter smile. "But of course when the scandal with Mrs. Blith broke out ..."

"He tried to extort a large amount of money from her," explained the man by the window.

"A very considerable sum," continued Dr. Williams. "This Mrs. Blith had an only daughter who was a paralytic."

"Infantile paralysis," someone specified.

"It was a great blow for the church," Dr. Williams resumed. "He was arrested and at the trial he confessed everything."

"Frankly, I liked that," declared a very pale young man who was wearing dark glasses. "At the trial he behaved himself like a true Christian. This Dugay ..."

"His real name is Dugay," someone interrupted. "He's originally from Canada."

"His name's Dugay; I know this for a fact," the young man continued. "At the trial he admitted everything. Just like a true Christian, honestly confessing his sins. He impressed me. And then did you see what he did later, after he got out of jail?"

"Then it's not him" shouted Dumitru, suddenly stooping to pick up his hat from the floor. I'm talking about a Dr. Martin, preacher and miracle-worker."

"He was a scoundrel!" Dr. Williams exploded, losing his temper.

"But he gave evidence of great moral courage," the young man began again.

"Another person wouldn't have returned to the scene of his crime straight from jail. As you know, he's living in the same neighbourhood as Mrs. Blith."

"So he doesn't have to pay any rent!" interjected the man who had said that Dugay was of Canadian origin. "He lives at his cousin's place. That's nothing to his credit."

"And yet he dared to face people he had deluded," the young man persisted. "He has moral fortitude."

"But *where* does he face them? Where does he meet them? At a bar. At the Three Hundred."

"A brother-in-law of his owns the bar," someone explained. "The fact is, he works there part-time for clothes and food."

"I don't know what he does," Dr. Williams interrupted, trying to bring the discussion to an end, "and I don't wish to judge him. I'm not in the habit of frequenting bars. But people who've run into him at the Three Hundred have told me that they found him, if not actually drunk, then at any rate very nearly so."

"Allow me to add a word too," Dumitru interrupted, seizing his hat with both hands and holding it tight against his chest. "I also want to add a word. Let me, how do you say—get a word in edgewise!"

In his excitement he lost his train of thought and began to babble in an English that was even more difficult to follow. "Me and my wife, Thecla, too, we'll be all our lives thankful. When I saw then, in the church, that congregation of people kneeling and bowing their heads and praying for Thecla, then, so to speak, I *understood*. I understood all that had happened from the beginning to our wedding day. Because it was, I can say, a marriage for love. We were both poor, and I spoke bad English. I was a refugee boy; I hadn't begun yet to catch all the fine points of the English language. I was from Dunăre. I swam across the Danube as best I could, in order to escape, swimming. I spoke very badly, and yet we understood each other. Thecla, she was educated. She had been to college. I can say that she taught me to speak correct English. And because we loved each other so much, we were married. But Thecla, she suffered from asthma. Every day, absolutely every day, attack after attack. Dr. Martin said, 'Go home in peace, and thank God for his great mercy. Your wife has been healed!' And as he was saying this, I *knew* it was so. That's why I didn't want to telephone. I *knew* that she was healed. Why should I put God to the test, why should I doubt his omnipotence? Only after I returned home about ten days later ... about ten days after I'd entered this holy church, believing that I was coming to a festival—did I see that this healing was only a small part of the miracle. The wonder of wonders was just now beginning."

He paused momentarily, gazing happily toward the table, an extraordinary smile illumining his face.

"That's why I want to tell you," he began again, "and I beg your pardon for daring to say this to you, educated gentlemen, enlightened and good Christians, but still I have to say that this Dr. Martin did work miracles. Believe me! I swear by all I hold dear. God was with him!"

* * *

He was not hard to recognize, although he had changed much in those four years. He was thinner, his hair was almost gray, his forehead wrinkled. Only his eyebrows had remained black and his eyes had kept their lustre of other days, although sometimes they were clouded by brief spells of absent-mindedness. He was sitting at a table by the window, reading, with a glass of beer in front of him and a pile of magazines and newspapers nearby on a couch.

"Good afternoon, Dr. Martin," Dumitru said solemnly and bowed slightly. "You won't remember me …"

The other man lifted his eyes from the newspaper and looked at him absently.

"No, I'm sorry," he said. "And besides," he added after a moment, "my name isn't Martin. It's Dugay."

"I'm Dumitru. It's a name that's very hard to pronounce. But you see I'm of Romanian origin. Sit still, and I'll show you something. Perhaps then you'll remember."

He had planned this move before entering the Three Hundred. He had taken the photograph out of his wallet and had it handy in his coat pocket. With a sudden gesture he held it out.

"A beautiful woman," Dugay observed, disinterestedly, laying the picture on the table. "She hasn't changed a bit. I believe she sang in the choir at Syracuse."

"No, she doesn't sing," Dumitru interrupted him gently. "She's my wife, Thecla. She is 2,000 miles from here. But she is as she is today, because of you … If you will allow me, I'll sit down a little while on a chair," he added shyly. "I'm rather tired. Business all day …"

He pulled out his handkerchief and wiped his forehead. Dugay looked at him again, this time a long, concentrated stare, and then seized the half-full glass and emptied it quickly.

"I'm having another beer," he said. "Will you join me?"

Without waiting for an answer he got up and headed for the bar. He returned after a few minutes carrying a tray with two bottles of beer and two glasses. "I'm serving myself because I'm somewhat at home here," he said, beginning to fill the glasses.

"I know," said Dumitru, smiling. "I found out at the church."

"At which church?"

"The Church of Salvation. I went there to find out your address."

"The Church of Salvation," Dugay repeated, smiling bitterly. "A beautiful name. It took me two years to understand that name."

"I had come for the Festival," Dumitru began. "The church was jammed and you were speaking from the pulpit. You finished what you had to say, and then you began to work miracles."

"It's true that it has a very beautiful name," Dugay interrupted in a dreamy voice. "The Church of Salvation. Perhaps I still don't understand it, even after two years of theology. Do you understand what it means: the Church of Salvation?"

"As far as I can understand, it means to me, the holy church where God takes pity and saves people."

"But how? How?" asked Dugay, as though overcome by a sudden fervour. "How is it possible for anyone to be saved in a church? God has withdrawn from the world, disappeared. For us, for mankind, it is as though he were dead. I could say, without a trace of impiety, that God has died, simply because he's no longer with us, he's no longer accessible. He has withdrawn, hidden himself somewhere. That 'somewhere' doesn't belong to our world; it's what philosophers call the transcendent. For us human beings, transcendence is a form of death. So, if for us God has died, how can a person now be saved in a church?"

For some time Dumitru endeavoured to follow him, but soon he tired of it. Gradually his face lit up again. He picked up his glass cheerfully and brought it to his lips.

"May God give you good fortune," he said. "Good fortune and health. But it was no use for you to try to frighten me by saying that God is dying. I don't let myself be fooled so easily as that!"

Dugay sipped from his glass, then tried to look at his companion. But apparently the effort seemed too great because he quickly dropped his eyes to the table, hesitated a moment over the picture, then stared off into space. "What did you say?" he asked after a pause. "It seemed as though you said something about God."

"I said that you don't fool me with your jokes," Dumitru repeated, forcing himself to pronounce the words quite correctly. "I was there, wasn't I, in the Church of Salvation when you performed the miracles? I also have proof. Look at this photograph," and he pointed, holding his finger close but being careful not to touch it. "Look at it closely," he repeated, lowering his voice. "This is the best proof that God was with you four years ago in the church. Look at it closely!"

Dugay took the photograph and held it very close to his face, as though he had become suddenly near-sighted. "I understand what you mean. You mean to say that man, *in himself*, is the best proof of the existence of God, that man is made in the image and likeness of God. Isn't that it?"

Dumitru sighed sadly. "It's a shame you don't remember … But, of course, you performed so many miracles. Hundreds, thousands of people—you cured them through concentration and faith. How *could* you keep all of them in your mind?"

"Yes, it's true," said Dugay, laying the photograph on the table. "I've about lost my memory. I was almost certain that this girl was in the choir at Syracuse. But that's another story. Let's go back to the image and likeness of God. Agreed: man reflects the image of God. Now, look closely at him—at man, I mean, not God. Look at him: do you find him like that in real life? Don't you see how he's degenerated? ... No, don't look at the photograph," he said, observing that Dumitru had kept his eyes focused on the picture of his wife.

"Look at the people around you. No, no, my good man!" he exclaimed, covering the photograph with his palm, "I'm not talking about this likeness of your wife!"

"But it's precisely a matter of *this*," Dumitru said, defending himself. "This photograph, as you see it, is the best proof that God was with you when you did the miracle."

Dugay sat for a moment staring vaguely toward the bar; then he picked up his glass of beer resignedly and took a long sip from it. "We're at a stalemate," he began after an interval. "I don't understand you, and you don't understand me. So let's start over again from the beginning. What did you say your name was?"

"Dumitru. It's very hard to pronounce."

"Good. At least we're sure about one thing. You're Dumitru. And the girl in the picture is your wife, and she never sang in the choir at Syracuse."

"No, Thecla doesn't sing."

"Right. Now, tell me, please, where does God come in? Because if there was one thing I understood in jail—if I understood anything out of all those hundreds of books on theology I read in jail—it was this: that God does *not* intervene in the world. I might say something more, but I don't dare say it: that he does well not to intervene because his long absence, his policy of non-intervention in history, more likely signifies something else: simply that God has permanently withdrawn, that is, in a word, he has *died*."

"God forbid!" Dumitru exclaimed in horror, crossing himself. "Don't say that Dr. Martin, don't even say it in jest; it's a great sin!"

"But what else is there to talk about?" asked Dugay. "This is the only vital problem, the only one which has any meaning. After I did time in prison—after I *woke up*, I mean—I discovered that I had access to theological mysteries, and only this problem seemed to me to be worth discussing."

Dumitru listened very attentively. "Did you also do miracles in jail?" he inquired suddenly.

"Miracles?" Dugay asked in surprise, raising his head slowly. "Who said anything about miracles?"

"Miracles through concentration and prayer," Dumitru explained. "You did them at the Church of Salvation. I was there and saw you with my own eyes. People of all ages, suffering from all sorts of illnesses—and you healed them one after another, as many as you laid your hands on."

"Yes, but I *paid* for that," Dugay interrupted him, speaking slowly and deliberately, underscoring his words. "That was *before*. And for all my sins of that time, I have paid. I spent two years in prison, and when I got out, they tossed me on the rubbish heap. Today I'm nothing. I no longer have an identity. If it weren't for theology to hold me in the world, I'd vanish into nothingness. I'd dissolve. And now you come along, reminding me of what I was before, when in my irresponsibility and depravity I pretended to heal people."

"You healed with God's help," Dumitru corrected him. "Through concentration and prayer."

Dugay gave him a long, pensive look, then picked up his glass, filled it, and drank thirstily. "Actually, what is it you want of me?" he asked at length.

"I came to thank you for all you did for us. Since she suffered from childhood and is cured, it would not be ..."

"Who suffered?"

"Thecla, my wife," said Dumitru, pointing to the photograph.

Dugay seized it again and looked at it for a long while, intently and with exasperation. "It's a terrible thing to lose your memory," he said. "I simply can't recall her."

"Well, you never saw her anyway," Dumitru explained. "She wasn't at the church. She stayed home, 2,000 miles away. I brought you just the picture, Now, what's more wonderful is that this photograph was an old one. It was at least ten years old. As you see her here, she seems to be a girl of eighteen or nineteen, but when you cured her, she was almost thirty."

"And what was her trouble?"

"Asthma. Since she was a child. She had attacks every day, every day."

"It was suggestion," Dugay interrupted, irritated. "She was cured through the power of suggestion. Doctors do this too."

"Yes, but what's so wonderful," Dumitru said smiling mysteriously, "is that this photograph was *ten years old*. I don't know if you understand me—?"

"No," Dugay admitted. "I'm sorry. I'm rather tired."

"No, no!" Dumitru apologized. "It's my fault. When I talk about these things that happened to us, about how God has blessed us … in a word, when I remember what happened four years ago, I lose the thread. I can't find the right words …"

"Lucio!" Dugay called, lifting his arm. "Lucio!"

At the bar a young man slowly turned his head. He had a thin black beard and was dressed in corduroy pants and a jersey sweater. When he caught sight of Dugay he shrugged his shoulders resignedly and slowly started toward the table with a half-full glass in his hand.

"Come here and lend us a helping hand," Dugay invited. "What do you make of this problem. *Apparently*, it's a matter of a photograph. But a strange sort of divinity seems to be telling me that it's really something else!"

Lucio sat down on a chair, picked up the picture, and leaned back looking at it. After an interval he put the picture down on the table, took his glass in hand, and directed a pensive gaze toward Dumitru. But he quickly changed his mind, set the glass down, and picked up the photograph again, this time holding it in both hands, as though he were afraid it might escape him.

"It was ten years old," Dumitru began, "But I liked it, because I'd never seen her as she looked there."

"Why do you speak in the past tense?" Lucio interrupted, lifting his eyes from the photograph.

Dumitru blinked his eyes and said nothing. He had not understood and was embarrassed.

"Why do you say, 'I liked it', 'it showed', 'she was'?" Lucio persisted. "Why don't you say, 'I like it', 'it shows', 'she is'?"

"Oh!" said Dumitru, brightening. "I understand what you mean. I said, 'I liked, it,'" Dumitru continued, being careful to pronounce the words correctly, "just because I was telling Dr. Martin how the miracle happened four years ago. Thus, I was speaking about what happened *four years ago*. I told him that I had come *then* to the Church of Salvation with this photograph. And I liked it because it was *ten years old*. It showed Thecla as I had never seen her: as a girl of eighteen or nineteen."

"But that's the way she looks now too, in this picture," Lucio interrupted. "Why then do you speak in the past? *This* girl in the picture is not an old woman."

"But this is just what I want to tell Dr. Martin!" shouted Dumitru, a triumphant expression lighting up his face. "I mean that, as she looks in this photograph, I had never seen her; and for just that reason I liked it so much, because she was, so to speak, a stranger to me, a young girl of eighteen or nineteen whom I had never met, and whom I never could have met, even if I had wanted to, because at the time she was eighteen or nineteen I had not yet arrived in America. But after the miracle, that is, four years ago, or to be more precise, *a few months after* the miracle at the Church of Salvation, she, Thecla, began to resemble this photograph which, *now* as I speak, is *fourteen years old*! In other words, then, in the church I had this ten-year-old photograph with me, and with this *ten-year-old* photograph Dr. Martin made the miracle; and now, while I'm speaking, it is the same photograph, but it is *fourteen years old*! In other words, even presuming that she was cured of asthma by suggestion, what do we make of this photograph? Because then, already four years ago, it was a ten-year-old picture! Do you see what I mean?" he asked with a supreme effort.

Lucio had listened in fascination, and he was still smiling and nodding his head dreamily when Dugay put his hand on his shoulder.

"I'll tell you what I understood," Dugay began in a trembling voice. "I understand that I shall never be able to say: now I've paid enough and I've been released; I'm a free man without a past. Whoever said that the past is dead was an idiot. Behold it here, beside us: a living reproach! I thought that my only connection with the Church of Salvation was my meeting with Mrs. Blith—a meeting which meant, at one and the same time, my death and my resurrection, because only since I was in prison have I considered myself a man—a good-for-nothing man, but a man nevertheless. But lo and behold, something else happened at the Church or Salvation: once upon a time there came this man, Dumitru."

"I came for the festival," Dumitru said apologetically. "The Festival of the Baltic Associations. I had the dates mixed up."

"Yes, it's just as he says!" Dugay exclaimed almost pathetically. "*He came there by mistake*! Can anyone boast that he has had more bad luck than I? I thought and hoped that the past was dead, that once I had paid for my meeting with Mrs. Blith that everything connected with the Church of Salvation had been forgiven and forgotten. But here is this man, Dumitru, who has come here from somewhere in the wide world—where *did* you come from, Dumitru?" he asked, turning toward the immigrant.

"I'm from Dunăre, in Romania. I crossed the Danube by swimming, and I fled."

"He came from Dunăre, and one fine day he happened upon the Church of Salvation. He came here with this photograph," he added, lifting the picture from the table.

"She suffered terribly from the asthma," Dumitru ventured to interject.

"With this photograph!" Dugay exclaimed, holding it over his head. "And I, I performed a miracle with this photograph. I, a religious charlatan, a third-rate actor and after-dinner speaker, I performed a miracle with a photograph!"

"Walt! A.B.! Junior!" Lucio called, signalling to a group at the bar. "Come join us in a theological discussion!"

"You can make fun of me if you want—I deserve it," Dugay continued with a bitter smile, watching the line of young men coming towards him with glasses in their hands. "I deserve it, heaped up and running over. I thought I had gotten off lightly, with two years in jail and public disgrace. I believed the past was dead, as dead as the idol we call God—which has nothing to do with the true God whom we shall meet someday when he wills, and without our knowing when—and then you'll see that *he'll* teach us no more theology! But this Dumitru proves to me that my past is not dead, nor is the God of the Church of Salvation and of the other churches. Boys!" he exclaimed in a voice of deep discouragement, speaking to the whole group, "misfortune pursues me! I wanted to write a doctrine or God composed exclusively of eschatology. No one has written such a thing, nor will you find it in any of the great theologians of our time. And then Dumitru shows up with this photograph," he said, picking up the picture again and showing it to the others, "with this photograph of his wife who was ill with asthma, and because the attacks of asthma disappeared, he proclaims a miracle and makes me responsible for it! Can you imagine any greater misfortune?"

One of the young men reached out and took the photograph. Dugay leaned his elbows on the table, rested his head in his hands, and closed his eyes.

"Yes, but you see, I told you that it was not only the asthma," Dumitru said, daring to break the silence. "I said that the photograph was *ten years old.*"

"I don't exactly understand why you call this misfortune," said Junior.

"It was a cure by suggestion. You did others too, and it can happen to anyone. What does this have to do with eschatology, or even the existence or non-existence of God?"

Dugay opened his eyes and looked at him in surprise, as if he had not expected to hear Junior of all people talking in this way. Junior had taken his pipe out of his mouth and was turning it around now slowly between his fingers, waiting.

"Then you haven't understood at all!" Dugay burst out. "Don't you see that I can't free myself from the past? As long as this man believes in me *as I was then,* as long as he's convinced that the charlatan I was then can work miracles, I'm not free. I carry him on my back. He's a corpse I carry on my back. With Mrs. Blith things are clear: she knows I'm a rogue, and I paid for her finding it out. But Dumitru believes that I cured his wife ..."

"You didn't do it alone. God was with you ..."

"You see? I have to carry him with me piggyback until he's persuaded to the contrary. But how can I persuade him to change his mind? I'm a good-for-nothing man, but I'm still a man. Can I wish his wife to become ill again just to convince him that it wasn't some sort of miracle?"

Dumitru tried to laugh, but he did not succeed. He was silent, perplexed, his hand over his mouth.

"If I believed in the devil," Dugay continued, "I could say that miracles are the work of Satan. But I don't believe in the devil."

Dumitru tried again to laugh. He picked up his glass and drained it in one swallow. "You're going to a lot of trouble for nothing, Dr. Martin, trying to lead me into temptation. Now, since I'm rather tired, I speak the bad English, but don't think that I'm greener than I am. I told you that this photograph was ten years old."

He hunted for the picture with his eyes and discovered it at the end of the table, in Walt's hand.

"As it shows Thecla there, I had never seen her. But lo and behold, God had mercy on me and I met Dr. Martin. And God, through Dr. Martin, took the asthma with one hand …"

"Your attention for a moment!" someone at the bar said, clapping his hands. The lights were turned down and in the middle of the room a young woman in black slacks appeared. She went to the microphone and announced her number. "'Simple Song,' based on a poem by E. M. Forster."

"With one hand he took away the asthma," Dumitru repeated, lowering his voice, and with the other he made her resemble herself …"

"Shh!" several persons hissed from neighbouring tables.

"Silly old Boney, Sat on his pony;" sang the girl.

"He made her resemble herself *in the photograph*," Dumitru whispered.

Lucio put his hand on Dumitru's shoulder and leaned near his ear. "Listen now," he whispered. "What comes next is really good!"

"Sat on his pony," sang the girl, "Eating his Christmas Pie."

* * *

The photograph passed from one table to another.

"He met her at a Baltic festival," a young man explained to a girl beside him—a man with a round face and wide-set eyes which gave him the air of an exotic puppet. "She was suffering from asthma, and they'd been married just that week. They were married at the Church of Salvation, where Dugay was speaking. But I didn't understand very well what Dugay's role was in this whole business—why it's such a catastrophe for Dugay ..."

They followed Dugay with their eyes as he passed among the tables wearing the immaculately white jacket of a bartender, carrying a tray in a curious manner, half-resting it on his shoulder. They tried to signal him, but he did not see them.

"He met her at a Baltic festival," said one of the girls, turning and holding out the photograph to someone at a neighbouring table.

"Who *is* the man?" asked the other girl.

"You can't see him very well now—he's asleep. He's the one sleeping with his head on the table, beside Lucio."

"But he seems old compared with her," said the first girl. "She looks like a child."

"Nineteen," the young man specified. Then he lifted his hand in the air and called, "Dugay!"

Dugay approached slowly and threw himself down, exhausted, on the free chair in front of them.

"What's happened?" the young man asked. "Who is that guy?"

"I'll carry him on my back all my life," said Dugay in a dry voice, seemingly choked by emotion. "I shall carry a cadaver on my back for the rest of my life. Goodbye doctrine of God, goodbye new eschatology!"

"But why? Why do you say you're carrying him on you back?" asked one of the girls.

Dugay raised an arm wearily in the air, then let it fall with a look of bitter resignation. A few moments later he got up with considerable effort from his chair and began to set the empty glasses on the tray.

"Shall I bring you something more?" he asked. But without waiting for a reply he started towards the bar carrying the tray in such a way that it bounced slightly in a rhythmic cadence beside his shoulder.

"I'm going to see what this is all about," said the young man, getting up suddenly and crushing his cigarette in the ashtray. Dumitru was sleeping peacefully with his head resting on his left hand on the edge of the table.

"Now tell me, Lucio, who is this guy? What's the matter with him?"

"He's from Dunăre," Lucio began dreamily. "He's abandoned Nature and started in the direction of Culture. He's come to us—and to semantics, sociology, and Zen. He was snatched suddenly from the plump warm arms of Mother Nature ..."

"False!" Junior interrupted. "He has nothing to do with Mother Nature. He's a Christian. He was born a Christian and has remained one. He knew the Spirit. He confessed the Logos. He was, in a way, on the road to salvation."

"Perhaps he was," A. B. spoke up, "but he was a long way back—on the road to salvation, I mean. He was lagging far behind. Perhaps two or three centuries, maybe more."

"In other words, he was a laggard on the road to salvation," Lucio quipped, smiling melancholically. "Perfect. The formula is perfect. He was lagging far behind. But unfortunately for him, History intervened—that force in which the Universal Spirit is incarnated—and lo and behold, he crossed the Danube and landed here among us, in the first ranks of the cultural *avant-garde*: amidst semantics, sociology, and Zen."

Dumitru awoke, and after listening for a few moments he tried to locate Dugay with his eyes among the crowd. But soon he became dizzy and took his head in his hands. "I'm very tired," he said, "What did you give me to drink? I can scarcely hold my eyes open."

"Yes," Junior was saying. "History brought him to us. He is, we might say, a surprise gift from History."

"But why do you say that he had lagged behind on the road to salvation?" inquired one of the young men who recently had joined the group at the table.

"Because he doesn't have access to a universal language," Lucio explained.

"How do you make culture with the archaic interjections and vocabulary of a Danubian parish? And then, how can you be saved if you don't have access to the Universal Spirit, if you don't possess a universal language? But happily for him, the process of transformation through culture has begun. By hook or crook, he's catching hold on a universal language, American English, through newspapers and television. He begins to bite into it, to chew it, to swallow it—he fills himself with it. And now this language, the American language, is somewhere in his stomach, his breast, his blood. You sense that it's there. You sense that our friend has begun to be transformed, that he has the Universal Spirit within. But the process of transformation is not yet finished. Because, you see, he isn't able yet to express mysteries. But what good is this universal language, this American language, if we can't express mysteries? And our friend has awakened our curiosity with a mystery which we cannot penetrate because Dumitru can't express it. As nearly as I can make out, it has to do with a photograph which is, simultaneously, ten and fourteen years old. Now, so far as I'm concerned, this mystery of simultaneity fascinates me."

"But where *is* the photograph?" Dumitru shouted all at once, after having searched his pockets frantically for it. "Where's Thecla's photograph?"

"Don't worry," Lucio assured him, "it's here somewhere; It's circulating around the tables."

Dumitru made an effort to rise.

"Sit still, don't move," one of the young men signalled him. "I'll go look for it."

The two girls approached the table, drawing up their chairs. "Have you found out anything?" one of them asked.

The young man shrugged his shoulders. "I don't understand very well. As usual, they were discussing philosophy."

At that moment Dugay appeared with an empty tray and threw himself down on the chair, exhausted.

"Dr. Martin," Dumitru exclaimed jubilantly. "The photograph! I want to explain it to you too?"

Dugay sighed deeply and picked up a glass at random from the table and drained it. "What else can I bring you here?" he asked. "After the dancing starts, I can't come whenever I want."

"Six bottles," said A. B., after counting off the number in the group on his fingers.

"Dr. Martin, the photograph! Don't forget about the photograph," Dumitru persisted, pronouncing the words with great difficulty.

With his eyes he followed Dugay departing, carrying the loaded tray beside his shoulder. Then he leaned over the table a little and spoke to one of the girls.

"But what did they give me to drink? I can scarcely keep my eyes open!"

The girl looked at him in amusement, smiled, and shrugged her shoulders.

"I'm very tired," Dumitru continued, massaging his temples. "And I'm sorry that these gentlemen believe that I don't know what I'm saying. I'm telling them the truth."

He was getting ready to rest his head on the table again when the young man returned with the picture and held it out to him. Dumitru took it with a trembling hand and showed it once again to everyone around the table. Then, smiling mysteriously, he carefully replaced it in his wallet.

"From now on, I shall not show it to you," he said. "But you saw how she had her hair—I mean what sort of coiffure she had then, that is, fourteen years ago. She has it that way now, too. And since then she hasn't changed. She has stayed this way. As she was at nineteen."

He tried to smile, put his hand to his forehead, and remained silent for some time.

"I'm rather tired. It's very hard for me to explain. But this was a miracle too. That she became as I had never seen her before. And since then she hasn't changed."

"I think I know now what you're trying to say," Junior broke in. "You mean that after she was miraculously cured, your wife cut her hair again in the way she wore it when she was nineteen. Is that right? Isn't that what you mean?"

Dumitru shook his head sleepily. "*As I had never seen her,*" he murmured.

"Maybe he means something different by all this," Lucio said thoughtfully.

"Maybe what he means to say is that after she was cured of asthma, his wife *became young*. She began to look like she did at nineteen. Is that right?" he asked him. "Is that what you've been trying to tell us?"

A blissful smile illuminated Dumitru's face. "A few months after the miracle," he began, pronouncing the words with great difficulty. He stopped, pulled out his wallet, and began to search anxiously. "It was ten years old, and a few months after the miracle ..." At last he found the picture and showed it to them again, holding it with difficulty over their heads.

"Look closely at her," he said again, trying in vain to pronounce his words correctly. "She was this way fourteen years ago. And she began to look this way again about four years ago, a few months after the miracle. As I had never seen her before."

"But if what he says is true," Lucio declared, "it means his wife's become ten years younger!"

"Fourteen years!" Dumitru broke in. "Fourteen years, minus a few months."

"And so it truly *was* a miracle," Lucio continued, fascinated. "And since Dugay swears he wasn't mixed up in this affair ..."

"But he was!" Dumitru interrupted him again. "God was with him!"

"Then, because it truly *was* a miracle, then there's no other explanation for it but that our friend Dumitru performed it!"

"God!" protested Dumitru, holding his arm straight up in the air. "God, through Dr. Martin!"

"Therefore, this friend of ours, Dumitru, is a maker of miracles, a saint!"

Dumitru protested, raising both arms in the air. "God?" he shouted.

"He is, consequently, a new saint," Lucio continued. "A new Saint Dumitru!"

　　　　A FOURTEEN-YEAR-OLD PHOTOGRAPH

"Do not take the name of God in vain," Dumitru tried to say, but after the first words the room began to reel and he lay his head on the table.

"Leave him alone," someone said, placing a hand on his shoulder. But Dumitru stretched out his arm slightly on the table, shoving the glasses, and everyone realized with relief that he was asleep.

Lucio made his way to the microphone. "Your attention for a moment, please," he began, "and I ask you also, please don't applaud, because you might waken him. Your attention for a moment. It is my rare, exceptional privilege to announce that we have a saint among us."

A hush fell over the room.

"A maker of miracles is a saint. Now our friend, Dumitru, whom the spotlight will show you in a minute, not only cured his wife of asthma, but he made her younger by ten years—or by fourteen years according to another version. This new saint, St. Dumitru, is the man whom the spotlight will now indicate."

Several got up from their tables in the back and came to the middle of the room to get a better look.

"As you see, he's asleep. So please don't wake him up by applauding. He's sleeping, not because he drank too much, but because he's exceptionally tired. He came from far away. He came all the way from Dunăre. And we've tired him with our questions. We pumped him because we wanted to find out how, and under what circumstances, fourteen years can be the same as—if not less than—ten years."

A few laughs were heard, but the next moment Dugay approached Lucio and took the microphone from him. "Why are you making fun of him?" he asked sharply. "He hasn't done anything. If he believes in idols and illusions, it's not his fault."

The spotlight suddenly shifted and Dugay was bathed in light, but it seemed not to intimidate him. Still holding his tray, looking quite pale, he gazed out across the tables as though he expected someone to rise up suddenly near the door.

"It's our fault—we've known about the true God, but we haven't confessed him. Dumitru, with his naive faith and his vain idolatry is nearer the true God than all of us. And he will be the first to see him—the true God, when he shall show his face anew. Not in the Church, nor in the University, but he will show himself suddenly, unexpectedly, here among us, perhaps on the street, perhaps in a bar. Yet we won't recognize him, and we won't bear witness to him."

All at once Dumitru awoke. He looked eagerly at Dugay, his whole face lit with a smile.

"Speak, Dr. Martin!" he whispered. "Speak with fire and sincerity, like a prophet!"

At the Gypsies'

IN THE TRAM THE HEAT WAS SCORCHING, oppressive. Making his way hastily along the aisle, he said to himself, "You're a lucky man, Gavrilescu!" He had noticed an empty place by an open window at the other end of the car. Seating himself, he produced a handkerchief and slowly mopped his forehead and cheeks. Then, folding the handkerchief and putting it around his neck under his collar, he began to fan himself with his straw hat. The old man facing him stared for a long time, with the concentrated look of one who was trying to remember where he had seen him before. Placed very carefully on his knees the old man held a tin box.

"It's terribly hot," he said abruptly. "I can't remember such heat since 1905!"

Gavrilescu shook his head, continuing to fan himself with his hat.

"It certainly is hot," he said. "But when a man is well-bred, he endures everything more easily. Colonel Lawrence, for instance. Do you know anything about Colonel Lawrence?"

"No."

"What a pity. I don't know much about him either. If he were to get on this tram, I'd question him. I like to talk with cultured people. Those young folk, my man, are surely students—eminent students. I waited with them at the tram stop, and I listened to them. They spoke about someone named Colonel Lawrence, and his adventures in Arabia. And what memories! Without consulting them, they quoted whole pages from the Colonel's books! There was a sentence that I liked, a very fine sentence, about the heat that he, the Colonel, encountered somewhere in Arabia, that was like a blow on the head, like a blow on the head from a sword ... Too bad that I can't remember it word for word. That terrible heat of Arabia was like the blow of a sword. Like being struck on the head with a sword, rendering him speechless."

The conductor listened to him, smiling, then handed him his ticket. Gavrilescu, replacing his hat on his head, began to search in his pockets.

"Forgive me!" he murmured, after a few moments, failing to find his wallet. "I never know where I put it!"

"It doesn't matter," said the conductor with unexpected good nature. "There's plenty of time. We haven't even reached the Gypsies' yet ..." and turning toward the old man, he winked. The old man blushed nervously and tightened his grasp on the tin box, which he was holding with both hands. Gavrilescu held out a bill and the conductor began to count the change with a smile.

"It's a disgrace!" whispered the old man a few moments later. "It shouldn't be allowed."

"Everybody talks," said Gavrilescu, taking off his hat and resuming his fanning. "And, really, it seems to be a beautiful house, and the garden! ... What a garden!" ... he repeated, shaking his head in admiration. "Look, there it is now!" he added, leaning forward a little in order to see better.

Several of the men turned their heads with studied casualness, as though they only happened by chance to look out of the windows.

"It's a disgrace," the old man reiterated looking straight ahead. "It should be forbidden."

"Those are old walnut trees," continued Gavrilescu. "Their shade is so cool and refreshing. I have heard that the walnut only begins to cast such shade after thirty or forty years. Is that true?"

But the old man pretended not to hear. Gavrilescu turned toward a nearby passenger who was looking thoughtfully out of the window.

"Those trees are at least fifty years old," he began. "There's so much shade. In heat like this, it's a pleasure. Lucky fellows ..."

"Fellows? Girls, you mean," said his neighbour without raising his eyes. "They are women."

"So I've heard," continued Gavrilescu. "I've been taking this tram three times a week, and I give you my word of honour, not once have I failed to hear them discussed, the Gypsy girls, I mean. Do you know any of them? I wonder, where did they come from?"

"They came from everywhere," said his neighbour.

"They've been here for twenty-one years," interrupted someone else. "The very first time I came to Bucharest these Gypsies were already here. But the garden was much larger. That was before the college was built ..."

"Well, as I was telling you," Gavrilescu began again. "I ride this tram regularly three times a week. To my regret, I am a piano teacher. I say, to my regret," he added, trying to smile, "because I am not meant for such work. I am an artist by nature."

"Now I know you," the old man spoke suddenly, turning his head. "You are Domnul Gavrilescu, the piano teacher. I have a grandchild, and you gave him lessons five or six years ago. I kept asking myself where I had seen your face ..."

"Yes, I am," returned Gavrilescu. "I give piano lessons, and travel a lot by tram. In spring, when it's not very hot, and there's a breeze, it's a pleasure. I stay by a window like this, and as the tram goes by, I see all the flower gardens. As I told you, I ride on this line three times a week, and I continually hear talk of the Gypsy women. Many times I have asked myself:

'Gavrilescu,' I've said to myself, 'supposing they *are* Gypsy women, where do they get so much money? A house like that, a veritable palace, with gardens, and old walnut trees—that represents millions.'"

"It's a disgrace!" the old man exclaimed again, turning away his head in disgust.

"And there's another question that I ask myself," continued Gavrilescu. "Judging from how much I make, a hundred lei for a lesson, it would take ten thousand lessons to make a million. But then, you see, things are not that simple. Suppose I have twenty lessons a week, I'd have to teach five hundred weeks, that's nearly ten years, and I'd have to have twenty pupils with twenty pianos. But what of the problem of summer vacations, when only two or three pupils stay home? And what about Christmas holidays, and Easter? All those lost hours are also lost from the million. So that one should not speak of five hundred weeks with twenty hours, and twenty pupils with twenty pianos a week, but much more; far, far, more!"

"That's true," said one of the men sitting near him. "These days, no one learns to play the piano any more."

"Ah!" exclaimed Gavrilescu suddenly, striking his forehead with his hat. "Something is missing, and I don't know what! Oh! The portfolio! I forgot the portfolio with the music. I was speaking with Madame Voitinovici, Otilia's aunt, and I forgot the portfolio! What miserable luck!" he added, taking the handkerchief from his collar and thrusting it into his pocket. "Well, Gavrilescu, nothing to do but go back to Preoteselor Street, and in all this heat …"

He looked around him desperately, as though he expected someone to stop him. Then he stood up abruptly.

"It's a good thing I thought of it," he said, removing his hat and bowing slightly from the waist.

Then he went out quickly onto the platform, just at the moment when the tram stopped. Stepping down, Gavrilescu met again the heat and odor of melting asphalt. With difficulty he crossed the street, in order to wait for the tram from the opposite direction.

"Gavrilescu," he whispered, "Be careful, you seem to be getting old! You're weak-minded, you're losing your memory!

I repeat: Take care, you can't do this sort of thing. At forty-nine a man is in the prime of life!" ... but feeling tired and exhausted, he collapsed limply on a bench in the full sun. He took out his handkerchief and started to wipe his face.

"This reminds me of something," he spoke to himself in order to sustain his courage. "A little effort, Gavrilescu, a little effort of memory. Somewhere, on a bench, without any money in my pocket. It was not quite so hot, but it was in summer ..." He glanced around him at the deserted street, the houses with their closed shutters and blinds pulled down, seemingly abandoned.

"The people have gone to the baths," he said to himself. "Tomorrow or the next day, Otilia will go, too." And now he remembered: He had been in Charlottenburg; he was then, as now, on a bench in the sunlight, but then he had not eaten, and he hadn't a penny in his pockets. "When you are young and an artist, you can endure everything more easily," he mused.

He stood up and took a few steps into the street to see if he could catch sight of the tram. As he walked it seemed as if the heat radiated from a fire, and, staying close to the wall of a house, he took off his hat and began to fan himself.

About a hundred meters up the street, there seemed to be an oasis of shade. It fell from the dense, leafy boughs of lime-trees growing in a garden elevated above the pavement. Gavrilescu looked at it hesitantly, fascinated. Once more he turned his head in the direction of the tram, then set out determinedly, with great strides, keeping close to the walls of the houses. As he neared the trees, the shade appeared to him to be a little less thick. However, the gardens seemed refreshing and Gavrilescu began to inhale deeply, throwing his head back a little. "What I need is a whole month of days like this with the linden trees in flower!" he said dreamily. He approached the gate with its grillwork and looked into the garden. The gravel had recently been wetted, and he saw rows of flowers, while in the background a pool was surrounded by small dwarf figures. At that moment he heard the tram pass by with a dry grinding sound, and he turned his head. "Too late!" he exclaimed, smiling. "*Zu spät!*" and raising his arm he waved his hat many times, as he had done in the North Station when Elsa left to spend a month with her family in a small village near Munich.

Then, resigned, unhurried, he began to walk ahead. He arrived at the next stop, took off his coat, and prepared to wait, when suddenly he was struck by the bitter fragrance of the leaves of the walnut tree, crushed between fingers. He turned his head and looked about him. He was alone. As far as he could see the pavement was deserted. He did not venture to look at the sky, but he was conscious, above his head, of that same white light, incandescent, dazzling, and he felt the hot flame of the streets striking him upon his mouth and cheeks. He started out then along the path, resigned, with his coat under his arm, his hat pulled down on his forehead. When he caught sight of the distant thick shade of the walnut trees, he felt his heart begin to beat faster, and lightly hastened his steps. He had almost reached the garden when he heard the metallic complaint of the tram behind him. He stopped and greeted it with a sweeping flourish of his hat.

"Too late!" he exclaimed. "Too late!"

The shade of the walnut trees surged forward to meet him unexpectedly, strangely cool, and Gavrilescu stood momentarily bemused, smiling. For a moment he seemed to be in a forest in the mountains. Bewildered, with something like reverence, he commenced to peer at the tops of the tall trees, the ivy-covered wall of stone, and sensing an infinite sadness around him, he felt overcome by apathy.

Many were the years during which he rode on the tram past this garden, without its ever having aroused sufficient curiosity in him to prompt him to get off and take a closer look at it. He stepped forward slowly, effortlessly, tipping his head back in order to see the crowns of the towering trees. And abruptly he found himself in front of the gate, where, as if she had been standing concealed for a long time, waiting just for him, a young girl stepped forward, beautiful, very brown of skin, wearing a necklace of gold and large golden earrings.

Laying her hand on his arm, she asked in a low voice, "Please, won't you come in to the Gypsies'?"

She looked at him with an expansive smile on her lips and in her eyes, and seeing that he hesitated, pulled him gently by the arm into the courtyard. Gavrilescu followed her, fascinated; but after a few steps he stopped, as though he wished to say something.

"Don't you want to visit the Gypsies'?" the girl asked again, lowering her voice still further.

She looked directly into his eyes briefly, deeply, then took his hand and led him quickly toward a little old hut hidden in large bushes of lilac and dwarf-elder. He accepted her guidance without question. She opened the door and pushed him gently forward. Gavrilescu entered into a curious half-light, as though the windows might have been made of panes of blue and green glass. He heard, far away, the approaching tram, and its metallic grinding seemed so unbearable to him, that he raised a protective hand to his forehead. When the noise had died away, he discovered near him, seated at a low table with a cup of coffee before her, an old woman looking at him with curiosity, waiting for him to collect himself and take notice of her.

"What is your heart's desire for today?" she asked him. "A Gypsy, a Greek, a German …?"

"No," Gavrilescu interrupted her, raising his arm in a gesture of protest. "No German."

"Then a Gypsy, a Greek, a Jew," replied the woman. "Three hundred lei," she added.

"Three piano lessons!" he exclaimed, beginning to search in his pockets, "and that's not counting the tram there and back."

The old woman sipped the coffee, deep in thought.

Suddenly she asked him, "You are a musician? Then you will like it here!"

"I am an artist," said Gavrilescu, rummaging in turn among many damp handkerchiefs in one pocket of his trousers, and putting them back methodically one by one, in the other pocket. "For my sins, I have become a piano teacher, but my ideal was above all pure art. I live for my soul … I'm sorry," he added, troubled, laying his hat on the little table, and beginning to place in it the objects which he removed from his pockets. "I can never find my wallet when I need it."

"There's no hurry," said the woman. "We have time. It is not yet three …"

"I am sorry to contradict you," Gavrilescu interrupted her, "but I believe that you are mistaken. It must be nearly four. I finished Otilia's lesson at three."

"Then the clock must have stopped again," murmured the old woman, once again lost in thought.

"Ah, at last," exclaimed Gavrilescu, showing her his wallet triumphantly. "It was there, where it should be!"

He counted the bills and held them out to her.

"Take him to the cottage," said the woman, rising, glancing at him.

Gavrilescu felt someone take his hand, and turning around, startled, he found the girl who had lured him through the gate once again by his side. He followed her timidly, carrying his hat full of articles under his arm.

"Now, remember," the girl said to him "Don't mix them up: a Gypsy, a Greek and a Jew."

They crossed the garden, going away from the front of the building with the roof of red tile, which Gavrilescu had noticed from the street.

The girl stopped and gazed deeply into his eyes for an instant. She laughed briefly, then was silent. Gavrilescu had just begun to transfer the various items from his hat to his pockets.

"Ah," he exclaimed. "I am an artist. If it were up to me, I should stay here in these woods," and he pointed with his hat toward the grove. "I like nature. And when it is hot like this, here one can breathe air as pure and cool as in the mountains ... but where are we going?" he asked, seeing that the girl approached a wooden fence, and opened a little gate.

"To the cottage. That's what Baba said ..."

Again she caught his arm and pulled him after her. They entered a neglected garden, with roses and lilies lost among the weeds and thickets of briars. He began to feel the heat again and Gavrilescu hesitated, disappointed.

"I've deceived myself," he said. "I came for the coolness, for nature ..."

"Wait until we go into the cottage," the girl interrupted, pointing out with a motion of her arm a little old house, on a patch of land, which had been cleared at the back of the garden.

Gavrilescu put his hat on his head and followed her morosely. But when he reached the entrance hall he felt his heart begin to beat more and more vigorously, and he stopped.

"I'm so nervous," he said. "I can't account for it."

"Don't drink too much coffee," whispered the girl, opening the door and pushing him inside.

He could not see how large the room was since the curtains were drawn, and in the semi-darkness he found it difficult to distinguish between a number of folding screens and the walls, vaguely discernable beyond them. He started to go ahead, walking on carpets that seemed to become thicker and thicker and more buoyant, as though he might be stepping on hidden springs, and with every step the beat of his heart quickened, until he was afraid to go farther, and stopped.

At that moment he felt happy, suddenly, as if he were young again, and the whole world was his, even Hildegard.

"Hildegard!" he exclaimed, addressing himself to the girl. "I haven't thought of her for twenty years. She was my great love. She was the woman of my life! ..."

But when he turned his head, he noticed that his companion had gone. Then he sensed a faint and exotic perfume assail his nostrils, and at once heard a clapping of hands, as the room was gradually illuminated in an incomprehensible manner, as if the curtains were being drawn back slowly, very slowly, one after another, allowing the light of the summer afternoon to penetrate the shadowy room. But Gavrilescu just had time to observe that none of the drapery had moved, when he found himself gazing into the eyes of three young girls who stood several feet in front of him, lightly clapping their hands and laughing.

"So you have chosen us," said one of them. "A Gypsy, a Greek, and a Jew ..."

"But you must, if you can, guess us," said the second.

"You must see if you know who is the Gypsy," the third girl added.

Gavrilescu's straw hat fell from his head, and he stared at them fixedly, petrified, as though he did not see them, but looked past them at something else beyond the screens.

Suddenly he whispered, "I'm thirsty," and he brought his hand to his throat.

"Baba sent you the coffee," one of the girls said. She disappeared behind a screen and returned with a round wooden tray which held a cup for coffee, and a pot. Gavrilescu picked up the cup and held it high, then extended it with a smile.

"I'm terribly thirsty," he said softly.

"This will be boiling hot, it's straight from the pot," said the girl, filling his cup. "Drink it slowly …"

Gavrilescu tried to sip it, but the coffee was so hot that it burned his lips, and he set the cup on the tray, discouraged.

"I'm so thirsty!" he repeated. "If only I could drink a little water."

The other two girls disappeared behind a screen and returned quickly with two full trays.

"Baba sent you sweets," said one of them.

"Rose jam and sherbet," added the other.

But Gavrilescu caught a glimpse of the jug full of water, and although he saw beside it the large bottle-green glass, he gulped, seized the jug with both hands and lifted it to his mouth. Gurgling, he drank for a long time, with his head thrown back. Then he sighed, set the jug on the tray, and took one of the handkerchiefs from his pocket.

"Ladies!" he announced, starting to wipe his forehead. "I was very thirsty. I have heard of someone, Colonel Lawrence …"

The girls looked at each other knowingly, then all three burst into laughter. This time they laughed whole-heartedly, and with more and more spirit. At first Gavrilescu looked at them in wonder, then a broad smile lit his face, and finally he also began to laugh. For some time he continued to wipe his face with his handkerchief.

"If you don't mind telling me … I'd like to ask …" he said at last. "I'm curious to know what amused you."

"We laughed because you called us ladies," said one of the girls.

"And here we are at the Gypsies' ..."

"That's not true!" another interrupted her. "Don't pay attention to her, she wants to trick you. We laughed because you were confused and you drank from the jug instead of from the glass. If you had drunk from the glass ..."

"Don't listen to her!" interrupted the third girl. "She wants to deceive you, too. I shall tell you the truth: we laughed because you were afraid."

"That's not true, that's not true!" the other two broke in. "She wants to test you, to find out if you *were* afraid."

"He *was* afraid! He *was* afraid!" repeated all three.

Gavrilescu took a step forward and raised his arm solemnly.

"Ladies!" he cried in an injured tone. "I see that you don't know with whom you are dealing. I am not just anyone. I am Gavrilescu, artist; and before coming here, for my sins, a poor piano teacher, I lived in a poet's dream, Ladies," he exclaimed, pathetically, after a pause, "at the age of twenty I knew I was in love, and I loved Hildegard!"

One of the girls moved an armchair near him and Gavrilescu sat down with a deep sigh.

"Ah!" he began after a long silence. "Why do you remind me of the tragedy of my life? Because, you understand, Hildegard never became my wife. Something happened, something terrible happened ..."

The girl handed him his cup of coffee and Gavrilescu began to sip it thoughtfully.

"Something terrible happened ..." he resumed finally. "But what? What could have happened? It's strange that I can't remember. It is true, I haven't thought of Hildegard for very many years. I became accustomed to the fact. I told myself: Gavrilescu, what's done is done! Artists are like that, unfortunately. Then suddenly, just before coming in here to you, I remembered that I also have known a noble passion. I recalled that I loved Hildegard!"

A glance passed between the girls, and they started to applaud.

"I was entirely right," said the third girl. "He was afraid."

Gavrilescu raised his eyes and regarded them with a long, melancholy stare. "I don't understand what you mean ..."

"You are afraid," uttered one of the girls in challenge, taking a step in his direction. "You were afraid when you came in ..."

"That is why you were so thirsty," the second one spoke up.

"And then you turned to talking continually," added the other.

"You have chosen us, but you are afraid to guess us."

"I don't understand at all," Gavrilescu attempted an appeal.

"You must guess us first," continued the third girl. "Guess who is the Gypsy, who is the Greek, who is the Jew ..."

"Try it now, if you say that you are not afraid," the second girl resumed. "Guess who is the Gypsy?"

"Who is the Gypsy? Who is the Gypsy?" like an echo, Gavrilescu heard the voices of the other two.

He smiled, and examined them again with a searching look.

"I like this," he began, feeling suddenly well-disposed. "I must say, if you realize that I am an artist, you probably think my head's in the clouds—that I wouldn't even know how to point out a Gypsy ..."

"Don't change the subject," interrupted one of the girls. "Guess us!"

"I must say," resumed Gavrilescu, obstinately. "You think that I don't have enough imagination to guess how to recognize a Gypsy, especially when she's young, beautiful, and naked ..."

Surely, then, when he looked at them, he could not fail. That one who had taken a step toward him, who was entirely naked, very dark, with black hair and eyes—she was without a doubt the Gypsy. The second, also naked, but draped in a sheer pale-green veil, had a body unnaturally white and shining like mother of pearl, while golden slippers adorned her feet. She could be no other than the Greek.

Unquestionably the third girl was Jewish. She wore a long skirt of dark red velvet, whose tight bodice revealed her bared breasts, while her rich hair, burning red, was gathered and plaited in a crown on the top of her head.

"Guess us! Which one's the Gypsy? Which one's the Gypsy?" cried all three.

Gavrilescu rose from the armchair and extending his hand toward the naked girl with a stern expression on his face, uttered solemnly: "Because I am an artist, I suppose I must take even this childish game seriously, and I respond: *You* are the Gypsy!"

In the next moment, he felt his hands grasped, and the girls began to whirl him around in a ring, shrieking and uttering shrill, high-pitched sounds in voices that seemed to come from a great distance.

"You didn't guess! You didn't guess!" he heard as if in a dream.

He tried to stop, to pull away from those hands which were whirling him about so tempestuously, as if in a fey dance, but it was beyond his power to disengage himself. The warm scent of their young bodies and their exotic perfume reached his nostrils remotely; and he heard on the carpet the rhythmic beat of the girls' dancing feet all around him and at the same time throbbing through him. He felt borne lightly by the dance, among the armchairs and screens, toward the back of the room, but after a while, ceasing to resist further, he was no longer aware of anything.

Awakening, his glance fell on the naked dark girl as she knelt on the carpet in front of the divan, and he sat up.

"Did I sleep long?" he asked her.

"You have not really been sleeping," the girl said soothingly. "Perhaps you were dozing."

"But, my God, what have you done to me?" he asked, lifting his hand to his forehead. "I feel quite giddy."

He looked around him in astonishment. It seemed as if he were no longer in the same room, and yet he recognized, located asymmetrically among the armchairs, divans, and mirrors, the screens which had so impressed him on entering. He could not comprehend their arrangement. Some very tall ones, almost touching the ceiling, he would have confused with the walls, if, here and there, they had not been bent toward the middle of the room, forming sharp corners. Others, mysteriously illuminated, seemed like windows, half covered with curtains, opening into interior corridors. Still more screens of many colours and curiously painted, or covered with shawls and embroideries that tumbled in folds indistinguishably onto the carpets, formed, so to speak, in the manner in which they were arranged, alcoves of various shapes and sizes. But a few moments closer examination of one such alcove was quite enough for him to understand that it was an illusion, that in fact what he saw was two or three separate screens, which, reflected in a large mirror like green-gold water, seemed to be joined together. Just at the moment when he recognized this illusion, Gavrilescu felt the room begin to whirl about him, and he raised his hand again to his forehead.

"My God, what did you do to me?" he repeated.

"You didn't guess," whispered the girl smiling sadly. "And yet I signalled to you with my eyes that I was not the Gypsy. I am the Greek."

"Greece!" exclaimed Gavrilescu, rising abruptly to his feet. "Eternal Greece!"

His fatigue dropped from him as if he were under some spell. He heard his heart begin to beat faster, and an indescribable beatitude flooded his body with a feeling of warmth and exhilaration.

"When I was in love with Hildegard," he continued, exalted, "we dreamed only of that—to go together on a journey to Greece."

"You are a fool," the girl interrupted him. "You should not dream, you should love."

"I was twenty years old and she had not quite reached eighteen. She was beautiful. We were both beautiful," he added.

He noticed then that he was dressed in a strange costume with full Turkish trousers and a short tunic of yellow-gold silk. He looked, wondering, in the mirror, recognizing himself with difficulty.

"We dreamed of going to Greece," he resumed finally, his voice more subdued. "No, it was much more than a dream, it was something that became very real, because we decided to leave for Greece very soon after the wedding. And then something happened … but what? In God's name, what happened?" he said to himself after a pause, raising his hands to his temples. It was like this, a hot day like today, a terribly hot summer day. I saw a bench and went directly toward it, and then I felt the heat striking my head, striking me like a sword on the top of my head … No, that is the story of Colonel Lawrence, that I learned today from the students while waiting for the tram. Ah, if I could only have a piano!" he broke off, despairingly.

The girl raised herself nimbly from the carpet, and taking his hand, said to him softly, "Come with me!"

He followed rapidly after her among the screens and mirrors and after some time their steps became more and more rapid, so that Gavrilescu soon felt that he was running, and wanted to stop a minute to catch his breath, but the girl would not allow it.

"It is late," she whispered as they ran, and again her voice seemed like a faint sibilance, coming to him from very far away.

But this time he did not grow giddy, although in his flight he had to avoid innumerable divans and soft pillows, and chests, as well as trunks covered with carpeting, and mirrors large and small cut now and then into strange shapes and sizes, which appeared suddenly before them, apparently standing isolated on the carpet. Quite unexpectedly, as they went out of a kind of corridor composed of two rows of screens, they entered a large and sunny room. There, leaning against a piano, the other two girls were waiting for him.

"What made you so late?" the girl with the red hair asked them. "The coffee is cold."

Gavrilescu drew a deep breath and taking a step toward her flung both arms high, defensively.

"Oh, no," he said. "I can't drink any more. I have had too much coffee already. Ladies, although I am an artist, I lead a well-regulated life. I don't like to waste my time in coffee-houses."

But the girl, giving no indication that she had heard him, turned toward the Greek.

"What made you so late?" she asked again.

"He remembered Hildegard."

"He shouldn't have been allowed to," spoke up the third girl.

"I beg your pardon. Permit me …" intervened Gavrilescu, approaching the piano. "This is a strictly personal question. No one can prevent me. It was the tragedy of my life."

"Now he is starting over again," said the red-headed girl. "Again he is confused."

"Permit me!" Gavrilescu broke in. "I am not at all confused. It *was* the tragedy of my life. I recalled it as I came in here. Listen!" he exclaimed, moving nearer to the piano." I shall play something for you and then you will understand it."

"He mustn't be allowed to do it," he heard the two girls whispering. "Now he will never guess us."

For a few moments Gavrilescu was lost in concentration, then he bent his shoulders over the keys, and poised his hands for a brilliant attack.

"I have remembered!" he exclaimed suddenly. "I know what happened!"

Nervously, he got up from his chair and began to pace the floor, head bent, looking at the carpet.

"Now I know," he repeated many times, in a whisper. "It was just like now, during the summer. Hildegard had gone with her family to Konigsberg. It was terribly hot. I lived in Charlottenburg, and I went out to walk under the trees. They were tall old trees with thick shade. And it was deserted. It was very hot. No one dared to go out of the house. And there, under the trees, I caught sight of a young girl who was sobbing, crying with her face buried in her hands. And I was astonished, because she had taken off her shoes and propped up her feet on a little valise that stood before her on the gravel. 'Gavrilescu,' I said to myself, 'there is an unhappy human being.' She seemed so innocent!"

He stopped walking and turned abruptly toward the girls.

"Ladies!" he exclaimed pathetically. "I was young, I was goodlooking, and I had the soul of an artist. It broke my heart to see a girl abandoned in that way. I stood and spoke to her, I tried to console her. Thus began the tragedy of my life."

"And now what is to be done?" asked the girl with the red hair, speaking to the others.

"Wait a bit and see what Baba says," the Greek girl suggested.

"If we wait longer he will never guess us," said the third girl.

"Yes, the tragedy of my life," continued Gavrilescu. "Her name was Elsa. But I was resigned. I said to myself, 'Gavrilescu, it was meant to be.' What a bad time! This is the lot of artists, to be without luck ..."

"You see," the red-headed girl said again. "Now he is confused again."

"Ah, destiny!" exclaimed Gavrilescu, lifting both arms high in the air and turning toward the Greek.

She looked at him with a smile, clasping her arms behind her back.

"Eternal Greece!" he exclaimed, "Never will I see you!"

"Stop it! Stop it!" cried the other two girls coming up to him. "Remember that you chose *us*!"

"A Gypsy, a Greek, a Jew," said the Greek looking meaningfully, deeply into his eyes.

"This is what you wished. You have chosen us."

"Guess us!" cried the girl with the red hair. "And you will see how beautiful it will be!"

"Who is the Gypsy? Who is the Gypsy?" asked all three, suddenly surrounding him.

Gavrilescu retreated quickly and leaned against the piano.

"You mean ..." he began after a pause. "So this is your scheme, here at your place. Artist or common mortal, you've got to guess the Gypsy. And why, please? Who gives the order?"

"This is our game, here at the Gypsies'!" the Greek girl said. "Try to guess. You won't be sorry."

"But I am not in the mood for games," continued Gavrilescu with fervour. "I have remembered the tragedy of my life. Because, you see, now I understand very well: if, on that evening in Charlottenburg, I had not gone with Elsa into the bistro ... or, even if I had gone in, but if I had had money with me, and had been able to pay for what I consumed, my life would have been different. But it happened that I had no money, and Elsa paid. And the second day I walked everywhere, looking for somebody who would lend me the money to pay my debt. But I found no one. All my friends, all my acquaintances had gone on vacation. It was summer, it was terribly hot ..."

"Again, he is afraid," whispered the girl with the red hair, bending over and glancing at the carpet.

"Listen, I have not told you everything," cried Gavrilescu, pleading. "In three days I didn't find any money and I went every evening to see Elsa at her hotel, to apologize for not having the money. And then we went together to the bistro. If only I had been strong, and refrained from going with her to the bistro! But what would you have had me do? I was hungry. I was young, good-looking. Hildegard was away at the baths, and—I was hungry! I tell you truly, there were days when I went to bed without any dinner. That is the life of an artist ..."

"And now what do we do?" the girls questioned him. "For time passes, time passes."

"Now?" exclaimed Gavrilescu, holding out his arms again. It is good and hot. I like being here with you, you are young and beautiful, and you stay here with me, ready to serve me with sweets and coffee. But I am not thirsty any more. Now I feel good, I feel perfect, and I tell myself, 'Gavrilescu, these girls expect you to do something for them. Please them; If you must guess them, guess them. But be careful, Gavrilescu, if you fail again, they will dance with you and you won't wake up again today.'"

Smiling, he went around the piano in such a way that it formed a barrier between him and the girls.

"That is to say, you wish me to tell you who is the Gypsy. Very well I'll have to tell you ..."

The girls lined up excitedly, without a word, looking into his eyes.

"I have to tell you ..." he resumed after a pause. Then he pointed abruptly and melodramatically toward the girl in the pale green veil, and waited. The girls stood like statues, incredulous.

"What has he done?" the red-headed one asked at last. "Why can't he guess?"

"Something happened to him," said the Greek girl. "He remembered something, and was distracted; he rambled in the past."

The girl he had pointed out as the Gypsy stepped forward, took the tray with the coffee, and passing by the piano, whispered, with a sad smile: "I am the Jew." Then she disappeared silently behind a screen.

"Ah!" exclaimed Gavrilescu, striking his forehead with the palm of his hand. "I should have known. She had a far-away look in her eyes. And that veil she was wearing; it was really a veil—but it revealed everything! It was thus in the *Old Testament*."

Suddenly the girl with red hair burst into laughter. "You did not guess, sir!" she cried, "you did not guess the Gypsy!"

She passed her hand through her hair and shaking it several times, let the red braids fall down over her shoulders. She began to dance, whirling slowly around in a circle, clapping her hands and singing.

"Say, girl of Greece, how would it have been?" cried she, shaking her braids.

"If you had guessed her, it would have been very beautiful," whispered the Greek. "We should have sung to you and danced for you, and taken you through all the rooms. It would have been very beautiful."

"It would have been very beautiful," repeated Gavrilescu, with a sad smile.

"Tell him, girl of Greece!" cried the Gypsy, stopping in front of them, but continuing to clap her hands rhythmically and tapping more and more vigorously with her bare foot on the carpet.

The Greek girl crept close to him and began to talk. She spoke quickly, in a whisper, shaking her head now and then, or putting her fingers to her mouth, but Gavrilescu was unable to understand her. He listened to her, smiling, looking about him absently, whispering at intervals, "It would have been beautiful ..." He kept hearing the Gypsy's foot tapping the carpet with a dull sound, subterranean, until the strange wild rhythm seemed beyond his power to endure, and then, with an effort, he rushed to the piano and began to play.

"Now, you also tell him, Gypsy!" cried the Greek.

He heard the Gypsy girl as she approached, as though she were dancing on a gigantic bronze drum, and a few moments later he felt on his back a fiery breath. Gavrilescu bent lower over the piano, and his hands pounded with all his strength, almost with fury, as if he wished to break the keys, to tear them out, and to dig with his nails a hiding place for himself in the belly of the piano, and so to be further away, deeper inside.

He thought no more of anything, save the stolen melodies that seemed new, unrecognized, to which he listened as though for the first time; although as they came one after another into his mind, they hinted at something remembered vaguely from much earlier times. Somewhat later he stopped. He noticed that he alone remained in the room, and that it had become almost dark.

"Where are you?" he cried, rising frightened from the stool.

He hesitated a few moments then went toward the screen behind which the Jewish girl had disappeared.

"Where are you hiding?" he cried again.

Slowly, walking on tiptoes, as though he wished to take them by surprise, he crept behind the screen. Here he was astonished to see that another room began, and it seemed to lengthen into a winding hall. It was a curious room, formed by the squat and irregular screens, and slightly undulating walls, which kept disappearing and reappearing in the darkness.

Gavrilescu took several tentative steps, then stopped to listen. It seemed that even in that moment, he heard rustling and hurrying steps on the carpet, passing very near him.

"Where are you?" he called.

He listened to the echo, trying to penetrate the darkness with his gaze. He thought that he perceived them, all three, hidden in a corner of the corridor, and he set out toward them with his arms extended in front of him, groping. But after some time he realized that the direction that he had taken was wrong, for he discovered the hall opening out for several meters on the left, and he stopped again.

"You are hiding in vain; I am sure to find you!" he cried. "You had better show yourselves willingly."

Then he listened, tense, with his eyes upon the corridor. He heard nothing more. But here he began to feel the heat, and decided to return and wait for them at the piano, playing it. He remembered very well the direction from which he had come, and knew that he had not taken many more than twenty to thirty steps. He extended his arms and advanced slowly and cautiously. But after a few steps his hands touched a screen, and a few moments later he drew back frightened, realizing that the screen had not been there before.

"What has come over you?" he cried. "Let me go!"

He seemed to hear subdued laughter again and rustling, and then he took courage.

"Perhaps you think that I am afraid," he began after a short pause, forcing himself to appear more composed. "Permit me, permit me! ..." he added hastily as though he expected to be interrupted.

"If I have consented to play your game of hide and seek with you, I have done it because I take pity on you. That is the truth: I take pity on you. I saw you in the beginning, innocent children, closed up here in a cottage at the Gypsies', and I said to myself, 'Gavrilescu, these girls want to play a trick on you. Let them think that you have been taken in. Let them believe that you do not know how to guess who the Gypsy is.' That's the game! That is the game!" he cried as loudly as he could.

"And now that we have played enough, come out into the light."

He listened, smiling, with his right hand resting on the screen. At that moment, very near him, he heard footsteps running away in the darkness. Suddenly he turned and extended his arms in front of him.

"Whom did I touch?"

But after he had turned around many times, flinging his arms about aimlessly, he stopped to listen, and this time he did not hear the slightest sound anywhere.

"Never mind," he said, expecting to meet the girls hidden in the darkness after a few more steps. "I'll wait. I see you don't know yet with whom you have to deal. Later, you will be sorry for it. I could teach you to play the piano. You would be enriched by musical culture. I would interpret for you the *Lieder* of Schumann. What beauty!" he exclaimed fervently. "What divine music!"

Again he felt the heat, more oppressive than before, and he began to wipe his face with the sleeve of his tunic. Then, discouraged, he set out toward the left, feeling his way continually along the screen. He stopped at intervals and listened, then set forth again, hastening his steps.

"You certainly put me in mind of children!" he burst out suddenly, seized abruptly with rage. "Pardon! I said children from politeness. You are something else. You know well what you are. You are Gypsies. Without any culture. Illiterate. Which of you knows where Arabia is? Which of you has heard of Colonel Lawrence?"

The screen seemed to have no end. He knew not how much lay ahead, and the heat became even more insufferable. He took off the tunic, and after wiping his face and the back of his neck furiously, he put it over his bare shoulder, like a towel, and groped again with his hands, searching for the screen. But this time he found a wall, smooth and cool, and he pressed himself against it, extending both arms. He stayed for some time in this position against the wall, breathing deeply. Then slowly he began to move without leaving the wall, dragging himself along it. Some time later he discovered that he had lost the tunic, and because he was sweating constantly he stopped, took off the trousers and began to wipe his face and his whole body. Just then something seemed to touch his shoulder; he leaped frightened to one side, with a short outcry.

"Let me go!" he exclaimed. "I tell you, let me go!"

Again someone, some thing, a nameless being or object, touched his face, his shoulders; and then he began blindly whirling the trousers around and around above his head. It was getting hotter and hotter. He felt drops of sweat running down his cheeks and he was breathing heavily. All at once the trousers slipped from his hand, snatched away unexpectedly, disappearing somewhere far off in the darkness. Gavrilescu remained a moment with arms raised, clenching his fists spasmodically, hoping that he would find, momentarily, that he was mistaken, that he still held the trousers in his hand. Suddenly he felt naked and shrank crouching, bowing his head, with his hands on the carpet, like a runner preparing to take off at full speed.

Groping with the palms of his hands on the carpet around him, he started to go forward, hoping fervently that he might find the trousers. Here and there he discovered objects that he found difficult to identify. Some he thought at first resembled small boxes, but when he ran his hands over them, they proved to be large gourds enveloped in kerchiefs; others which seemed to be cushions or bolsters from the divan, appeared on closer inspection to be bowls or old umbrellas filled with bran, or clothes baskets full of newspapers. He could not quite decide just what they might be, since he kept running across other objects in front of him, and his attention turned to them. Now and then large pieces of furniture loomed in front of him. Gavrilescu avoided them prudently since he did not recognize their forms and was afraid of overturning them.

He could not tell how long he went on in this manner, crawling on his knees, or dragging himself on his belly in the darkness. He gave up all hope of finding the trousers. That which vexed him the most was the heat. He felt like he was crawling over the tin roof of a house on an extremely torrid afternoon. He felt the air in his nostrils grow hot, and the objects he touched burned him. His whole body was wet with sweat, and at times he had to stop to rest. Then he stretched out as much as he was able, extending his feet and hands in the form of a cross, face down, his cheeks sticking to the carpet, breathing deeply, panting, greatly agitated.

Once it seemed to him that he dozed, awakened by an unexpected breath of fresh air, as though a window had been opened somewhere, letting in the coolness of the night. He was immediately aware, however, that this was not so, but that it was something else, something he could not explain, and for a moment he lay baffled, feeling his sweating back grow cool. After that he could not remember what happened. He was too frightened to call out because of what it might bring forth, and he came to his senses as he was running frantically in the darkness, bumping into a screen, knocking over mirrors and all manner of little objects strangely scattered about the carpet, frequently tripping and falling, but getting up quickly and setting out again in flight. When he surprised himself by leaping over boxes and going around the mirrors and screens, he realized that he had entered into an area of half-light in which he began to distinguish contours. At the end of the hall a window appeared to open, unusually high up in the wall, allowing the glow of the summer twilight to float in. When he entered the corridor the heat became unbearable. He had to stop in order to breathe, and with the palms of both hands he wiped the sweat from his forehead and cheeks. He heard his heart beating as though it would burst. Going on ahead he arrived in front of the window where he stopped again, frightened. Voices came to him, and laughter, and the noise of chairs dragging on the inlaid floor, as if an entire group of people was rising from the table and coming toward him. At that moment he saw his naked body, thinner than he had known it to be, with bones protruding through his skin, and his abdomen swollen and drooping, as he had never before seen himself. There was no time to turn back. By chance his hands found a drapery and he began to draw it about himself.

He thought it would be easy to pull it down, and propping his feet against the wall, he leaned back with all his weight. But then something unexpected happened. He began to feel the drapery drawing him toward it, with increasing power, so that in a few moments he found himself stuck against the wall; and although he tried to undo himself, pulling at the drapery with his hands, he was not successful. Very soon he felt himself wrapped up, squeezed tightly all over, like being tied and thrust into a sack. Again it was dark and very hot, and Gavrilescu realized that he could not hold out much longer, that he would suffocate. He tried to cry out, but his throat was dry, wooden, and what sounds he could produce seemed as if smothered in felt.

* * *

He heard a voice that he seemed to recognize.

"Say something, sir, tell me more."

"What more is there to say to you?" he whispered. "I have told you everything. That was all. I came with Elsa to Bucharest. We were both poor. I began to give piano lessons ..."

He raised his head slightly from the pillow and looked at the old woman. She was seated at the small table with the carafe of coffee in her hand, ready to fill the cups again.

"No, thank you, I can't drink any more," he said, raising his hand in protest. "I have drunk enough coffee. I'm afraid that I won't get any sleep tonight."

The old woman filled her cup, then set the carafe on a corner of the table.

"Tell me more," she insisted. "What else did you do? What did they do? What else happened?"

Gavrilescu remained a long time in thought, fanning himself with his hat.

"Then we began to play hide and seek," his voice changed suddenly, and he spoke somewhat harshly. "They surely didn't know with whom they had to deal. I am a serious man, an artist, a piano teacher. I came in here simply from curiosity. I'm interested in things that are new and unusual. I told myself, 'Gavrilescu, here is an occasion for enriching your knowledge.' I didn't know it would be a question of naive and childish games. Imagine! I saw myself suddenly naked, and heard voices. I was sure that from one moment to the next … You understand what I'm trying to say?"

The old woman nodded her head and sipped the coffee languidly.

"What a time we had looking for your hat," said she. "The girls hunted all over the cottage until they found it."

"Yes, I recognize it; it was my fault," continued Gavrilescu. "I didn't know that if I didn't guess them by daylight, I'd have to look for them, catch them, and guess them in the dark. No one told me anything about that. And, I repeat, when I saw myself naked, and felt the drapery wrap itself around me like a shroud—I give you my word of honour that it was like a shroud …"

"What a time we had putting your clothes on you!" said the old woman. "You didn't want us to dress you at all."

"I tell you, that drapery was like a shroud, it wound all around me; it wrapped me up and squeezed me until I couldn't breathe any more. And it was hot!" he exclaimed, fanning himself more vigorously with his hat. It's a wonder I didn't suffocate!"

"Yes, it was very hot," said the old woman.

At that moment he heard, far off, the metallic grinding of the tramway. Gavrilescu raised his hand to his forehead.

"Ah!" he exclaimed standing up with difficulty near the sofa.

"How time flies! Here I am talking, and with one thing and another, I forgot that I have to go to Preoteselor Street. Can you imagine that I forgot my portfolio with the scores? I told myself this afternoon, 'Gavrilescu, take care, it seems as if ... as if ...' Yes ... I told myself something like this, but I don't quite remember what ..."

He took several steps toward the door, then turned, shrugged his shoulders slightly, and said, lifting his hat, "I'm glad to have made your acquaintance."

In the courtyard he was unpleasantly surprised. Although the sun had set, it was hotter than it had been in mid-afternoon. Gavrilescu took off his coat and slung it over his shoulder; and continuing to fan himself with his hat, he crossed the courtyard and went out. Leaving the tree-shadowed wall, he again encountered the intense heat of the pavement, and the odor of dust and softened asphalt. He walked dejectedly, his shoulders drooping, intermittently glancing up ahead of him. At the stop no one else was waiting. When he heard the tram approaching, he raised his arm and signalled it with his hand.

The car was almost empty and all the windows were open. He sat down in front of a young man in shirt-sleeves, and when he saw the conductor coming, he began to look for his coin purse. He found it sooner than he had expected.

"This weather is most unusual!" he exclaimed. "I give you my word of honour that it is worse than in Arabia. Perhaps you have heard of Colonel Lawerence ..."

The young man smiled absently, then turned his face toward the window.

"And what would be the time?" asked Gavrilescu of the conductor.

"Five after eight."

"Just my luck! I'll find them at dinner. They'll think I came so late on purpose in order to have dinner. You understand, it wouldn't be right for them to think that ... You understand what I mean? On the other hand, if I tell them where I was Madame Voitinovici is so curious, she'll keep me there talking until midnight."

The conductor smiled at him, and winked at the youth.

"Just say that you were at the Gypsies', and you'll see she won't ask you anything more."

"Oh, no. Impossible! I know her well. She has so much curiosity. It would be better not to say anything."

At the following stop several young couples got on and Gavrilescu moved near to them so that he could better hear what they were saying. When he found an opportunity to enter into their discussion, he quickly raised his arm.

"If you will permit me—I must contradict you. I, for my sins, am a piano teacher, but I was not made for that ..."

"Preoteselor Street," he heard the conductor announce, and standing up suddenly, he bowed and hurriedly traversed the length of the aisle.

He set out slowly, fanning himself with his hat. In front of number 18 he stopped, arranged his tie, ran his hand through his hair, and entered. Slowly he climbed the stairs to the first floor, then rang the bell. A few moments later the youth from the tram arrived.

"What a coincidence!" exclaimed Gavrilescu, seeing the youth stop nearby.

The door opened suddenly and on the threshold appeared a woman still young, but with cheeks pale and withered. She was wearing a kitchen apron, and in her left hand she held a jar of mustard. Looking at Gavrilescu, she frowned.

"What is it?" she asked.

"I forgot my portfolio," Gavrilescu began timidly. "I was talking and I forgot it. I had to go through town and couldn't come earlier."

"I don't understand. What kind of portfolio?"

"If you are already at dinner, don't disturb yourselves," Gavrilescu continued hastily. "1 know where I left it. It is near the piano." And he tried to go in, but the woman would not move from the doorway.

"What do you want, Domnule?"

"Madame Voitinovici. I am Gavrilescu, Otilia's piano teacher. I have not had the pleasure of meeting you," he added politely.

"You have the wrong address," said the woman. "This is number 18."

"Permit me ..." Gavrilescu began again, smiling. "I have known this apartment for five years. You might say that I'm part of the family. I come here three times a week."

Leaning against the wall, the young man listened to the conversation.

"What did you say her name is?" he asked Gavrilescu.

"Madame Voitinovici. She's Otilia's aunt. Otilia Pandele ..."

"She doesn't live here," the youth interrupted him. "We live here, the Georgescu family. She, the lady in front of you, is my father's wife. She was born a Petrescu ..."

"Please be more polite," said the woman. "And don't embarrass me in front of all kinds of people!"

Then she turned her back and disappeared into the hall.

"Please excuse this scene," said the youth, trying to smile. "She is my father's third wife. She carries on her shoulders all the mistakes of former marriages—five boys and a girl."

Gavrilescu listened to him, troubled, fanning himself with his hat.

"I'm sorry," he began, "I'm very sincerely sorry. I didn't mean to upset her. Truly, it isn't a proper time to come. It's time for dinner. But you see, tomorrow morning I have a lesson in Spirii Hill. I need my portfolio. I have Czerny II and III in it. They are my scores, with my important personal interpretations in the margins. I always carry them with me."

The youth, still smiling, looked at him.

"I don't think I have made myself clear," he interrupted. "What I am trying to tell you is that *we* live here, the Georgescu family. We've lived here for four years."

"Impossible!" exclaimed Gavrilescu. "I was here a few hours ago. I gave Otilia a lesson from two to three. Then I chatted with Madame Voitinovici."

"In number 18, Preoteselor Street, first floor?" astonished, the young man smiled in amusement.

"Exactly. I know the house very well. I can tell you where the piano is. I could lead you there with my eyes closed. It is in the living room near the window!"

"We have no piano," said the young man. "Try another floor. Although I assure you, you won't find her on the second floor either. The family of Captain Zamfir lives there. Try the third. I'm sorry," he added, seeing that Gavrilescu appeared to be frightened, fanning himself with his hat in great agitation. "I should like it if an Otilia did live in this house ..."

Gavrilescu hesitated, staring into the youth's eyes.

"Thank you," he said finally. "I'll try the third floor. Although I give you my word of honour that at a quarter after three I was here ..." and he extended his arm emphatically, pointing along the hallway.

He began to climb, breathing hard. On the third floor he wiped his face for a long time with a handkerchief, then rang the bell. He could hear the sound of little feet approaching, and soon a small boy of about five or six years opened the door.

"Ah!" exclaimed Gavrilescu. "I am afraid I have confused the floors. I'm looking for Madame Voitinovici ..."

A young woman appeared in the doorway, smiling at him, "Madame Voitinovici lived on the first floor," she said, "but she moved. She went to the country."

"Has she been gone long?"

"Oh, yes, quite long! In autumn it will be eight years. She went as soon as Otilia was married."

Gavrilescu brought his hand to his forehead and began to rub it.

Then he cast a glance at the woman with a meek smile.

"I think you are somewhat confused," he began. "I mean Otilia Pandele, in class 6-a at the high school, the niece of Madame Voitinovici."

"I knew both of them well," said the woman." When we ourselves moved here, Otilia had just become engaged. You know, at first she was involved with that Major. Madame Voitinovici would not give her consent, and she was right, there was too great a difference in their ages. Otilia was a child, not yet nineteen. Happily, she met Frâncu, the engineer Frâncu. Perhaps you have heard of him?"

"The engineer Frâncu?" repeated Gavrilescu. "Frâncu?"

"Yes, the inventor. He wrote for the newspapers ..."

"The inventor Frâncu," repeated Gavrilescu, dazed. "How strange!"

Then he stretched out his hand, patted the boy on the head, and, bowing slightly, he said, "Please pardon me. I think I have confused the floors."

The young man was waiting for him, smoking, leaning against the wall.

"Did you find out anything?" the youth asked.

"The lady upstairs claims that she is married, but I assure you that it is most confusing. Otilia is not even seventeen. She is in Class 6-a in high school. I stood and talked with Madame Voitinovici. We spoke of many things, and she didn't say a word about it."

"That's strange."

"It's very strange," said Gavrilescu, taking courage. "I tell you, I don't believe it. I give you my word of honour. But I give up, it's no use to insist. Everything is very confused. I'll have to come again tomorrow morning."

And with a bow, he started to descend the stairs with determination.

"Gavrilescu," he whispered, as soon as he reached the street, "Take care, you are beginning to get weak-minded. You are losing your memory. Confusing addresses ..."

He noticed the tram approaching and hastened his steps. As he seated himself at the open window, he felt a light breeze.

"At last," he exclaimed, addressing the woman in front of him. "It seems ... it seems as if ..." but he smiled in confusion, not knowing how to finish his sentence. "Yes," he resumed, after a short pause. "Lately, I told a friend, it seems as if I were in Arabia. Colonel Lawrence, if you have heard of him ..."

The lady continued to look out of the window.

"Now, at this time, between one and two," Gavrilescu began again. "It is finally night. Dark, I mean. The coolness of the night ... at last ... one can breathe ..."

The conductor stopped in front of him, waiting, and Gavrilescu began to look through his pockets.

"After midnight, one can breathe," he said to the conductor.

"What a long day!" he added, slightly nervous, when he did not succeed in finding his wallet. "What a sudden turn of fortune! ... Ah, at last," he exclaimed, and opened it quickly.

"This is not used any more," the conductor said, handing the bill back to him. "Exchange it at the bank."

"But what's the matter with it?" wondered Gavrilescu, turning the bill in his fingers.

"They took it out of circulation a year ago. Change it at the bank."

"How curious!" said Gavrilescu, looking at the bill more closely. "This morning it was good. And the Gypsies took them. I had three like this and the Gypsies took them all ..."

The lady went slightly pale, and rising ostentatiously moved to the other end of the tram.

"One mustn't speak of the Gypsies in front of a lady," the conductor rebuked him.

"Everyone talks," Gavrilescu defended himself. "I travel three times a week on this tram, and I give you my word of honour ..."

"Yes, it's true," a passenger intervened. "We all talk, but not in front of the ladies. It's a question of good manners. Especially now that they have made them light the place. Yes, yes, the city consented, but they have to light the garden. I, I can tell you, am a man without prejudice, but lighting the Gypsies' place I consider to be a provocation."

"That's strange," said Gavrilescu. "I heard nothing about it."

"It was in all the newspapers," intervened another passenger. "It's a disgrace!" he exclaimed, raising his voice. "It shouldn't be allowed!"

Several people turned their heads, and under their reproving glances, Gavrilescu turned away his eyes.

"Look again, maybe you have some other money," said the conductor. "If not, get off at the next stop."

Blushing, not daring to raise his eyes, Gavrilescu began again to search through his pockets. Happily, his coin purse was right on top among the handkerchiefs. Gavrilescu counted out some money and handed it to the conductor.

"You have given me only five lei," the conductor said, showing it to him in his hand.

"Yes, to Vama Poștei."

"It doesn't matter where you are going, but the ticket costs ten lei. Where in the world do you live?" added the conductor sternly.

"I live in Bucharest," said Gavrilescu, looking up with pride. "And I ride the tram three to four hours a day, and I have done this, day in and day out, for years, and I've always paid five lei."

By now, almost everyone in the car was listening with interest to the conversation. Several passengers moved nearer, taking the adjacent seats.

The conductor tossed the money in his palm many times, then he said, "If you don't want to give me the rest, get off at the next stop."

"The tram fares have been higher for some three or four years," mentioned someone.

"Five years," corrected the conductor.

"I give you my word of honour," Gavrilescu began, pathetically.

"Then get off at the next stop," the conductor interrupted.

"Better pay the difference," someone advised him. "It's a long walk to Vama Poștei."

Gavrilescu looked in his purse and held out five more lei.

"Strange things are going on in this country," he muttered, after the conductor went away. "They make decisions overnight, in twenty-four hours—more exactly, in six. I give you my word of honour ... Oh, well, what's the use of insisting? It's been a terrible day. And what is more serious, I can't live without the tram. At the least I am forced to travel three to four hours a day by tram. And yet a piano lesson is a hundred lei, a bill such as this. And now even this bill is no good any more. I must go and change it at the bank."

"Give it to me," said an older gentleman. "I'll change it tomorrow at the office."

He took a bill out of his wallet, and held it out. Gavrilescu grasped it with great care, and looked at it attentively.

"It's pretty," he said. "Have they been long in circulation?"

Several of the passengers glanced at each other and smiled.

"About three years," said one.

"It's curious that I haven't seen one until now. Really, I'm quite absent-minded. I am an artist by nature."

He put the bill in his wallet, then allowed himself to glance out of the window.

"So now it is night," he said. "At last!"

Suddenly he felt tired, exhausted, and resting his head on his hand, he closed his eyes. He remained thus until they reached Vama Poștei.

He tried in vain to open the door with his key, then for a long time pressed the button of the bell. After pounding vigorously on the dining-room window, he returned to the front door and began to beat it with his fist. Immediately, at the open window of a neighbouring house there appeared in the darkness a man in a nightshirt who called hoarsely, "What's all the fuss, Domnule? What's come over you?"

"Excuse me," said Gavrilescu. "I don't know what's happened to my wife. She doesn't answer. I've broken my key, and I can't get into the house."

"But why do you want to get in? Who are you?"

Gavrilescu went to the window, and greeted the man. "Although we are neighbours," he began, "I don't think I have had the pleasure of knowing you. My name is Gavrilescu and I live here with my wife, Elsa."

"Then you have the wrong address. Domnul Stănescu lives here, and he is not at home, he's away at the baths."

"Pardon me," Gavrilescu interrupted him. "I'm sorry to have to contradict you, but I think you are confused. Here at number 101 we live, Elsa and I. We have lived here for four years."

"Stop it, gentlemen, at once. We can't sleep!" called someone.

"What in God's name is going on?"

"He pretends to live in Domnul Stănescu's house."

"I'm not pretending," protested Gavrilescu. "This is my house, and I don't allow anyone in it. And above all, I want to know where Elsa is, what has happened to her ..."

"Ask at the police station," spoke up someone upstairs.

Gavrilescu raised his head in fear, "Why at the police station? What has happened?" he cried excitedly. "Do you know something?"

"I don't know anything except that I wish to sleep. And if you are going to stand there all night and talk ..."

"Pardon me," said Gavrilescu. "I also need sleep. I am, I can tell you, very tired ... I have had a terrible day. The heat is almost Arabian. But I don't understand what has happened to Elsa. Why doesn't she answer? Maybe she has fainted!" And returning to the front door of number 101, he began again to pound with his fist even harder.

"Haven't I told you, Domnule, that he is not at home? That Domnul Stănescu has gone to the baths?"

"Call the police!" the sharp voice of a woman was heard. "Call the police right now!"

Gavrilescu stopped abruptly and leaned against the door, breathing hard. Suddenly he felt very tired and he sat down on the step, his head in his hands. "Gavrilescu," he whispered, "Something very serious has happened, and they won't tell you. Think hard, try to remember."

"Madame Trandafir!" he exclaimed. "I should have thought of her at the start. Madame Trandafir!" he called, standing up and going toward the house facing him.

Someone who was still at his window, said in a more subdued voice, "Let her sleep, poor thing."

"It is urgent!"

"Let her sleep, God forgive her, she has been long dead."

"Impossible!" declared Gavrilescu. "I talked with her this morning."

"Perhaps you confuse her with her sister, Ecaterina. Madame Trandafir died five years ago."

Gavrilescu stood for a moment stupefied, then he thrust his hands into his pocket and pulled out several handkerchiefs.

"It's strange," he whispered finally.

He turned slowly, and climbing the three steps of number 101, he picked up his hat and put it on his head. Once more he tried the latch. Then he stepped down and left unsteadily. He walked slowly, without thinking, wiping his face automatically with the handkerchief. The tavern on the corner was still open, and after walking about distractedly he decided to go in.

"We are not serving any more," said the waiter. We close at two."

"At two?" said Gavrilescu, wondering. "But what time is it now?"

"It's two. It's even a little after."

"It's terribly late," Gavrilescu whispered, mostly to himself.

On approaching the counter, he thought he recognized the face of the tavern-keeper, and his heart began to beat faster.

"Aren't you Domnul Costică?" he asked.

"I am," said the tavern-keeper, taking a long look at Gavrilescu. "You look familiar," he added, after a pause.

"It seems … it seems as if …" began Gavrilescu, then he lost the thread of his thought and was silent, smiling in confusion. "I was here many times," he resumed. "I had some friends. Madame Trandafir …"

"Yes, God forgive her …"

"Madame Gavrilescu, Elsa …"

"Oh, what a time she had!" the tavern-keeper interrupted. "I don't know to this day what happened to him. The police searched for several months and couldn't find a trace of him, neither alive nor dead. It was as though he had been swallowed up by the earth. Poor Madame Elsa, she waited and waited for him and finally she went to her family in Germany. She sold her things and left. They didn't have much, they were poor. I myself thought of buying the piano."

"You mean to say she went to Germany?" asked Gavrilescu in a daze. "Did she leave a long time ago?"

"Very, very long ago, a few months after Gavrilescu disappeared. It will be twelve years in autumn. It was written in the newspapers …"

"How strange!" whispered Gavrilescu, beginning to fan himself with his hat. "And if I told you … if I should tell you that this morning—and I give you my word of honour that I don't exaggerate—this very morning I was talking with her— even more, we ate lunch together. I can tell you what I ate …"

"She must have come back," said the tavern-keeper, looking baffled.

"No, she didn't come back. She didn't go away, not at all. Everything is most confusing. Now I'm very tired, but tomorrow morning I shall put things in order …"

Bowing slightly, he went out.

He moved forward slowly, with his hat in one hand and the handkerchief in the other, stopping for a long while at each bench, to drink in the coolness of the gardens. Finally a horse and carriage drew up behind him.

"Where to, sir?" asked the driver.

"To the Gypsies'," answered Gavrilescu.

"Then get in. I will take you for forty lei," said the driver, stopping the carriage.

"I'm sorry, but I don't have much money. I've only a hundred lei left, and a little change; and I'll need the hundred lei to get in to the Gypsies'."

"It's more," said the driver, beginning to laugh. "You won't get in for a hundred lei."

"That's what I paid this afternoon. Good night," he added, starting out again.

But the carriage remained in step with him. The driver took a deep breath. "That is the 'queen of the night'," he said. "It's in the general's garden. That's why I like to come here at night. Customers or no customers, I go by here every night. It's appalling how I love flowers."

"You have the soul of an artist," said Gavrilescu with a smile.

Then he sat down on a bench and waved his hand. But the driver drew up near him and stopped the carriage directly in front of the bench … He took out his tobacco case and began to roll a cigarette.

"I love flowers," he said, "horses and flowers. In my youth I drove a hearse. What beauty! Six horses clothed in black and trimmed in gold, and flowers, flowers, an infinity of flowers. Well, my youth has gone. Everything was taken away. I have become a night cabbie with only one horse."

He lit his cigarette and drew a puff lazily.

"You say you are going to the Gypsies'?" he began at last.

"Yes, it is a personal matter," Gavrilescu hastened to explain. "I was there this afternoon and I left a rather complicated situation."

"Ah, the Gypsies," declared the driver, sadly. "If there were not the Gypsies," he added, lowering his voice. "If there were not ..."

"Yes," said Gavrilescu. "Everyone talks; in the tram, I mean. When it passes in front of the gardens, everyone talks of the Gypsies ..."

He rose from the bench, and started again along the way, with the cab keeping in step with him.

"Let's go this way," said the driver, pointing with his whip to a small street that opened into the road. "This way we pass by the church. The 'queen of the night' is also in flower there. Actually, it's not like that at the general's, but you'll see, you won't be sorry."

"You have the soul of an artist," said Gavrilescu, dreamily.

In front of the church they stopped together to breathe the fragrance of the flowers.

"It seems as though there must be something else as well as 'queen of the night'," said Gavrilescu.

"Ah, there are all kinds of flowers. If you were to be buried today, there are still many flowers. And now, near morning, all these flowers pour out their fragrance anew. We came by here often with the hearse. It was a beautiful sight!"

He gave a short whistle to his horse and moved along with Gavrilescu.

"Now we haven't much farther to go," he said. "Why not get in?"

"I'm sorry, but I haven't the money."

"Just give me the change. Get in ..."

Gavrilescu hesitated a moment, then with an effort he climbed in. But as soon as the cab moved off, he leaned his head against the cushion and fell asleep.

"It was beautiful," began the driver. "The church was rich, and all the people good ... young ..." He turned his head, and seeing that Gavrilescu was sleeping, he began to whistle softly, and the horse quickened his gait.

"Here we are," cried the driver, letting himself down from the carriage. "But the gates are closed ..."

He began to shake Gavrilescu, who awakened with a start.

"The gates are closed," repeated the driver. "You'll have to ring."

Gavrilescu took his hat, arranged his tie, and descended. Then he began to search for his coin purse.

"Don't bother looking," said the cab driver. "Give it to me another time. I may as well wait here," he added. "At this time, if I have any customers at all, they'll all be here."

Gavrilescu lifted his hat, then approaching the gate, he looked for the bell and pushed the button. Just at that moment the gate swung open, and, entering the courtyard, Gavrilescu went toward the hut. In the window he could see a faint light. He knocked timidly on the door, and seeing that no one answered, he lifted the latch and entered. The old woman was sleeping with her head on the low table.

"It is I, Gavrilescu," he said, touching her lightly on the shoulder. "You've made things frightfully complicated for me," he added, seeing that she woke and began to yawn.

"It is late," said the old woman. "There isn't anyone else."

But, after a long look, she recognized him.

"Ah, it's you, the musician. Only the German girl is left. She never sleeps."

Gavrilescu felt his heart beat faster, and shivered slightly.

"A German girl?" he repeated.

"A hundred lei," said the old woman.

Gavrilescu began to search for his wallet, but his hands shook so much that when he found it among the handkerchiefs, it slipped to the floor.

"Forgive me," he said, bending over and straightening up with difficulty. "I am very tired. It was a terrible day ..."

The old woman took the bill, stood up from the stool, and at the doorway pointed out the large house.

"See that you don't get lost," she told him. "Go to the right in the hall and count seven doors, and when you reach the seventh, knock three times and say, 'It is I, Baba sent me.'"

Then she smothered a yawn, covering her mouth with her hand, and closed the door. Breathlessly, Gavrilescu walked slowly toward the house that gleamed silvery beneath the stars. He climbed the marble steps, opened the door, and stood for a moment in indecision. Before him there stretched a dimly lighted hallway, and Gavrilescu again felt his heart begin to pound as though it would break. He began to go forward, deeply moved, counting the doors in a loud voice as he passed them. Presently he noticed that he was counting "thirteen; fourteen," and he stopped, puzzled. "Gavrilescu," he whispered, "be careful. You are complicating things. Not thirteen, not fourteen, but seven. That's what the old woman said, to count seven doors ..."

He wanted to return and start counting again, but after a few steps he felt drained of strength, and stopping in front of the first door at hand, he knocked three times and entered. It was a large and simple, almost poorly furnished, living room. He saw in front of the window, looking toward the garden, a young woman in shadowy silhouette.

"Excuse me," began Gavrilescu with difficulty. "I counted wrong."

The shadow detached itself from the window and came toward him stepping softly, and suddenly a long-forgotten fragrance stirred his memory.

"Hildegard!" he exclaimed, letting his hat fall from his hand.

"I've waited so long for you," the girl said, coming closer. "I looked for you everywhere."

"I was at the bistro," whispered Gavrilescu. "If I had not gone with her to the bistro, nothing would have happened. Or if I had had some money of my own. But *she* paid, Elsa, you understand. I felt obligated—and now it is late, isn't it? It is so very late ..."

"What difference does that make?" said the girl. "Let's go."

"But I don't have a house any more. I have nothing. It was a terrible day. I talked with Madame Voitinovici and forgot my portfolio of scores ..."

"You always were absent-minded," she interrupted him. "Come on."

"But where? Where?" Gavrilescu tried to cry out. "Someone else has moved into my house, I've forgotten his name, but it is someone I don't know ... and he isn't at home either, so that we can explain to him. He has gone to the baths ..."

"Come with me," said the girl, taking his hand and pulling him gently into the hall.

"But I have no money," continued Gavrilescu in a whisper. "All of a sudden they have changed the money, and the tram costs twice as much ..."

"You are still the same," said the girl, beginning to laugh. "You're afraid."

"Of all my acquaintances, there is no one left," continued Gavrilescu, whispering. "Everyone is at the baths; and Madame Voitinovici, from whom I should have been able to borrow, people say that she has moved to the country ... Ah, my hat!" he exclaimed, intending to return.

"Leave it," countered the girl. "You don't need it now."

"But you don't know, you don't know," Gavrilescu insisted, pulling his hand away from the hand of the girl. "It's a very good hat, it's almost new."

"Can it be true?" wondered the girl. "Do you not yet understand? Don't you understand what has happened to you, recently, very recently? Is it true that you don't understand?"

Gavrilescu looked deep into her eyes, and sighed.

"I'm very tired," he said. "Forgive me. It was a horrible day. But now I seem to be starting to feel better."

The girl pulled him lightly after her. They crossed the courtyard and he went out without closing the gate. The cab driver waited for them, slumbering, and the girl pulled Gavrilescu gently after her into the carriage.

"But I swear to you," began Gavrilescu, in a whisper. "I give you my word of honour that I don't even have a penny ..."

"Where to, miss?" asked the driver, "and which way? At a trot or faster?"

"Take us toward the forest, by the longer route," said the girl. "And drive slowly. There's no hurry."

"Hey, Junior!" called the cabdriver, whistling quietly to his horse.

Hildegard held his hand in hers, but she leaned her head back on the cushion, with her eyes on the sky. Gavrilescu regarded the girl with a penetrating look, concentrated.

"Hildegard," he began at last. "Something *has* happened to me, and I don't really know what. If I had not heard you speaking to the driver I should think I was dreaming."

The girl turned her head toward him and smiled.

"We are all dreaming," she said. "This is how it begins. As in a dream ..."

The Bridge

ALL SORTS OF THINGS HAPPEN. There was that motorcyclist, for instance. I was standing in front of the cabin, and I followed him with my eyes. I wondered how long it would take him to get bored. Four times he climbed the steep slope, and every time he reached the top, he would turn the machine around and coast down, noiselessly, to the valley. The fifth time, the inevitable happened: the accident, I mean. I carried him, bleeding and unconscious, to the cabin. After I'd splashed some water on him, he revived, and to my surprise, he seemed to recognize me.

"I thought you weren't going to come," he said. "I waited for you last year too, about this same time." I didn't understand.

"I believe you're confusing me with someone else," I said. "This cabin's not mine. A friend's letting me use it for a week."

He smiled. "I know that's the rule of the game: that you pretend not to know me. But I'm Emanuel." And he began to tell me stories—all sorts of strange happenings, quite improbable tales. I interrupted him several times.

"But these things *aren't true*. I know very well they *can't* be true! You've made them up."

"Including the accident?" he asked with a smile. "I invented the accident too?" He pressed the handkerchief to his upper lip, which was bleeding, and looked at me with candour, but with just a hint of irony. I hesitated. It was hard for me to tell him the truth, that he was suffering from amnesia. Finally, I had to make the decision. If he should faint again, I'd be obliged to take him to the hospital—and that would mean complications, many complications.

"It's just a mistake," I said gently. "By some error you've come here. You've confused me with someone else, but you belong to another world, another society. Perhaps you're a writer, or maybe an adventurer; in any event, you're a man of mysteries, with fabulous happenings in your past and more ahead of you. I myself move in a modest, settled, uninteresting world. You have no way of knowing me. I repeat, this lodge isn't mine; it belongs to a friend. This is the first time I've been here."

He kept staring at me and blotting his lip with the handkerchief. I let him go, although I knew full well he'd get lost. He was an amnesiac. What chance did he have of finding those who were waiting for him, and who had waited for him to come the year before? He was amnesiac, and the "rule of the game"—I believe those were his words—required that he not be recognized at first. Hence, he had to return a second or even a third time, but how would he know whose place he'd visited already, and whose he hadn't, if he had amnesia? He left, and I knew very well he'd lose his way. I began to feel sorry for having let him go. He was an interesting fellow. What perseverance he'd shown in climbing that hill on his motorcycle all those times, and coasting down into the valley—far down, all the way to the bridge."

"Yes, all sorts of things *do* happen," Onofrei interrupted me. (I knew why he interrupted me: through an oversight, I'd referred to a bridge.) "All sorts of things happen. This past spring, while walking on Strada Domniței, I caught sight of a lieutenant of the Roșiors* emerging from a courtyard. I stopped where I was, on the curb, to look at him. He was so handsome that one could speak about him only in terms of negative theology. This is the way a person would have to describe him, I said to myself: to use a language other than that of everyday. The language of theology, for instance, or of metaphysics. I said to myself: a cavalry officer represented in terms of negative theology constitutes in itself a mystery, a paradox, a *coincidentia oppositorum*, as Nicolas of Cusa would

---

* An elite cavalry unit of the Romanian army, whose uniforms were red. Existed from 1868 until 1941 [tr.].

say. I liked the way I was thinking. I'd been lifted up suddenly into another world; I had penetrated a universe of essences and archetypes. A smile of happiness crossed my face, and perhaps that smile encouraged him—the young man standing next to me on the pavement, I mean. 'I admired him too,' he said to me. (I realized immediately that I was dealing with an intellectual.) 'I can tell you that he's more than a handsome man, so handsome that he can be described only in terms of negative theology. I'm acquainted with him. He craves culture. He's read the *Upanishads*. And I can tell you something else: he and two students are looking for a house. That is—I don't wish to be misunderstood—he and the two students want to rent a house—a whole house, not just an apartment. A house with a courtyard, a garden, a veranda. Probably he didn't like this house,' he added after glancing again at the front of it. 'From what I know of him, he prefers a more spacious place ... For holding lectures, parties.' I listened in fascination. He knew him very well; he understood him. 'Of course, he likes to come home riding horseback. That's why he chose a regiment of the Roșiors. But the colonel forbade it. Such a handsome man, in the Red uniform of the Roșiors, on these streets with so many autumn leaves, on streets looking so melancholic toward sunset ...' 'And all the girls watching him from their windows,' I added. 'The colonel was right.' 'No, it wasn't that,' he continued. 'It was because of the melancholy, the sadness of our Bucharestian twilights. If you will allow me, sir,' he addressed me very politely, 'we have the fortune or the misfortune to live in the most melancholic city in the whole world.'"

"Then I know him!" Gologan interrupted. "I met him once too. He likes to strike up conversations with strangers on the street. He's an odd one."

"Well, I'm grateful to him," continued Onofrei, "because it was through him that I met the lieutenant. The lieutenant and the two students ... When I said *coincidentia oppositorum,* I wasn't exaggerating. Of course, Cusanus used this expression as a definition of God. But, you understand, I'm not saying that the lieutenant resembles or can be compared with God, or that he participates in a mode of being comparable to that of the Deity. No, I'm not saying that. But I assure you that it's impossible to speak about a person of his kind except in terms of negative theology. Not only has he read the *Upanishads,* but when he read them, *he put certain problems to himself.* I believe you understand what I'm alluding to: *Neti! Neti!* ultimate reality, being, and finally *ātman.* When I went to see him for the first time, escorted by my friend Blanduzia ..."

"I don't believe that's his name," Gologan broke in. "If it's the eccentric I'm referring to, the one who talks about the melancholies of Bucharest, and so forth, his name is Gorovei—Iancu Gorovei."

"I'm sure he's called Blanduzia," Onofrei insisted.

"Actually, it's not important," said Gologan, shrugging his shoulders.

"On the contrary, I believe it's *very* important. We ought to know if we're talking about the same person ... Now, I was speaking of Blanduzia, my friend, and also the lieutenant's. When I went to see them for the first time in their new residence on Strada Preoteselor, I was very impressed. I must add that the lieutenant and the two students live a very different life from ours. I can go further and say that they have transformed their existence into a ritual. For example, they all know that the lieutenant doesn't like to wait for his dinner. So, then, by common consent, they have devised this ceremonial in the evening, when he returns home from being with his regiment—I've told you already why he can't ride home on horseback—his orderly is waiting for him at the corner. When he sees him getting off the tram, he hurries back to the house and shouts from the courtyard, 'He's coming!' The first student opens then the first bottle of wine. The second student hastens to lock the drawing room door with a key. I have to tell you why he locks it: in the drawing room, at that hour, there will be three, four, often more young women: single ones, wives, widows, divorcées; and the lieutenant, in agreement with everyone in the house, has decided to—ah, but probably this is one of their secrets, and I shouldn't tell you. Although, the existence they live as a ritual starts at this point. 'Ritual' in the sense of a secret, a mystery, a sacrament. It's strange, when you stop to think about it."

We all waited, respectfully, curious for him to continue, but Onofrei smiled vacantly.

"It *is* true," began Zamfirescu, "all sorts of things happen. Things we often forget. I once found myself staring at an old woman. I believe she was blind. A young girl was leading her by the hand. But the *way* she was leading her! They had just come out of the gate, when the girl stopped. She had an open book in her right hand; holding it up, she began to read from it. The old woman listened with rapt attention, almost with reverence, straining to understand. She held to the girl's left hand while listening. I was reflecting on that fact—that she was holding to her left hand—when suddenly I remembered that all these things had happened once long ago, and I'd forgotten them. Really, it's just as I'm telling you. Some time before—maybe a month, maybe more, several years, I don't know—I had found myself in front of a house. I can't say why I'd stopped just there, but it seemed as though I was waiting for something. A little later, I understood. In that house there lived an old woman who was dying. She had been near death for a long time, but she couldn't die among strangers. She wanted to go back home, to die at her own place in the country, to be buried in her own ground. But how could she go home? She could scarcely move. I was asking myself—I was posing this problem to myself, I mean—when a girl of about fourteen or fifteen, the daughter of a neighbour, said that she would go with her and lead her. And then, in a way that seems to me incredible, the old woman got up from her bed, took the girl's hand, and they set off. They started down the road together. 'But we don't have a passport,' said the girl. 'I must take a map and a book—a book to read from, to orient myself.'

"Gentlemen, I had before me a scene of rare beauty. An old woman, already weary and seated on a bench—and a girl, reading to her from a book. A scene of rare beauty. The girl read wonderfully, carefully intoning every word, raising her voice slightly whenever there was something having to do with home. Yes, that book—I don't know its title or who wrote it—that book had, really, a very simple theme. It was about home, about going back home—to your own home, I mean, wherever that home might be. It seemed to me it resembled something familiar. For a few moments, I wondered if it was a new *Odyssey*—that is, a more beautiful one, written especially for women, old people, and children. But I soon realized I was mistaken. And this is why: shortly after that, a young man appeared. I must add that the girl who had seemed only about fourteen or fifteen, now, in the light of day, looked several years older. No more than nineteen or twenty, but now she had become a beautiful woman. And of course, that young man, come from God knows where, when he saw her reading from the book, stopped out of curiosity and—I well understand him—began to flirt with her, after a fashion. I say after a fashion, because the young man was quite discreet. I remember perfectly how he began: 'Ah!' he exclaimed, 'You're an idealist, a teacher, a poetess! You like to read. I have books too.' Then he added with polite modesty, 'And I have ideas.'"

"I know him!" interrupted Onofrei. "That's Blanduzia. Although he's a youth of rare modesty, he doesn't hide the fact that he has books and ideas. His friendship with the lieutenant of the Roșiors and the two students is founded on this fact: they share the cult of noble worlds, of ideal universes. I told you that their existence is lived on a lofty plane—I'd even dare to call it metaphysical or theological. Because, actually, what do these young men seek, if not ultimate reality, which for us human beings is obscured, camouflaged, under countless illusions and errors? They seek it, and I would venture to add, sometimes they find it. If you could listen to the lieutenant discoursing about *ātman* or, even more tragically, about the myth of Adonis!—you'd understand to what I'm referring. Not to the fact that he's every bit as handsome as Adonis, but, unfortunately, to his personal tragedy—a tragedy, moreover, of a metaphysical order. I believe I told you already: it all started with the *Upanishads*. When the lieutenant asked himself the question, 'Who am I?' and replied, correctly, 'I, the true I, am *ātman*, which is identical to *brahman* (in Sanskrit: *aham brahmāsmīti*, or to use another expression, *ayam ātmā brahma*), something burst deep inside his being. This is what some call the metaphysical rupture. In his case, the trauma was total. As Adonis was wounded by a wild boar, that is, indirectly castrated by the will of Aphrodite, a great goddess whose lover, son, or husband he was—just so was the lieutenant traumatized by his encounter with ultimate reality, with that mystery of the *brahman*—*ātman* identity. But don't misunderstand me. I don't mean for you to think it's a case of a physiological accident or even a psychosomatic one. I said that his tragedy is of a metaphysical or theological order. It doesn't matter how many women the lieutenant goes to bed with. When the first student met him, he was sleeping with twelve. Now, since I've known him, it's eleven. But please don't see in this numerical difference a terrible omen. It's a much more serious thing. By continuing to behave like a Don Juan, the lieutenant is acting like an Adonis. You understand what I mean: spiritually, he's already detached. For him, now, only the spirit counts. His tragedy is of a spiritual order. But, as you can imagine, this has brought about a radical change in his manner of living. His drawing room, for instance, which was devoted to parties and lectures before, has now become—what shall I say? It would be an exaggeration to call it a sanctuary, but it's something on that order: a place reserved for meditation and ceremonies. You'll ask me: but what about the women, all those beautiful young women: single, married, etc.—waiting for him in the drawing room every evening, in the room the student locks with a key as soon as he hears the orderly call from the courtyard, 'He's coming!' Well, if you know how to phrase this question correctly, then implicitly you've found the answer. Please don't dwell on the door or the key—these symbols are obsolete for a man of the spiritual stature of the lieutenant. You have your answer in the definition I gave at the beginning: the lieutenant can be described only in terms of negative theology. You have your answer in the concept of *coincidentia oppositorum*. Meditate on this detail: eleven women—but detached. In other words ...”

Onofrei stopped again, and smiled knowingly, mostly to himself. Then he continued:

“Have you ever found yourself in a situation from which there is absolutely no way out—an absurd situation, because it has no beginning and, consequently, can have no end, nor can any solution be found on the plane of immediate reality? Or, to use another image, have you found yourself in a room with absolutely no exit, without doors, without windows, in which you awoke without knowing how you got there, and from which there exists no possibility, on the rational plane, of escaping?"

He stopped speaking again, and looked at each of us in turn, continuing to smile.

"I've asked you the question," he said. "Now I'm waiting for your reply."

"I know what you're alluding to," began Gologan. "It really happened to me, just as you said. I found myself in a situation with no way out. I was with several friends, at the house of someone you never met, Stavroghin—the famous Stavroghin, the one with the imported foods shop and the delicatessen. Although it's been almost thirty years since then, I remember it quite well. Several of us who were friends had gathered there after a christening. The baptism had taken place in the morning, but, of course, in another house, in another environment—lycée professors, priests, pensioners—quite far away, in a squalid neighbourhood. We were at Stavroghin's house, and anyone who never knew him can't imagine what this meant in those years. I only need to tell you that the import store was on the ground level; on the second floor a part of the Stavroghin family lived—it's too complicated to give all the whys and wherefores—but on the other two floors, the third and the fourth, Stavroghin lived with another part of his family, but he also lived alone—because, you see, he was an eccentric, he had money, he had his store and his delicatessen; actually, he could afford anything. So there were several of us friends, as I said, at Stavroghin's after the christening. When, all of a sudden, we heard the doorbell ring, and the master of the house himself went to answer it. We all were curious. Who could it be? Because, you understand, no one knew we were here, at Stavroghin's house. Everyone supposed we were at the christening, in another neighbourhood, at the far side of the city, in the slum. Stavroghin opened the door and lo and behold, there was an old man, very properly dressed and polite. He looked at us one after another, and it was evident that he could scarcely believe his eyes. 'Pardon me,' he said, addressing Stavroghin, 'With whom do I have the honour of speaking?' 'Stavroghin,' he replied, introducing himself. 'And these, certainly, are friends of yours. I can say, then, that I'm in luck. I tried on all the other floors, but without success.' 'The others are at a baptism,' Stavroghin explained. 'I thought so,' said the old man. He went up to each one of us and gave us his hand, introducing himself as Herghelie. Here, ordinarily, we have meetings,' he added. 'On one of these floors. Last year they couldn't all come. The Baron, for instance, was snow-bound on a train at Valea Largă. You remember all the talk about it at the time.'

Of course, we all remembered very well.

'And so the Baron couldn't come. But we had a surprise we hadn't anticipated. Mme. Pelikan, whom you see here, was with us this past year also, although she had written us that she couldn't come.'

He approached her and gently kissed her hand. Then he presented us, so to speak, *en bloc*: 'The friends of Stavroghin.' We approached her, one by one, each kissing her hand, and she, in turn, introduced us to her friends: all grand, elegant ladies, many of them foreign. It was curious to hear so many strange languages in Stavroghin's apartment. But you can imagine what straits Stavroghin found himself in with all those good people, most of them foreigners, and he scarcely able to speak French. (He knew Greek a little better, but not *much*, as we realized that evening especially.) It was fortunate that preparations had been made for the christening party: champagne, caviar, and so forth. Soon Stavroghin went downstairs to the store with two of us and brought up a case of champagne and some haddock and fresh fruit. All the chairs and sofas were now occupied—we had given them to the ladies and we, Stavroghin's friends and the others, stood along the walls or leaned on the furniture. But what interesting conversations! What houses had these people not visited! They met customarily in buildings with more than one floor. And they explained to me why. But it's curious—now, when I'm telling you about it, I can't recall the reason. And even more curious, I ran into a woman I'd met at the Swiss Legation, with whom, I confess, I'd tried to flirt, but without success. Of course, she recognized me immediately, and she had enough tact not to remind me of what I'd tried to do. On the contrary, this time she seemed more friendly.

'I see that you lead a very interesting life,' I said to her. 'The life of the embassy, fashionable get-togethers, always with distinguished people.' 'Oh, yes,' she replied, 'I have a great weakness for houses with an upstairs. You climb up, you go down; you climb up, you go down, but you never get too much of it. You never get *bored*, I mean.'

And then, all of a sudden, I remembered that, this time, *I hadn't climbed the stairs* to Stavroghin's apartment. I didn't know how I had gotten here, but I knew very well that I *hadn't climbed any stairs*! I approached Stavroghin.

'Now tell me,' I whispered, 'how did we get up here? To the best of my knowledge, you don't have an elevator.' 'No, I don't have one,' Stavroghin confessed. 'I wonder myself how I got here. I remember very well that we went down to the store a little while ago. I recall quite clearly that we went down the stairs; but I don't know how we came back up.' 'In other words, if we want to go down, we can do it any time,' I said. 'You can rest assured of that.' I felt easier immediately. Nevertheless, I asked, 'What if we returned to the christening?' 'It's a long way from here,' Stavroghin answered. 'At the other end of town.' 'There may be interesting people there too,' I said, trying to persuade him. 'But I have to take care of *them*,' Stavroghin said, motioning to the room filled with guests. 'The Baron's arrived,' I observed. 'He'll take care of them.' And at last I persuaded him. But you understand the situation we were in. Without beginning and without end. Because none of us remembered having climbed *up* the stairs. Fortunately, as for going downstairs, we could do that without any trouble. So, I understand what you mean," he added, looking at Onofrei.

"I don't think it *is* the same thing," said Onofrei. "In your case a way out existed, because you could go downstairs."

"Not only that," Zamfirescu interjected, "but you had to do with a distinguished group, a fashionable society, embassy people who were already initiated. I mean, people who had already discovered the secret of multi-storied buildings: to go up and down, up and down. The old woman, the girl, and the young man of whom I was speaking were, I should say, lost in the world. They hadn't discovered anything yet. That's why they were having such a hard time. Later, I don't know how many months after that episode, I met them again in a railway station. I think they were waiting for a train. The old woman was in a seat, holding onto the girl by the hand—the left hand—and the girl was reading to her. Ah, but how many things had happened to them in the meantime! To listen to what the girl was reading would break your heart. So much had happened to them since they'd set out! The boy, who had lived at home with her, with whom the old woman had spoken earlier—that boy had grown up, he had all sorts of problems now and was contending with many hardships. Of course, the girl was reading to know where she was. As I told you, they had no passport. Therefore, they needed a map to be sure of the direction. Fortunately, they had taken the right one. But how much sadness in the pages she was reading then, waiting on the station platform! ... Moreover, the girl was alone now. The young man who had engaged her in conversation in front of the house had disappeared."

"He didn't disappear," Onofrei broke in. "He's Blanduzia, and he never left Bucharest. He has a great weakness for that city. And since he became friends with the lieutenant and the two students, his life is almost wholly devoted to perfecting himself inwardly. The discussions that I've been fortunate enough to attend, I shall never forget. Even with all those women locked up in the drawing room, the atmosphere is truly elevating. In vain, the women, sometimes, start to pound on the door with their fists, to call out, to threaten. The men don't even seem to hear them. And you understand why: the life of those superior men is sanctified daily through ritual. When they sit at table, their whole attention is concentrated on the Supper. Moreover, it's their only meal together, because the lieutenant eats lunch with the regiment and the students at the canteen. But their evening meal is a ritual, and no one has the right to distract them.

"You might suppose that at the second course, the second student would open the second bottle of wine. I supposed it was that way too, but I was wrong. *The second bottle of wine is opened by the lieutenant.* The orderly stands beside him, ready to take the bottle once he has opened it and fill the glasses. But the lieutenant must uncork the second bottle. I don't know if you understand what I mean.

"I asked you a little while ago if you'd ever found yourselves in a situation where there was absolutely no way out. The most adequate image of that is of a room with neither windows nor doors—or, even more apt, this one: you reach the end of a tunnel and come to the wall of the mountain, and then, when you try to turn around, you can't. You can't move your body even a little, because the wall is right against your back, and you feel it above your head too, very close, threatening to crush you—and yet you say, '*There must be a way out! An exit must exist*!' Well, gentlemen, I assure you that an exit *does* exist—but, of course, on a different plane. And I will dare to be specific: on the plane of *unreality*. You understand what I'm referring to: negative numbers, paradox; basically, the negation that denies negation, and pulls you out again into the light at just that moment when you, a poor man devoid of imagination, consider yourself imprisoned forever within that sarcophagus of stone, sealed in that narrow, icy crypt in the heart of the mountain. Now you understand why the lieutenant opens the *second* bottle of wine. I've given you the key: think of the history of religions, of what you might call the 'secret of the first repetition.' Think of the mystery of this expression: *the second time,* an expression apparently banalized through an excessive usage and therefore a profanation of language, but which preserves, nevertheless, well-camouflaged, fragments of a primordial revelation. *The second time*: that is, *born* a second time, reborn, raised from the dead—in a word, *born into the world of the spirit.* The second bottle of wine is as different in quality from the first as from a third or fourth. It doesn't matter how many bottles of wine they empty each evening on Strada Preoteselor. But you understand that the solution to the situation that apparently is without exit is found in the second bottle, the one the lieutenant opens. If I should say that it is a matter of a transfiguration, I'd be exaggerating. Because, *apparently*, nothing is transfigured. The orderly is still there, with a tray of glasses, and the students continue their discussion, sometimes raising their voices. The lieutenant has unfastened the collar of his tunic, and sometimes he recites verses, other times he meditates or even recalls childhood memories. But, I repeat, all these things are only apparent.

"In reality, once he has uncorked the second bottle, you begin to sense how everything around you is gradually transformed. At first, you're not aware of it. You hold your glass in your hand, you sip it with genuine pleasure, you listen to the conversation, and you seem to sense something unusual, somewhat unreal, in the surroundings; you drink again—and you can't believe it. You begin to hear footsteps, whispers, stifled laughter. You turn your head in surprise. Yet there's no one behind you. But you're ill at ease; you look right, you look left, you look straight ahead, then you gaze at the lieutenant. He's talking about the regiment, about horses. Now you begin to understand. You imagine him going home at dusk, mounted on horseback, handsome as an Adonis, and yet detached, wounded; you imagine you hear the hoofbeats of the horse on the carpet of withered leaves, when the light is fading imperceptibly, and the streetlamps are lighted and the kerosene lamps in the houses are lit, and you ask yourself, then, what's the use? What meaning can all this have? Why was I born, if I can't understand it, if I can't comprehend it? No, the colonel was right to forbid him to ride home mounted. One can't fight melancholy unprepared.

"You didn't realize when you sipped from your glass again; you kept listening to the lieutenant talking, you expected to stay there at the table another hour, perhaps even two—he seemed engrossed in his own charm—when suddenly you see him button his tunic and stand, appearing excited. Holding his glass, he declares: 'We acknowledge defeat. Come out now!' And they all start to laugh, and we see them there, behind us and in front of us—all those gorgeous young women; and you wonder if they're real, in flesh and blood, and you wonder how they got in. The ritual requires the second student to get up, blushing, and point to them, holding the key to the drawing room as high as he can reach. And then the girls start laughing again. Of course, if you don't live there, you don't know that the drawing room connects with the dining room, the rooms being separated only by a curtain. You don't know, because you didn't imagine such a thing. But if you have imagination, you immediately see the curtain—and then you understand this very simple thing—which, however, none of us could understand without help: you understand that there's a doorway and a curtain right in front of us. But you don't understand this until the *second time*. This is what I like to call the 'mystery of the first repetition.'"

He smiled happily and seemingly abandoned himself like an epiphany to our curious, fervent stares.

"Yes, it is indeed a mystery," I said. "You're right; not only do things happen, but they happen twice. I was speaking about a motorcyclist. A friend had loaned me his summer cabin. He had lent it to me for a week, and I was getting ready to leave when I heard the motorcycle again. I was afraid he'd have another accident, and I ran to the edge of the road, raised my arm, and called out to him, 'Emanuel!' He stopped and smiled with the same mixture of candour touched with irony. 'In other words, you recognize me!'

'Of course I recognize you,' I said. 'I was afraid you'd get lost, that you wouldn't find him.' He looked away. 'It's true I didn't find him,' he said. 'I went to other places too, on the motorcycle, but I didn't find him. And the people I happened to meet at the cabins and hotels didn't recognize me.' 'I'd like to help you,' I said, 'but I must know more about you. From what world do you come?' He gazed at me and smiled again. 'I thought that in our case, I had to ask *you* this question. From what world do *you* come if, even though you know I'm Emanuel, you don't recognize me? I believed that if you hadn't forgotten the rule of the game, you'd recognize me.' I covered my eyes for shame, sadness, regret, wishing the earth would swallow me. 'Vladimir!' I said to myself, 'how old are you now?' I knew how old I was: fifty-five. My life was approaching its end quickly, all too quickly. In a sense, I could say that I had lived my life. It was too late now. I couldn't begin it again. And I had lived it badly, or more precisely I had lived it as in a dream, without realizing what was happening to me. I had lived randomly, although in adolescence, in the first years of my youth, I'd heard of the story of Jehoshaphat and had started learning it. Moreover, for a few years, the most beautiful ones, I had gotten into the second part, the one that begins: 'At a mill, at Jehoshaphat's.' I liked it so much, I was so happy acting it out, that I was sure I'd never forget it, that I'd go on to play the third part, that I'd play it better and better until the end of my life. And now I was approaching rapidly, all too rapidly, the end—and I realized that I'd forgotten all about Jehoshaphat, that I'd lived my life without playing the part, that, actually, I hadn't lived; but others had lived through me, that I'd let myself be lived *by* others and *for* others …

"How completely can we forget the essential! I had carried him in my arms, all bloody, to the cabin, and I hadn't recognized him. I hadn't recognized him even when he told me he was Emanuel. I had taken him for an amnesiac. I had felt sorry for him. I was afraid he'd lose his way, get lost. And he had come to awaken me, to remind me of Jehoshaphat. He had tried everything to wake me up. Five times he had ridden up that steep slope on his motorcycle, and in the end he had resorted to the accident. He'd imagined that the blood might rouse me. Or one of his stories—so unbelievable, so fabulous. Or perhaps his name, Emanuel. But nothing awakened me … Fortunately, he came back—and then I recognized him. 'Do we still have time?' I asked him quickly. 'Isn't it too late?' 'It's late, and we have only a little time,' he answered. 'But the second part has been played before, and if you wish…' 'Where are the others?' I interrupted. 'I remember Prajan: he had a handsome brow, loved music and Goethe, and said he'd compose a divan … And I remember Elina, who called to us at the end of the second part: *Anyone who doesn't deny he recognizes a member, no longer remembers!* And I remember …' They've all gone astray,' Emanuel said. 'They've forgotten. Some grew weary and settled down. You remember the rule of the mill: When you enter a mill and see an empty chair, you ask yourself who put it there for you, and you go on. When you see someone sitting in a chair, you ask yourself—but wait, do you still remember what you're supposed to ask?'

He waited, and I felt my cheeks burning. I couldn't remember any more.

'Almost no one remembers towards the end of their youth,' he said with a smile. 'But others play out the second part. Some forget for a while, and then, all at once, they recall the second part and begin playing it again. But of course, those who have been doing it from the beginning, and who now are playing the third part, have gone on. You go from one garden to another, from one wood to another, but until you go outside a mill, the game is the same: you keep meeting other couples, other groups, and if you linger too long or forget one of the rules of the game, you go astray …'"

"That's right," Zamfirescu broke in. "If you forget, you go astray. I told you I'd forgotten about the episode with the old blind woman and the girl. I believed at first that she was blind. I believed this because I'd *forgotten*. In fact, as I realized once I'd remembered, the old woman was dying. Since then, every time I remember that detail, I meet up with them. Of course, the girl keeps reading, and thus the old woman learns interesting things, she understands what's happening to her; above all, she understands life. But how much those poor people have gone through since I encountered them the first time at the house! I see them sometimes in restaurants. People don't understand the situation, and touching the girl's arm, they smile with pity and slip a banknote between the pages of the book. The girl blushes, bows her head slightly, thanks them with a smile, and goes on—with the book in one hand, drawing the woman gently after her. It's hard for her to refuse, because the people have the banknotes ready, and she doesn't want to offend them. But neither the girl nor the old woman go to restaurants to beg. They pass through banks, schools, churches, and hospitals because their road takes them there—the road their map shows them.

"Sometimes these travels give rise to all manner of confusions. For instance, on the day the foundation stone was being laid for the city hall. You remember how much the newspapers made of it, because the prime minister was to be there. I represented the Society. I remember, the first speech had just ended, and the prime minister had picked up a brick—when they appeared. They didn't realize they were intruding on something. They'd come, probably, straight from inside the church. At that hour, the church was empty; no one would have been guarding it. And just as the prime minister was balancing the brick in his right hand, the old woman sat down on a chair directly in front of him, a step from the foundation trench, as if she had not seen him. And the girl immediately started reading from the book. Everyone removed their hats respectfully; obviously, they were impressed. They didn't understand what it was all about, but they supposed it had to do with ancestral customs. And, indeed, the girl read quite well. What an uplifting text it was: something about the Waters of Babylon, about the boat that waits for us there. The bishops wept as they listened to her reading, and even the politicians became pensive, with their eyes on the girl. She seemed even more beautiful now. And when she closed the book and gently drew the old lady to her feet, leading her on their way, the prime minister ran after her and kissed her hand. We knew he did this for his own advantage, for propaganda, but nonetheless we were all impressed. We liked the gesture, I mean to say.

"But what confusions followed! First, they couldn't find the brick, the foundation stone, on which there was an inscription—a short text having to do with the city hall. There were plenty of bricks there, ready for the prime minister to use, but he'd lost the one with the inscription. And the people, drawing back respectfully to make way for the women, created a commotion. Some of the bishops, in their sacerdotal robes, set off after the two. The brass band would have left too, if someone hadn't reminded them that they couldn't leave before the prime minister. Since I represented the Society, I had to keep my place beside the foundation—and I was sorry. I was in a quandary. I wanted to go after them, to listen to the girl reading. I knew the old woman tired quickly and would sit down on a chair, and the girl would open the book to read to her. But I couldn't leave until the brick was found. I tried to console myself with the thought that I'd meet them again, perhaps very soon."

"That's true," began Gologan. "It's a consolation to know that you'll keep meeting someone. I was telling you about Stavroghin. He died long ago, and his widow returned to Greece. The shop passed into the hands of a nephew—but the friends of Herghelie still meet all the time, gathering in large, luxurious houses with several stories, and so we too have the opportunity to meet him again—we, Stavroghin's friends, I mean. Several years after the baptism, I was at Aristide's home. It was the celebration of his silver wedding anniversary and he had invited, he said, three hundred guests. Luckily, they couldn't all come, because, I ask you, where could he have found room for all of them? It's true, he has three upper floors besides the ground floor, but who would dare to climb to the fourth story? That wide, majestic staircase of marble was crammed with people. With difficulty, excusing yourself, making your way with your elbows, you can reach the third floor—but you're exhausted when you arrive! You don't dare venture beyond. Nothing but English and Russian are spoken. Gentlemen with Vandykes, in tuxedos adorned with medals, women in long evening gowns—and what jewels, what splendid jewels! I was standing with my eyes focused on a diamond of extraordinary beauty, when someone took hold of my arm. It was the Baron.

'Did you know that until about two hours ago Mme. de Chenier was selling tickets at the Cinema Select?' he whispered to me, smiling. 'But she did what she had to do to get ready, and she came. It's true,' he added, 'that we're always glad to come to Aristide's. It all depends on Herghelie: if he has time to notify us a week in advance we come, even if we're abroad. That's what happened in Mme. Pelikan's case. She returned the day before yesterday from Stockholm.' 'But where's the lady, that good-looking blonde?' I began, embarrassed that I couldn't remember her name. 'I met her quite a while ago at the Swiss Legation.' 'Evangelina,' he smiled. 'Evangelina Farmaki. She should be here. It seems to me I saw her just a little while ago.'

And it happened that we found ourselves face to face a few moments later. I kissed her hand with genuine pleasure. 'I see,' I began, 'you're still leading the same distinguished, dazzling life.' 'Yes,' she said, 'but you observe that people get tired, bored, and then they try something else. They settle in resort towns, at spas, and stay there ten or twenty years. I imagine comfort attracts them more than anything else. The elevators, the rooms with baths and showers, the game rooms, but above all the tennis courts. Those lively balls, the racquets, the rhythmic sounds—because, isn't it true? When the ball is struck properly by the racquet, you hear a peculiar sound, quite a disturbing sound; you recall your childhood, your youth, and you understand that there are people capable of listening for ten or twenty years to the sound of tennis balls being struck by racquets, you understand that you aren't satiated with the same rhythm, over and over, the same mysterious, disturbing rhythm; and you think you could watch and listen for dozens, for hundreds of years and still wonder: *why? why?*'

I found her fascinating. I didn't get bored hearing her talk about spas, her fashionable life, so interesting and glamorous."

"I understand you," Onofrei interrupted. "Sometimes, in the case of certain people, under the guise of the most grating banalities, profound structures of reality are revealed to you. Structures, I mean, which are inaccessible to us otherwise, rationally. As I told Blanduzia, if Western thought, from the pre-Socratics to the present, has made no progress, but on the contrary, we could even say that it has become stuck in a rut with no outlet, this is due above all to the arbitrary, monstrous importance accorded to language. It has been believed, wrongly, that reality can only be understood through concepts, and since concepts are formed through language, we can perfect them only by perfecting and purifying language. But ultimate reality cannot be captured in concepts nor expressed in language. For our minds, ultimate reality, *being*, is a mystery; and I define a mystery as that which we cannot recognize, that which is unrecognizable. This, however, could mean one of two things: either that we can never know ultimate reality, or else that we can know it at *any time*, provided only that we learn to recognize it under its infinite *camouflaged appearances*, in what we call immediate reality, in what India calls *māyā*, a term I would translate as immediate *unreality*. You understand what I'm referring to: happenings, events, chance encounters, things that apparently couldn't possibly have any significance. I say *apparently*, but what if this appearance is only a snare laid for us by *māyā*, the cosmic sorceress, matter in the state of continuous becoming? That's why I spoke of *coincidentia oppositorum*, of that mystery in which being can coincide with nonbeing. I repeat, *can* coincide. But it doesn't always coincide, because if it did, it wouldn't be called a mystery any more.

"And what about the lieutenant? you will ask. How could the lieutenant, so young, so handsome, the sort of man he is: both Don Juan and Adonis—how could the lieutenant reveal this mystery? I believe I've answered this question several times, but I'll answer it once again.

"When he understood that *ātman* is identical with *Brahman*, the lieutenant understood that he had died to this world because he suddenly found himself detached from everyone and everything—and although this death meant his freedom, he was, as the Indians put it so well, a 'living corpse,' and, as it happens in such 'borderline cases,' sometimes he felt alive and other times he felt dead. In one such moment of the latter type, the lieutenant asked himself if there were not indeed some way out, some *exit*. And, of course, an exit did exist. He had to die a *second time*; he had to become again what he had been at first—a cavalry lieutenant—continuing, however (because herein lies the paradox of the *coincidentia oppositorum*) to remain what he had succeeded in becoming through the *Upanishads: ātman-brahman*. But how? How could he find this exit, how could he die a second time when, having become pure spirit, he had become immortal? If you know how to ask this question correctly, you've found the answer already. I spoke to you about a curtain, about a doorway. These terms give you the answer. I spoke about a group of beautiful young women who appear suddenly, from out of nowhere, in the dining room, and start laughing. These women give you the answer. One of them is the *Magna Mater*, the great goddess—call her Aphrodite if you will, although her names are innumerable. *One of them*, I said. Nearly always, in a group of beautiful young women, one will be a great goddess—but how do you recognize her? No one knows which she is; she doesn't even know herself. And now I give you the answer again: the lieutenant behaves as if he didn't know that he is really the lieutenant of the cavalry, as if he had forgotten that he is an Adonis wounded by the Great Goddess, an Adonis agonizing beside the trunk of a tree, a bleeding, dying Adonis ...

"But you see," Onofrei resumed again after a long silence, "herein lies the mystery: that the lieutenant never knows beforehand if he will die permanently, or if he will succeed in being resurrected. Every evening, therefore, in beginning the ritual, he takes this risk: that he may never awaken again—that he may never again be reintegrated into *this world*, I mean. Because, of course, he—*ātman*—being immortal, spirit, is indestructible. But *this* life has nothing to do with immortality. In this life you do not ask to be immortal or indestructible; all you ask is to be alive. And, of course, life, with its corporeal plenitude, beauty, virility, and fertility—all these you do not obtain through the spirit; *ātman* does not give them to you, but rather the Great Goddess—call her, if you wish, Aphrodite. She is the source of life, *this life*, in this world—the world to which the lieutenant, every evening, runs the risk of never returning again.

"You understand what I'm referring to: suppose he doesn't happen to find a great goddess among those beautiful women? Because, before the ritual, no one knows if the Great Goddess *is there* or *who she is*. Nor does she know this. Those women believe they are single, married, widowed, or divorced females. Still more serious: they would continue to believe this to the end of their lives, if there were not *someone*—in our case, the lieutenant—who would reveal their true identity to them. And what *is* their true identity? Four, five, ten or eleven of them are really what they look to be—just women—but one of them proves to be the Great Goddess. More precisely, *on that evening*, one of them incarnates—without her knowing it and without anyone else's knowing it—a great goddess. Of course, on the following evening, it may be another, and herein lies the mystery, that no one knows beforehand, not even the lieutenant. But fortunately …"

He stopped to catch his breath and looked at all of us, smiling.

"Fortunately," he added after a pause, "for our troubles, God has left to the world the red grapes and the vineyard."

Startled, I was about to clarify matters, to explain that he had misunderstood me, when Zamfirescu spoke up first.

"It's curious that you should speak about grapes and vineyards."

"It is indeed curious," Gologan echoed.

"I said that it's curious," Zamfirescu continued, "because the last time I ran into them, it happened just that way, I met them in a vineyard, one of the vineyards of my brother-in-law, Eufrosin. Let's see, when was that? I don't remember exactly, but it couldn't have been too long. It was after his second child had been born, so it was about two or three years. At a grape harvest at their vineyard, near Târgoviște. And of course, many people were there: friends, neighbours, some from Târgoviște, some from Bucharest. I recognized them at once: the old woman was sitting on a chair, the girl had begun to read, and little by little, the harvesters gathered around them. I approached, moved, eager especially to listen to her reading. But the curious thing is, I didn't hear her any more. Or perhaps

I heard her, but I didn't understand her. I didn't understand what she was reading. All the others, the grape-pickers, the workers, the visitors, listened reverently; apparently, they could hear and understand.

"'What is she saying?' I asked someone next to me in a whisper.

"He turned and stared at me. It was plain to see he was annoyed. 'Listen to her yourself. It's beautiful,' he answered, and turned his back.

"I stayed there several minutes longer, endeavouring to hear, to understand, and then I started back, dejected, toward the manor house. But I spied Eufrosin running, and I followed him. I found myself running too, because, although I called to him, he didn't hear me, or else he pretended not to hear. But when I caught up with him, he whispered to me: 'They're going to cross the bridge. The girl says they're going to cross there.'"

"You see!" Onofrei interjected, suddenly animated. "It happened just as I expected it would. There's always an exit, a doorway, a bridge—in your case a bridge. But you weren't worrying, because you were in a vineyard. I don't know if you understand what I'm alluding to," he said, looking at each of us in turn. "You were *in a natural mode* there, in a sense you were unconscious, because you hadn't begun to ask the question. But what are *we* to do, we who ask ourselves the question, and who therefore can no longer reintegrate the pure spontaneity, the natural mode of being? We who have lost the unconscious bliss of children and the uneducated? We *know* we must cross the bridge. I repeat, *we know*, and we also know what this could mean: to cross it and be unable to return."

I wanted to interrupt, but Gologan stepped in ahead of me.

"You're perfectly right," he began, troubled. "You're perfectly right to ask this question. But if God, for our troubles, has left to us the grapevine, why is life so hard? Why do we all struggle, from morning till night, and never prevail, but have to start all over again every morning, the same old thing, over and over? And it's hard not only for us, ordinary men, each with his own affairs and troubles, but also for superior people, like the friends of Herghelie, the Baron, Mme. Pelikan, Evangelina, and all the others. This to me seems incomprehensible. That superior people like them, cultured people, who go around in distinguished circles, travelling in foreign countries, can't settle down as they'd like, can't rest. For example, the Baron, who told me one St. Dumitru's Day: 'I don't say it's not beautiful here too, because they have a park with a fountain, a roomy, luxurious five-story house—but can you imagine being in the country now, getting ready for the grape harvest? Imagine you have your own vineyard, however modest it may be—but you know that it's yours, that you work it, that from the grapes you gather you'll make your wine; and then you rest there, in your vineyard, waiting, not hurrying, letting the wine age, leaving it for ten, twenty years, while you stay beside it, without a care, without a thought.'"

"You've misunderstood me," I interrupted Gologan, addressing myself mainly to Onofrei. "The vineyard to which we're going is at Gorgani, by the sea. And undoubtedly it's the most beautiful vineyard in that part of Dobrogea. About fifteen years ago, the District wanted to buy it, to give it to the Queen. But my uncles were opposed, and they did well to be. It's a wonderful place. Now, close to harvest time, it's like another world. You look on the vineyard from the terrace, you see how it stretches up the hillside, climbing, climbing, until all at once it disappears, dropping off to the shore; and from there you see nothing but the sea, as far as your eyes can reach—nothing but the sea."

"I'm sorry," said Onofrei, giving me a long look, "but I'm afraid we don't understand each other. Because, of course, in order to reach the sea, we must first cross the Danube. And we cross it on a bridge."

"Yes, at Cernavodă."*

"That's what I meant. There's a bridge for us too. And now we're approaching it, and whether or not we want to, we're going to cross it. But we've posed the question. Or, speaking only for myself, *I've* posed the question. And I can't forget I've posed it. Who will guarantee me that once I've crossed the bridge, I'll be able to return?"

"It's a solid bridge…," I began.

"I know what you mean," Onofrei interrupted. "You mean it's not a symbolic bridge. But I wasn't referring to a symbolic bridge nor to the symbolism of the bridge. I'm no great lover of symbols. Symbols have their place in the economy of the spirit, but symbolism, like language, holds you in an abstract universe. Now, the whole problem is: how to escape from the abstract universes which we ourselves have constructed? In itself, no symbol is important, but rather the concrete object in which it's manifested. Herein lies the whole mystery. The symbolism of the grapevine doesn't matter, but a single vine, one alone, which could also be something else, which could signify, for instance, the presence of the goddess. Notice that I said the *presence* of the goddess: her real, concrete presence, not an idea, not an image.

"This is, in fact, the lieutenant's problem: how to identify the Great Goddess among those five or ten beautiful young women who surround him every evening. But if you take into account the fact that between the grapevine with the clusters of red grapes and the Great Goddess a mysterious solidarity exists, that in certain cases the grapevine even grows upon her nude body, and in other cases the cluster of red grapes

---

*   The Cernavodă Bridge was built between 1890 and 1895, and was an exceptional work of engineering [tr.].

is even the mouth of the goddess, the mouth that gives life, riches, fertility, fortune, bliss—if you take account of all these things, you can imagine how the lieutenant, every evening, identifies the Great Goddess, camouflaged among all those women—married, widows, and so forth. It is a matter of a ritual, not a symbol. Symbolism has nothing to do with the drama the lieutenant relives daily, namely: how to reintegrate *this world*, after he has known the tragic accident of Adonis."

"I understand very well," I tried to interject.

"No, I don't believe you *do* understand," Onofrei continued. "Because if you did, you wouldn't have referred to the solidity of the bridge at Cernavodă. If I didn't recognize the solidity of the bridge over the Danube, I wouldn't be living in this world. But it is *this world* above all that interests me, because only *here* are the camouflaged mysteries found, and, this being so, only here in an incarnate existence do we have any chance of their being revealed to us. But if we accept on principle that mysteries are camouflaged in beings and objects, we must also accept this particular case: that the bridge at Cernavodă might camouflage a mystery. I say *might*, and I add: for *some* of us, at least. Of course, we can't know this beforehand. Now, what sort of mystery might it be? Symbolism helps you somewhat, but only to a limited extent. Symbolism tells you that the bridge signifies a passage to something else, to another world, another mode of being. But symbolism can't guarantee in advance what kind of *other world* you will integrate or what *other mode of being* you will attain.

"You understand, then, why I find myself in a situation comparable to that of the lieutenant, a situation apparently without an exit. Because, you see, we're approaching the Bridge, and in a few minutes the Danube will be flowing under our feet. And in a few hours, we'll reach the vineyard at Gorgani—but how? In what state? I mean, in what mode of being? As far as I'm concerned, I've been to those places before, but I remember them only vaguely, or, more precisely, I remember only the fact that I remember. Was it a dream? If I should succeed in remembering, I'd know if I dreamed it or not. But, gentlemen, I take this opportunity, since it could be the last, to say how charmed I am to have met you, and how happy I shall be to meet you again in Bucharest. And now, gentlemen, as I look at each of you, I feel a deep and unaccountable bliss; and I recall vaguely the journey we made once before, perhaps in a dream, perhaps in another time, but a journey precisely like this one: we four, in a first—class compartment; and now, as then, the puffing of the engine slackens because we're approaching the Bridge. I wouldn't want you to consider me a sentimentalist, but I venture to say that I'm happy, quite happy. The lieutenant has warned me about this also—that you feel an indescribable bliss at the moment when fear comes over you, when it suddenly engulfs your whole being, welling up from the depths, from the heart of the creature. And if in that moment you don't say to your-self, *an exit must exist*!—you're lost, you can never return; you'll remain buried alive in that crypt in the heart of the mountain, in that pitch-black chamber with neither door nor window. I feel that bliss, I feel fear engulfing me, and I say to myself and to you as well, *an exit exists*!"

He stopped speaking abruptly and stared at me with glassy, unseeing eyes. How long did this moment last? How long? I saw him get up and reach for his briefcase.

"I'd like to add something more," he said. "But since some-one's waiting for me, there's no time for that. Forgive me, if I permit myself to speak frankly, but what more could you understand now than you understood a half-hour ago, when I told you that, for me, the mystery is unrecognizable? Probably, some of you looked out the window and saw it—the Danube,

I mean. You saw the river while we were crossing it, you saw the Bridge, and you'll see the vineyard at Gorgani. In a way, I envy you; but on the other hand … What more can I say? Now that I've begun to know you, I can only say this: that all sorts of things happen to each of us, but unfortunately we forget them. And even when we don't forget, we don't know how to recognize them. With a little imagination, I'd be able to recognize you—and then I'd remember all I ought to remember."

Onofrei took his briefcase, shook hands with each of us warmly, and went out into the corridor. We didn't dare speak. But we all watched him leaving. And, as if by coincidence, when he reached the end of the corridor, the train stopped— and he got off. I hadn't suspected a station existed so close to the Bridge. I've never been able to remember its name.

The General's Uniforms

THE TWO ADVANCED ON TIPTOE, with great care. Whenever a floorboard squeaked they would stop immediately, holding their breath. In one of those moments, almost without realizing what he was doing, Ieronim pressed the switch on the torch, leaving them in the dark. Stumbling over a rope he could not see, he caught hold of a wardrobe to keep from falling. One of the cabinet doors opened slowly, making a long whine like a stifled moan.

"Don't be frightened," he whispered. "There's nobody in the whole house."

"Then why are we whispering?" the other asked.

Ieronim switched on the torch again and rotated the cone of light around the boy several times, yet without shining it directly in his face. There was no need for that; he could see it well enough: the pale countenance of a schoolboy, with eyes set unnaturally deep in their sockets, thin lips and short-cropped hair, the beginning of bangs on his forehead.

"You say your name is Vlad, is that right?"

"Vlad. Vladimir Iconaru."

"Take it from me, Iconaru, my friend," he said, leaning his head a little closer. "Never has anyone in any play, in any novel, in any poem—*never*, I repeat, has anyone ever dared to speak in a normal tone of voice when he was breaking into the attic of a strange house in the dead of night and especially when he's breaking in, as we are, with a very precise purpose: to find the trunk in which the widow of the war hero, General Iancu Calomfir, has reverently preserved the dress uniforms of her husband—to find, I say, the trunk, in order to break the lock and steal the two uniforms. I repeat, to *steal* two general's uniforms!"

"But you said you were relatives."

"We are. Moreover, my father was her favourite nephew. He was the favourite nephew of General Iancu Calomfir's widow. But what does that matter? We entered this attic with a false key in the dead of night, to search for certain objects and *steal them*. It's true, they're only art objects, perhaps with some historic interest, but of no real value: two uniforms."

"And a collection of coleoptera," Vladimir added.

Ieronim raised the light again, this time concentrating it above the boy's head. Then he signalled him to follow, but after a few steps he stopped.

"I haven't been in this attic for many years," he began in a voice which showed no emotion. "But I remember very well all these objects, all these wardrobes, trunks, and boxes," and he pointed to them, playing the light along the walls. "I remember, likewise very well, the location of the trunk with the uniforms: it's *there*, about ten meters in front of us, although I don't see it yet, because it's hidden by all those other trunks and boxes and those bundles of old newspapers. But there's one thing I don't remember, Vladimir Iconaru: I don't remember speaking to you about a collection of coleoptera. All I said to you was that *in this house* there are many insectaria, and in particular a very rich collection of butterflies."

"What a shame! Butterflies are beautiful, but what I'm really keen on is coleoptera."

Ieronim leaned his head back slightly and looked at him questioningly, surprised.

"Interesting," he observed after a few moments. "And I must admit, I wasn't expecting that. If someday I should write a treatise on ethics, I shall have to discuss your case. Because you are an interesting case: in a word, you agree enthusiastically to become a burglar for a collection of coleoptera, but you hesitate, or more precisely you're troubled by scruples, when you find out it's only a matter of butterflies!"

"I'm not hesitating," Iconaru protested, turning scarlet. "Because, actually, it's not stealing. You're a relative. It's a matter of the same family ... And now," he added, lowering his voice, "they're all dead."

"Why do you say *all*?"

"All who used to live in this house: the General, his widow, and their children who died one after the other—some fighting in the war, some in air raids. And didn't you tell me the day before yesterday that everyone was dead and the house deserted, and that no one has occupied it because the bombings left it dilapidated, and that they'll probably tear it down next spring?"

Ieronim looked at him again, a long time, with great sadness; then he switched off the light. "That's so," he whispered. "They've all died. Or," he added after a pause, "to be more precise, *almost* all. But what does it matter? We have no right to give up hope. When I saw you the other morning ..."

He turned on the torch and pointed the beam directly into the boy's face. Iconaru jerked his hand to his eyes.

"Pardon me," Ieronim continued, after putting out the light again. "I didn't mean to hurt you, but I wanted to look you in the eyes once more, before recalling it. No, it's not a matter of recalling, but of evoking. The way I like to imagine it, it's like listening to a chorus in a Greek tragedy. The Chorus which summarizes, evokes, or prophesies the actions of the hero and the punishments of the gods. And now, don't move! Listen! The stage setting is simple; you know what it is. A street in Bucharest in the year 1950. Early autumn. In the background, a vacant lot. I'm walking toward that open space for some purpose or other, when coming toward me I see a schoolboy, holding a dove in his hand."

"It was injured ..."

"Please, don't interrupt! I told you the Chorus is speaking now! There comes a pale-cheeked schoolboy, hunched over, holding a dove in his right hand and petting it from time to time with his left."

"It was injured, and I was afraid the cats would eat it."

"That's what you said at the time, too. But I recognized you immediately because *you were carrying a dove in your hand.* And I knew what I've known for a long time: that we have no right to give up hope ... By the way, is it still alive?" he asked after a moment.

"All that was wrong was a half-broken wing. Some no-good had hit it with a sling shot. But it healed. It healed quickly like all birds do."

"At any rate," Ieronim continued, "this was the beginning of our adventure. Because, as you realize—since I've made no secret of it—it is an adventure we're undertaking."

"You told me that you knew about an attic in an abandoned house, an attic full of trunks and boxes and all sorts of things—swords, helmets, toys, and old illustrated magazines."

Ieronim ran his hand nervously through his hair, as though trying to relieve his impatience.

"And how many other things, how many others!" he added. "And as I was speaking to you I was looking at you. If only you'd known how I was looking at you, to guess what would attract your interest! And yet, from time to time, I stole glances at the dove."

"I'd found it on the vacant tract. Someone had hit it with a stone ..."

Ieronim reached out suddenly in the darkness and laid his hand on the boy's shoulder.

"Don't imagine that I wanted to put you to a test or tempt you. But for me, a person who lives only for the theatre, the scene was too exceptional—I realized instinctively that it belonged in that mysterious scenario which I labour constantly, *yet vainly*, to reconstruct—if you know what I mean."

He withdrew his hand from the boy's shoulder, and continued in a different tone of voice.

"Listen: after I'd seen you coming across the field with a dove in your hand, I thought: if only I can climb those stairs with him, if I can ascend those attic stairs with him at night, in the dark, and feel him there beside me when I try the keys one after another—and then, all at once, one key fits and the door opens with a creak, and we enter this attic, here, which no one has entered for many a year, not since the last son of General Calomfir's widow died ... Listen! Don't interrupt me!" he said, lifting his arm, "because now comes the really dramatic scene. Listen, and visualize it! We have entered slowly, slowly, making our way toward the back where the trunk is located. And how much might happen? God, *think how much might happen*! A poor pocket torch. Scarcely any light, because I'd had it since the war, when I was a Boy Scout. At any moment it might fail and we'd be left in the dark. And we weren't even beside each other. I'd go ahead because I'd suspect that the battery was almost spent. And we'd find ourselves suddenly in the dark, lost in this attic full of trunks and boxes all covered with dust and cobwebs, and I wouldn't even dare to cry out, to call your name. I'd just whisper, 'Vlad'—Your name is Vlad or Vladimir, isn't it?—'Vlad, do you hear me?' But you wouldn't hear me because you'd lagged far behind me and, blind in the darkness, you'd become separated even farther from me and wouldn't be able to hear me. Even if I'd dared to raise my voice, you'd still not be able to hear me, because just then the wind would begin to blow, and in this attic, damaged by the bombings, the wind makes a sinister sound, as in the theatre when a storm is about to break."

He stopped abruptly, breathing hard, spent.

"I wouldn't get lost," the boy said calmly. "I wouldn't get lost because I'm used to the dark. I spent my childhood in the mountains. I'm not afraid of the dark or the wind."

"You mean to say, that's *all* you understood?" Ieronim broke in, a sudden sadness in his voice. "You understood that I wanted to frighten you, to put you to the test *in the dark*? Schoolboy Iconaru Vladimir, you have no imagination! You're not the only one, either. Almost no one has imagination any more. We live in difficult times. Who has time any more to imagine another world, with *another kind* of people—a more poetic world, and therefore a truer one?"

"If you thought I'd be afraid to be left alone in the dark ..."

"Please don't interrupt! We're at the theatre now, and we're approaching the main scene ... Eventually, I'd be able to find you. I'd find you clinging to one of the wardrobes, and then you'd understand what had happened; you'd understand why I separated from you and why I'd let you believe that the batteries had given out. There, with both of us clinging to the wardrobe, I'd tell you the history of the house, which is, in fact, the history of General Calomfir; his true history, which no one knows any more because, as you guessed too well, almost all of them have died."

"Then why haven't you told it to me?"

Ieronim shrugged his shoulders. "Something interfered. A mere trifle."

"You could have told me," Vladimir continued, "because I wouldn't have been afraid. And you can tell me now. I like to listen to stories. While I'm listening I keep asking myself, I keep wondering: when my turn comes, what will I tell? Shall I tell what happened to me one night at the sheepfold?"

Ieronim, annoyed, passed his hand through his hair.

"Something interfered, and the play vanished. It returned to non-being. It gave way to other problems, some of them banal, others—or more precisely, one of them—extremely important, of first rank. Can't you guess? You interfered—without intending to, I realize—when you introduced a moral idea, namely, the difference between coleoptera and butterflies."

"... and lepidoptera," Iconaru corrected him.

Ieronim turned on the torch again, carefully, lest he blind the boy, and gave him a long look.

"Let's go," he said, starting forward suddenly. "It's beginning to get cold."

* * *

He sensed someone was following him and he slackened his pace, expecting from one moment to the next to hear a call from behind. But the unknown person hesitated. He stopped and leaned the cello case against the wall of the corridor and began to search unhurriedly for his handkerchief. First he had to unbutton his overcoat, a labourious task.

"*Maestro!*" he heard all at once behind him. It was a remarkably clear and robust contralto voice. "Maestro, is it true that you're no longer giving private lessons?"

Antim turned his head and looked at her, trying to appear surprised. He pulled out his handkerchief and wiped his forehead absent-mindedly, then held it in his hand.

"It's true," he said. "I've decided not to give private lessons any more because ..."

At that moment he seemed to see her for the first time, and he looked at her deeply, wonderingly, almost in panic. He began wiping his forehead and cheeks rapidly with his handkerchief.

"Don't think my hand is shaky," he said, trying to smile.

"You're tired, Maestro."

"It is tiredness, but it's something else too. It seemed to me that I've seen that face somewhere—your face, I mean."

The girl stepped a little closer, hunching her shoulders slightly.

"I've never missed a concert, Maestro. I've followed you for five years, ever since I was at the Conservatory. And out of all the orchestra, I didn't look at anyone, or listen to anyone, except you, Sir!"

"No, I'm not thinking of that," he interrupted her, continuing to gaze at her and passing the handkerchief from one hand to the other. "Are you Romanian? I mean, have you always lived here, in Bucharest?"

The girl blushed instantly. "My parents are from the provinces, but I grew up here."

"Ah, then I was right. In a certain sense you're a 'foreigner'; you come from another place."

The girl nodded her head, smiling with embarrassment. At that moment Antim noticed with a start that she had a very large mouth and irregular teeth. These features gave her an air of wild, threatening, almost aggressive beauty.

"I had heard it, but I couldn't bring myself to believe it. It would be too terrible, I told myself, too terrible if it were true that the Maestro is no longer giving private lessons, just now, when I've found a job and have some money. Just now when I could take lessons! Only a few … Only a lesson or two a month," she added, seeing that he was silent, watching her restlessly, as though he were not listening to her, but was just following the movements of her lips and the gleam of her teeth, now moist, now dull.

He folded his handkerchief, put it into his pocket, and began to button his overcoat.

"I'm sorry," he said, picking up his cello case. "I decided to give up private lessons when I realized I *wasn't succeeding*. I've not been successful for two years, nor for four or five. I'm simply not succeeding."

He turned and saw that the lights were beginning to be turned off at the far end of the hall. "We must go, or we'll be in danger of finding the door locked."

Nevertheless he only strolled forward, holding his cello case in his left hand and trying with his right to turn up the collar on his coat.

"You understand what I mean. One fine day I realized that I wasn't succeeding in helping them, that is, in making them *excel me*."

The girl burst out laughing, and in a quick gesture of familiarity she approached him and took his arm.

"Maestro," she began fervently, "you can't imagine how happy I am. I've heard so much about you. What don't they say, what don't they relate about the Maestro Manolache Antim? But no one ever told me this, and I had no way of guessing it. All I knew was that in a certain sense you'd not had good luck."

Antim stopped and looked at her again over his spectacles, confused.

"You've not had luck with pupils, Maestro. Who has come to study with you? All sorts of prize students. First and second prize winners. Perhaps even a few third prize winners too. But the others, Maestro? The *others*?" she repeated, emphasizing the word and leaning very close to his face.

"What do you mean, the *others* ?"

"Yes, Maestro, the others, those consumed by ambition and plagued by misfortune—the majority, besides. Like Horia Gradișteanu, for instance, of whom no one ever heard because he committed suicide at eighteen. Or like Maria Da Maria ... Myself, Maria Daria Maria—I am she," she added, lowering her voice. "But at school they call me Maria Da Maria."

"We have to hurry, or else we're in danger of ..."

"Allow me to carry your cello," she interrupted him.

The gesture was so unexpected that he had no time to resist it. Embarrassed, he put both hands to his neck, trying to stuff his scarf under the turned-up collar of his coat.

"If I were ten years younger, I'd be angry!" he said.

"You'd be angry now too if it were someone else, a different sort of woman, I mean. It would make no difference whether she were a young woman or an older one. The difference must be sought, not in the age of a woman, but in her destiny."

She stopped suddenly and hugged the cello in her arms, clasping it tight against her body.

"Maestro!" she exclaimed in a choked voice, as though she were about to burst into tears. "Maestro, since you didn't know Horia, then you have before you the most gifted creature and the most proud, the most ambitious young person you have ever met in your life—and yet the one most plagued by misfortune! There have been whole days when I didn't dare cross the street: I *knew* a car would run me down. Maestro, I could *sense* the car from a distance, from ten meters away, I could feel it knocking me down and crushing my fingers. My *fingers*, Maestro, these fingers which, if misfortune had not followed me ... For a whole year I looked for a job that would allow me to take a few private lessons from you—any kind of job, however dull or disgusting, only that my fingers would be spared. A whole year I looked, and in the meantime I lived on the pity of one friend or another, because even the nightclub wouldn't keep me as a hat-check girl. And only now, very recently, this past week, I located a job—but what's the use? If bad luck hadn't hounded me, I'd have found a job two or three months ago and these fingers—you would have seen what they can do, and believe me, Maestro, you'd have been amazed!"

With an effort Antim pushed her slowly toward the door, trying to seem amiable and yet detached, pretending that he did not notice the tears slipping slowly down her cheeks.

"Good night, Vasile," he said to the doorman. "Excuse us for being so late," he added, tightening his scarf around his neck. "I didn't feel very well in the intermission. I've taken a chill. Autumn has come all of a sudden."

* * *

After breaking through the cobwebs with hastily made rolls of old newspapers, Ieronim tried to wipe the dust from the lid of the trunk. But soon he realized it was stuck like a layer of mud, smooth and dry, and he flung the roll of papers among the bundles by the wall. Entrusting the torch to Iconaru, he pulled a ring of old keys out of his pocket.

One by one he tried them at random, without much en-thusiasm. At intervals he shook the padlock violently, as if he wanted to confirm that it really was locked.

"Be more careful," whispered Iconaru. "You're making too much noise. Someone may hear us."

Ieronim looked at him in surprise, frowning. Then he nodded his head, as if he had suddenly realized that the boy was right.

"Then put out the light," he said as softly as he could. "Don't move or say anything for a few minutes. Let's see if anyone heard us."

At first they could hear nothing but the wind, just as in other moments when they had both kept silent in the dark. But soon the sound of a low moan reached them, like a sigh prolonged interminably and then suddenly stifled. After a few seconds, seemingly closer to them, the sound was heard again, this time deeper and followed by a short, frightened gasp, as if someone had passed by them quickly and were heading in the direction of the attic door.

"It's nothing," whispered Ieronim. "Not a ghost or a phantom, I mean. All the sounds we hear come from the skylight overhead. It won't close tightly any more, and the wind shakes it!"

"Shhh!" Iconaru interrupted, grabbing his arm. "Listen now!"

They heard the moan again, but in addition, from the direction of the attic door, there came another kind of noise, louder, as though someone were making his way with difficulty across the old, weakened floorboards, dragging a sack of firewood behind him.

"Perhaps someone heard us," Ieronim continued, lowering his voice even more, "and they're coming to look for us."

Both were silent, holding their breath.

"If someone should catch us," Ieronim began abruptly, doing his best not to raise his voice, "tell him the truth. We met by chance the day before yesterday and I told you about a collection of butterflies. But I told you especially about the theatre, about the secrets of dramatic art. Tell them about the uniforms: that we came intending to take them—you can even specify that we came intending to take them on loan for a week or two, because who would want to keep two general's

   THE GENERAL'S UNIFORMS

uniforms permanently? So, we're agreed then: we came to borrow them; but don't tell them why, for what purpose. For the theatre, tell them. It has to do with the theatre ... You're a schoolboy," he added after a short pause, with an almost solemn air. "You know how to keep a secret. Don't tell them anything except that the uniforms have to do with ..."

"It's no use trying to scare me," Iconaru interrupted him, suddenly switching on the torch. "Just because you saw me with a hurt dove in my hand, you think I'm a poor peasant boy, an ignoramus, a fool!"

Ieronim listened with surprise and grief, his right hand shielding his eyes.

"Don't talk that way any more—you're committing a sacrilege!" he whispered. "You mustn't speak that way about a wounded dove."

"Then why do you want to scare me into thinking that someone might come and catch us here in the attic and turn us over to the police?"

Ieronim slowly withdrew his hand from his eyes and smiled.

"Not for a single moment did I intend to frighten you. I just wanted you to imagine a *possible scene*, not an *event*."

"If you think I'm afraid of ghosts or the police ..."

Ieronim shrugged his shoulders and began to examine the keys one after another.

"I remember very well," he whispered. Suddenly he stopped speaking, looking at one key, holding it quite close to his eyes, wiping it, rubbing it with his handkerchief. Then he tried it carefully, almost trembling with excitement.

"This is it," he announced. "Now, watch closely!"

He removed the padlock, laid it on top of a bundle of magazines, and tried the lid gently. Then he motioned with his head, and Iconaru, passing the torch to his left hand, helped him to raise the lid with his right. It creaked so harshly that they stopped several times, frightened by this sinister, unexpectedly loud metallic noise. When at last they had succeeded in lifting the cover, they were surprised by the immaculate whiteness of the sheets and by the penetrating smell of camphor, naphtha, and basil.

"How evident, down to the last detail, the hand of Generăleasa! She packed things in a trunk the way others in olden-times built monasteries or erected pyramids. Now see how beautiful this sheet is! As white and smooth as if it had been put here yesterday or the day before; and look, put your hand here and feel how silky it is, as if it were a shroud!"

Carefully, almost beside himself, Ieronim slowly pulled back the sheet, rolling it up and shoving it into a corner. Vladimir held the torch much closer and played the beam from one end of the trunk to the other. Ieronim could not suppress a cry of surprise.

"I hadn't expected this! And yet, I should have thought ..."

For some moments they both gazed in silence at the pale green dress with the high collar of black lace.

"It's untouched," whispered Ieronim, "just as the dressmaker had brought it to her a few days earlier. She never got to wear it to the charity ball. She had ordered it specially for the party because she, Caty, was one of the vice-presidents of the Society. But she was terrified of air raids, and when the alarm sounded, she took the children to the shelter at the end of the street, on the corner of Popa Nan."

He stopped and took several deep breaths, as though endeavouring to suppress a sigh.

"Everything went up in smoke," he added. "Carpet-bombed. Not a house was left standing from Popa Nan to here, where we are, a distance of some two hundred meters. Generăleasa did everything she could to find them, but in vain. She even went to the Palace to obtain a special crew to excavate the shelter and search for her. Just to find her daughter! She wanted at any price to bury her in this new dress of hers ... In this dress," he added, taking hold of the collar with trepidation and drawing it slowly toward himself. "In vain. Nothing was found. Only ashes ..."

He stretched out his arm as far as he could, holding up the dress while Iconaru played the light over all of it, from top to bottom.

"But you see, I ought to have thought," Ieronim resumed, folding up the dress and laying it on top of the sheet. "I ought to have imagined that Generăleasa would have preserved it like a holy relic, because this was all that remained of Caty, her youngest daughter and up to that time the most fortunate of her children. Generăleasa had four children, and Caty was the only one happily married. (She didn't know that at the time of the bombing raid her husband, Vanghele—Captain Vanghele—was dying in a hospital in Iași.) The other two daughters had not been lucky in marriage. One was divorced and lived at Craiova; she was involved in an affair with the vice-president of a bank. While the other, Voica—it's better not to remember about her. Eventually, she did away with herself."

"May God forgive her," said Iconaru, crossing himself.

"May God forgive them all," Ieronim murmured softly. "One and all," he added mostly to himself, because his words were barely audible. "It was like a curse in a classical tragedy. Not one escaped."

Then all of a sudden he squared his shoulders and raised his head.

"How beautiful if it had been just that—a classical tragedy!" he exclaimed abruptly in a voice suddenly firm. "If it had been only a 'spectacle', if you know what I mean. If all of this had been just a part of a drama I imagined. And of course, if I had invented it, it would have been truer than all that really happened. The reason why theatre is *truer* is because you can leave one drama and go on to others. Or you can even step out of the play entirely. At any time I could address the Chorus and tell them, 'Enough, now! I've listened to you long enough. It's too much, too much tragedy! Let's all go to Caty and beg her pardon. Tante Caty,' I'd say, 'forgive me for killing you again, forgive me that I killed you this time with all those children, in an air raid!'"

He frowned and bent farther over the trunk. Hurriedly, yet intently, he began to rummage through it, picking up and laying aside what he found: peasant blouses, kerchiefs of fine silk and woolen scarves, peasant skirts, sashes.

"This was their great passion, to dress in peasant style. They'd collected costumes from all the peasant provinces. They were reared in the cult of the unity of the Romanian people, and so we must respect them for this passion, however naive it may seem to us. But at least they didn't dress up like shepherds and shepherdesses, as the Western European aristocrats of the eighteenth century did, in the ridiculous hope that they could recover the blessedness of the pastoral life in an environment of 'nature', that is, in the surroundings of artificial grottos, artesian wells, and pre-romantic ruins."

He realized all at once that Iconaru's arm was trembling.

"You've taken a chill, haven't you?"

He hunted among the costumes, selected two scarves, and laid them on the boy's shoulders.

"Have a little more patience, and when we come to the uniforms, we'll put them on."

"But the butterflies?" asked Iconaru, wrapping one of the scarves around his neck. When do we get to the butterflies?"

For some time Ieronim did not reply. He continued to search nervously and more hurriedly, laying aside girl's dresses, lace shawls, and blouses and jerseys of all colours.

"The box with the butterflies," Iconaru repeated. "Because, so far as I'm concerned, that's what I came for."

"More precisely, the *boxes* with butterflies; because there are many of them, a great many."

While he was speaking, Ieronim, in great excitement, took hold of a bridal gown and held it up as high as he could, in the beam of the torch, to admire it better.

"Whose might this have been?" he asked himself, curious, yet with a trace of sadness in his voice. "By its style and material it surely was used before my time ... Are you still cold?" he asked Vladimir. "Hold still until I put something on your back."

He found a Transylvanian peasant's skirt and laid it like a cape over the boy's shoulders. He was about to say something else when he saw a huge black spider which seemed to have emerged just then from under the trunk, and he stuck out his foot to crush it.

"Please, the boxes with the butterflies," Iconaru insisted.

"They're down below, in one of the rooms. And it's never locked. Only first we must dress in the General's uniforms and gird ourselves with a sword apiece, if we find them in their places, in the wardrobe"—and he pointed with outstretched arm toward the door—"and then we'll go down. Don't be afraid—no one can catch us. The Maestro is a distant relative of mine, a sort of uncle. 'Oncle Vania', I call him. And I know his habits well. He never returns home until two or three a.m., after the bistro closes.

But we'll have to be careful not to turn on the lights, because the neighbours might notice us. We'll have to be content with this torch."

He stopped speaking suddenly, and, displaying some fancy footwork, he pursued and smashed three more black spiders, one after another, which had darted in different directions, making little jumps as though they were flying.

"That's a shame," Iconaru said softly. "You didn't have to kill them. They weren't doing you any harm."

* * *

Several times, in front of the coffee house, Antim tried in vain to take the cello case from her hand. Finally, he threw up his arms in exasperation. Then, opening the door wide, he invited her to enter. To his surprise, the girl went inside with a firm step, her head held high, smiling and glancing all around as though she were looking for someone—or perhaps it was just to convince herself that she was not intimidated. It was past ten when they arrived and the coffee house (which was a bistro as well because in the evenings you could order crenwurst and eggs) was almost full. From several tables Antim heard people call out to him, but he pretended not to notice and headed straight toward the back of the room.

"Bravo, Maestro!" Iliescu congratulated him. Iliescu had not been assigned any role in the autumn theatrical season, and lest people think it had dampened his spirits, he came every evening to the coffee house, accompanied by a boisterous group of girls.

Antim shrugged and made a vague gesture with his left arm, showing weariness and resignation.

"I'm rather tired," he said. "This is a pupil of mine."

The girl walked on, her step just as firm as before but faster, because she saw a free table at the back in a secluded corner.

"Bravo, Maestro!" someone shouted again. "A good choice!"

"This is a pupil of mine," he replied with a bitter smile. "My last pupil. You'll soon be hearing about her."

They sat down facing each other and Maria quickly took his hand into hers and whispered, "Thank you, Maestro. Thank you for everything."

He withdrew his hand slowly and, turning his head, made a sign to the waiter.

"Don't thank me," he said, "because you don't know what's coming."

Smiling mysteriously, he took off his scarf, then sought his handkerchief and wiped his glasses. The waiter started to help him remove his overcoat, but he prevented him.

"I'll keep it on a while, until I warm up a little more."

Then he turned toward the girl.

"For the lady …" he began.

"For me, a cup of tea," Maria said. "And if you have a sandwich with ham or cheese—or with anything," she added quickly, smiling without lowering her eyes.

"And for me, along with the tea, bring a cognac. I seem to have taken a chill."

He adjusted his glasses and looked at her again, intently, searchingly.

"So, you're a foreigner. I repeat this because I've always felt I have important news, significant revelations, to learn from foreigners, from people who have come from other places. In my imagination they come from *another world*, even if they come only from Iași or Ploești. For that reason, I'm glad we've met. Without meaning to, without knowing it, you bring me news. I'm very curious to know: what sort of news? What tidings? What revelations ?"

The girl blushed quickly, then smiled. "I, Maestro?"

"Don't smile. Don't think I'm a crazy old man. Although I've felt rather feeble for some time, I'm really not so old and I'm certainly not crazy. But this has been my life: *exclusively* the result of encounters with men and women who were foreigners. It's too long a story to tell you in one evening, but I have to say at least this much: all the women with whom I ever believed I was in love were foreigners, they were from other places."

The girl lowered her eyes suddenly because it seemed that people at the neighbouring tables were beginning to listen.

"Maybe it's only a coincidence," Antim continued, "but what a strange coincidence, when I tell you that none of these loves was fulfilled. Moreover, I broke three engagements, although through no fault of my own. And all of this *on account of a story*. Yes, Maria Da Maria," he said, raising his eyes and looking at her, suddenly animated, "purely and simply for a story. It's true, a rather strange story and one written, probably, by a rather obscure author, because I've long since forgotten his name and no one has ever heard either of him or his story. You might call it a novella, although it was quite short, hardly more than a sketch."

He broke off speaking suddenly and stared dreamy-eyed, almost absently, as the waiter set down the cups of tea and the plate with the sandwiches.

"Thank you, Petrache," he said when the waiter, winking knowingly, placed the glass of cognac, full to the brim, close by him. "Please, don't stand on ceremony," he added, seeing that the girl had not made a move but was sitting with her eyes fixed on the plate. "Try the one with ham first."

He sipped alternately from his teacup and his glass.

"I believe I read it in school, when I was fourteen or fifteen," he began after glancing around as though to assure himself again that there was no familiar face nearby. "I never suspected then that I'd become a musician, although I'd played the violin ever since the age of five, and soon after that I had discovered the cello. But my passion then was natural science, especially entomology and above all butterflies. And I haven't recovered from this passion even to the present day. But after I read that story, my life was changed. I *had* to become a musician. I felt—I *knew*—that only art, in my case music, could cure me of my obsession. Because, actually, that's what it was: an obsession. I found myself reproduced, from beginning to end, in the hero of that story. It was as though all his adventures had happened to me. And what was it all about? It will seem absurd when I tell you: a matter of something that had happened in a former life."

"In a former life?" Maria broke in, looking deeply into his eyes, puzzled and somewhat alarmed. "So it was a story about metempsychosis?"

Antim picked up his teacup, then changed his mind and replaced it slowly, with great care on the saucer.

"There are many stories of metempsychosis in the world," he said, shrugging his shoulders and smiling. "But that wasn't what impressed me—the fact that things had happened in another life. What impressed me was this detail, which appears simple and rather commonplace, that two lovers broke their engagement because the young man, unintentionally, made a discovery one day. And of course he hurried to tell his fiancée, who, for motives hard to understand, felt herself insulted and left him. It's beyond my powers to understand what happened, why the girl was so upset."

Without being aware of it, Maria blushed.

"The story, I repeat, is a very simple one," Antim continued. He looked up and noticed that she had scarcely taken a bite from the second sandwich and seemed embarrassed, not daring to eat. "In a word, the events had taken place several centuries earlier, probably in the Middle Ages, somewhere in western Europe. And the hero of the story was a juggler, a clown, a sleight-of-hand artist, or whatever you want to call it."

He interrupted himself in order to drink more deeply of the cognac. After wiping his spectacles again, he sat for a few moments dreamily staring straight ahead without seeing her.

"And now, when you hear the story," he began in a firm tone of voice, "you'll be surprised it made such an impression on me. That young man, the fiancé of the girl, was, as I told you, a juggler, a clown. I remember now the climactic scene: he was costumed and was preparing to mask, that is to put paint on his cheeks, when he heard voices and laughter not very far away. Probably he was in a fair of some sort, in a tent, hidden by a curtain, getting ready to appear again before the spectators and make them laugh with his acrobatics and jugglery. When all at once, said the author, the young man became aware of his *decadence*—in a certain sense, his *treason*. All at once, at that moment, he understood that a juggler and clown like himself had been made to *entertain the gods*, to amuse them by means of his acrobatics and sleight-of-hand tricks, and now he, and everyone like him, was entertaining *people*."

"I don't understand," whispered Maria, paling slightly.

"It's hard to understand," Antim went on, signalling the waiter across the room, "because this was something that wasn't known then, in the fourteenth or fifteenth century, and I wonder how the juggler discovered it. Indeed, not everyone knows this fact even today. But that's the way it was. All the acrobatics, the juggling, and the jokes of clowns were, in the beginning, invented to amuse the gods."

He stopped, waiting for the waiter to approach.

"The same again; unless the lady wants a cognac too."

"No, thank you, Maestro," Maria said quickly. "Perhaps, at most, a little rum in the tea … But why would the gods have need of our jugglery?" she added a few moments later, with a smile.

"Don't ask me. I don't know the answer to that one. What is certain is that all the arts—vocal and instrumental music, the dance, sculpture, painting—all were invented to pay homage to the gods and serve them."

"Music, the dance, the theatre—this I understand," said Maria …

"But this idea does not, properly speaking, constitute the theme of the novella," Antim interrupted her. "The real drama begins after that, after the young man tells his fiancée about the discovery he has made: that he, the famous artist, the champion clown and juggler, has betrayed his *true vocation* which was, in a certain sense, *religious*, and has become, like everyone else in his guild, a simple craftsman performing at fairs, flattered and happy that he can amuse all kinds of people from the lords and ladies of the castle to their field workers and servants."

"And then," asked Maria, puzzled, "what happened? Why did they separate?"

"It's precisely this that I don't exactly understand. Maybe I don't remember the ending of the story any more. His fiancée, the author wrote, left him that very night—left for the wide world."

"But *why*?" Maria persisted, "Was she afraid that her fiancé, in the wake of his discovery, would no longer be, so to speak, at his best? That he would no longer be the foremost artist, admired and praised as he had been up to then? I don't know."

Antim was silent for some time, smiling wistfully.

"I should have liked a different ending, something more dramatic, even melodramatic. For instance, that he had surprised her when she was getting ready to run away, and that he had said he would search for her for the rest of his life, and that if he didn't find her, he would seek her in other lives, and that until she should come to him, he would never rest."

He broke off and looked intently, almost admiringly, at the deftness with which the waiter had set the glass of cognac in front of him without spilling a drop.

"Thanks, Petrache. You're a wonder!"

Antim put the glass to his lips and sipped carefully. Then he turned toward Maria.

"… But he didn't say anything," he continued. "Or, at any rate, if he did, I don't remember it. The end of the story was quite banal. Probably that's why I've forgotten it."

"It's a pity," Maria said softly.

"How many people I've asked!" continued Antim, becoming animated again. "When I was young, I would no sooner begin to be well acquainted with someone than I would ask him if perchance he had read that story, and I would summarize it. Sometimes I'd become very excited, because if I saw he was listening closely, frowning as though trying to remember, I would begin to hope: perhaps this time I'm in luck, and I'll learn the name of the author and the title of that novella, or at least I'll find out the ending … I made a fool of myself in those days, back in 1914 on the eve of the War."

He sipped a little from his cup of tea, then picked up the glass of cognac and held it in his hand a long while.

"But, as I was saying, this story changed my life. Not only because it *made* me become a musician, but especially because—it seems so ridiculous, so absurd, that I don't expect you to believe it—because, I tell you in all seriousness, every woman I ever loved (whom, of course, I couldn't help telling about the discovery the character in the story had made) left me. Not right on the spot, as in the story, but within a short while afterward."

Maria had listened to him in fascination, first turning pale, then blushing.

"But why would they be upset? Did they think I was naive, or too sentimental, or perhaps downright stupid—because who could take seriously a story written by an obscure author, and such an absurd one at that?"

"It wasn't so absurd," Maria said softly, "if it changed your life."

For the first time, Antim broke into a laugh. He laughed in a reconciled yet bitter way, as old men sometimes do.

"I'm glad I've convinced you, and convinced you so quickly," he said, still smiling. "You don't realize how right you are! On the one hand, I was unable to forge a permanent bond with any of the women I loved—who were, I repeat, all foreigners. On the other hand, that story wrenched me away from my butterflies and made me, eventually, a cellist: first in a quartet in Vienna, and now here, in the Philharmonic Orchestra. But why only this much? Why haven't I achieved what was predicted for me in my youth—what Casals, in fact, predicted in 1926: 'One of the greatest, among the first two or three cellists in the world'?"

"But, yes, Maestro," Maria interrupted, "you *have* attained it! That's what you are—one of the great ones!"

"I know what I'm saying," Antim went on, smiling bitterly. "You spoke about ambition, you said you're consumed by an ambition that's almost a disease. My congratulations, Maria Daria! If you believe in your genius, you have to be sick with ambition."

"But in my case ..."

"Don't interrupt me, since you don't know what I intend to say next. Perhaps, in a sense, I too was ambitious. Because, actually, I did agree to give concerts. I tried, so to speak, to *manifest myself*. But that was not enough. Success didn't matter to me—neither with the critics nor the public. It didn't matter to me for the simple reason that *I couldn't play for people*. That story radically changed my conception of art. I couldn't play for my fellow beings, for men. But then for whom? For the gods? But the gods don't exist. For God? But if you truly believe in God, it would be an impiety to play profane music for him ... to play *lieder*, waltzes, and love songs for him, as you might for some rich gentleman. But, if you don't believe in God, as I fear is true in my case, then for whom?"

"For the angels, Maestro!" Maria exclaimed passionately and almost pathetically. "For the angels!"

Antim burst into laughter anew. Blushing, Maria reached across the table and took his hand.

"You don't understand me, Maestro. When I say for the angels, I'm not talking about angels in churches or in heaven, in museums or on picture post cards. I play for the angels inside us—Because everyone has within him an angel—not a guardian angel, but an angel who sighs, locked in the darkness of the soul of each of us. Only rarely, very rarely do we succeed in realizing him and freeing him to take wing and mount up; and then, together with him, our souls, the souls of every one of us, are purified and uplifted."

Antim listened, troubled, blinking his eyes now and then as though struggling to awaken from a dream.

"Please, silence!" he burst out suddenly in a choked voice, almost unrecognizable. "Silence!" he repeated.

Embarrassed, Maria withdrew her hand and sat with downcast eyes. At the same moment Antim became aware of the fact that all the people around them had been listening, and with an effort he smiled.

"It's difficult to explain," he said. "But it has nothing to do with me."

* * *

They had dressed themselves in the General's uniforms and Ieronim had begun to put things back into the trunk, working quickly and yet very carefully and with much attention.

"Yours fits you marvelously," Vladimir whispered, "as though it were made for you. But mine hangs on me like street urchin's clothes."

"It'll keep you warm," Ieronim consoled him. "It's like an overcoat lined with wool."

"But see how it hangs! It reaches almost to my knees! And look at the sleeves!" he added, stretching out his arm.

"I told you; it'll keep you warm. You can take it off after we go down to the salon. It's easier to carry it on your back than in your hands. We don't have much time."

He laid the bridal gown on top of the other things, but then he realized with astonishment that there was no room for it in the trunk. For a few moments he was at a loss as to what to do.

"Maybe it'd be better if I roll up the sleeves," Vladimir said. "If you'll just hold the torch a moment ..."

Ieronim took it with one hand, and with the other, absent-mindedly, he began pressing down on the fringes of the dress.

"And yet I well remember that it wasn't folded or doubled over."

With the sleeves of the tunic turned up, Vladimir took the torch again, and the two of them examined the position of the gown.

"Since it won't be used any more," Vladimir began, "I say put it in any way you can. It's getting late."

Ieronim continued his efforts, pressing down first on the skirt, then on the upper part.

"I wonder how Generăleasa laid it in the trunk without doubling it over. Look, no matter what I do, however much I press on it, there's always some left on the outside."

"I say let's not waste any more time," Vladimir began, but he stopped speaking suddenly, frightened. Signaling Ieronim to be still, he put his finger to his lips and switched off the light. "I heard something" he whispered as softly as he could ...

After the first measures, Antim closed his eyes, and it seemed to him suddenly that he was dreaming, that he was with Casals again on that afternoon in May when, without prior arrangement, he had knocked timidly on the door and said, "Pardon me, please, but I'm an entomologist." Probably he had succeeded in disarming him that way, because fifteen minutes later Casals was listening to him very attentively with his customary frown and then he congratulated him. "You did well to give up entomology!" he said, laughing. Then he picked up his cello, and looking at him with obvious liking, winking at him in boyish fashion he replayed the same piece. And now Casals was playing again, the whole Opus 56, and he was playing it in this salon—this cold, damp, poorly-lighted, run-down, and half-ruined salon!

"Oncle Vania's come back!" Ieronim whispered. "I don't know what could have happened, because ordinarily he doesn't come home before two or three a.m. Besides, he doesn't play," he added. "He never plays after a concert."

"What'll we do?" Vladimir asked timidly. "What if he hears us?"

"Don't be afraid. When he's listening to music he doesn't hear anything else. He must have brought someone home with him from the orchestra, to check some passage. So he won't be staying very long. The others are waiting for him at the coffee house. They're waiting to play chess with him."

He added the last words very softly, mostly to himself, but without being able to control his irritation. He seemed to hear again Caimata, speaking in a pretentious, patronizing way, yet with respect and almost reverently. Whenever they met, he could talk of nothing else.

"It's hopeless, Ieronim," he'd begin, putting his hand heavily on his shoulder. "As brilliant as Conu* Manolache is in music, no one excels him at chess. He could become national champion any time. *Anytime*! But he doesn't want to. He's not interested. In the finals he lets himself be beaten, as though he wanted to spite us—*us*, his friends and admirers!"

Antim had long since opened his eyes, but he dared not look at her. Leaning slightly over the cello, Maria was smiling sadly as in a dream. Those incomparable measures which prepare so subtly for the finale surpassed his previous understanding of them. When the echoes of the last notes had died away, he sprang to his feet, went to her, kissed both her cheeks and then her hands.

"You were right, Maria," he began excitedly. "These fingers ..."

He was afraid that the tears would start to flow, so he took a few steps back and began to unbutton his overcoat, as if he had suddenly decided to take it off.

"Don't catch cold, Maestro," said Maria. "It's colder in here than it is outside."

Antim remained undecided for a few moments, standing with his coat half unbuttoned.

"You were right," he repeated, lowering his voice. "We've not had good luck, neither you nor I. We've lost so much time. You ought to have sought me long ago, come to see me. You'd have been famous by today."

"Thank you, Maestro," whispered Maria, shyly wiping away her tears with the back of her hand.

"Won't you play something else? But this time one of your favourites."

* An archaic form of deferential address for children and young boyars, sometimes used affectionately but humorously.

Maria looked at him, a broad smile lighting her face. Then she leaned slightly over the cello and waited.

"We could put things back in the trunk," Iconaru whispered, "even like this in the dark. They're just ladies' things and they don't make any noise …"

Antim was dreaming again … "I'm an entomologist," he repeated, "but when I was about fourteen or fifteen I read a strange story, quite an odd one, in some ways an absurd tale—and that story *forced* me to become a musician."

Casals listened to him, smiling all the while, and to his amazement, he did not seem surprised. "Actually, this happens to all of us, to all artists," he said. "On the one hand we *betray*—we betray an ideal—because any ideal ultimately is inaccessible. But on the other hand …"

Suddenly Maria stopped and looked up toward the ceiling in fright.

"Pardon me, Maestro, but I can't go on … I'm afraid! I think there's someone walking around in the attic!"

Antim began to laugh without, however, managing to hide his vexation.

"I always hear things like that at night, especially in autumn when the wind's blowing. This house is falling down. You can see that for yourself," he added, pointing toward the far end of the salon.

In the shadows several boards could be seen nailed along the walls, haphazardly covered with faded, frayed, moth-eaten draperies.

"He's not playing any more," Ieronim whispered. "That means he's getting ready to leave. Hand me the torch a moment."

He turned it on and shading the light with his left hand he headed toward the door on tiptoe.

"It's not the wind, Maestro," said Maria, listening, with her head slightly tilted back. "Someone's walking in the attic. And a little while ago I heard whispering too."

Antim listened for a few moments, then abruptly left the room. After switching on the hall light he went to the foot of the wooden stairs that led to the attic and shouted in a surprisingly harsh voice, "Ieronim! Come down here immediately! *Tu entends*? Immediately!"

He returned with the culprit in hand, and presented him.

"My nephew, Ieronim Thanase. Perhaps you remember hearing of him about ten years ago when he was a child prodigy and played at the Municipal Theater. He was the most precocious actor we ever had."

Ieronim walked erect, with his head held high, smiling, but in front of Maria he bowed, and with an exaggerated politeness kissed her hand.

"Kiss both her hands," Antim commanded, "because she is a very great artist! Maria Daria Maria, from this day forward my pupil, but a pupil in name only, because she had surpassed me even before she met me."

"Maestro ..." Maria began in chagrin.

"She is, of course, a foreigner. Her parents are from the provinces. When I met her this evening, I wondered what revelation she had to give me. I didn't suppose that it would be this: her genius!"

"Maestro," whispered Maria again.

Ieronim continued to kiss her hands, first one, then the other, gently yet insistently.

"Enough now," Antim said, laughing. "*Ça suffit*! You will listen to her also and you will be convinced: she is going to be, if she is not already, the most brilliant cellist of our time!"

He adjusted his glasses and looked at his nephew in sudden curiosity, measuring him from head to toe.

"What are you doing dressed in the General's uniform?"

Ieronim turned toward Maria and scrutinized her gravely.

"Can you keep a secret?" he asked her finally. "At least for a week or two, until the performance?"

Then, without waiting for a reply, he turned back to Antim.

"Because, in a week or two, we're playing *Hamlet* at the Experimental Theater—our theatre. I want to interpret Hamlet's father, and how could I express the condition of a ghost more vividly than in this uniform of a Romanian general, the uniform of a hero of the First World War?"

"It's absurd!" Antim interrupted, smiling with amusement. "It's absurd … but nothing you do surprises me."

Ieronim started toward Maria resolutely, almost menacingly.

"Is it *really* so absurd?" he asked her, looking into her eyes. "Simply because nothing like it has ever been done before? But a uniform of a Romanian general tells *us* more clearly and more directly than could any other baroque costume—the alleged garb of a prince from a fictitious Denmark—it tells us that we have to do with a dead man, or specifically with death, with something which has been and can be no more—which can be no more because a tragedy has intervened."

Maria stared at him, smiling as she listened.

"It will be hard," she said in an unexpectedly kind voice, "it will be hard to convince the spectators that you're the ghost of the assassinated king. The way you look now, in that Romanian general's uniform: young and slim and, as you know, more handsome than a man has a right to be, you seem more like a romantic hero out of Byron or Pushkin."

Ieronim paled slightly, and a sudden sadness darkened his countenance.

"In other words, all you've understood is that I'll appear on the stage in the role of the ghost, that I'll walk on in this general's uniform as you see me now! And yet I specifically stated that we're staging *Hamlet* in *our* theatre, which is an experimental theatre. Hasn't it entered your head that I'll be masked in such a way that no one will recognize my face? But what if I were to tell you that I'm going to play the part of *Hamlet* too? As you will recall, at the beginning of Act I both Hamlet and his father are on the stage—that is, I shall be there twice, and at the same time!"

He approached Maria, took her hand and squeezed it excitedly in his hands.

"Princess Maria, Oncle Vania says that you're a genius. Then you understand what it was like for me all those years when I was the spoiled *wunderkind* of the Municipal Theater. They destroyed me, Maria Daria; they drained me of any trace of talent. And for this only was I born—for the spectacle. But they mutilated my imagination, they hardened my intellect, they corrupted all the gifts with which the Fates endowed me in the cradle. Cursed precocity! ... And when I could no longer be a *wunderkind* because I was more than five feet three, they forced me into juvenile leads. It was the only time in my life when the thought of suicide tempted me. But then I revolted and abandoned it all. I tried to forget everything they had taught me—and, I assure you, Princess, I succeeded in forgetting. I became more ignorant, more naive, more *pure* than ever an actor was in the whole history of the theatre. And after that I started all over again, from the beginning. I recreated the *spectacle*; I reinvented dramatic art."

He began pacing nervously, restlessly, in front of them.

"This is what each of us must do, we people of today in the second half of the twentieth century: we must reinvent everything, from language to Pascal's wager, from love to institutions, from ethics to gymnastics."

"Pardon me," Maria interrupted. "I didn't mean to offend you. I don't know you, and when I tried to imagine you in the role of the ghost of an assassinated king—But now I'm beginning to understand you."

"I congratulate you," said Antim good-naturedly, smiling and taking a seat in the armchair. "As much as I admire his intelligence, I cannot boast that I always understand him."

Ieronim paused in front of him and went through the motions of a genuflection playfully.

"Because you, Oncle Vania, don't like drama, pure *spectacle*, in a word: tragedy. Nevertheless, we two have experienced it as few of our contemporaries have. You don't like tragedy, although you continue to live here *in this house*," and he pointed with outstretched arm to the far end of the salon. "That's why you like chess so much. When you play chess you think, you imagine, you make correct or incorrect moves; you pay for your errors and you lose the game. But *that's* not tragedy!"

Antim maintained his smile.

"Alright, alright, you've convinced me!" he tried to interrupt. "Besides, you know why I play chess: I do it out of desperation … Like everyone else," he added, lowering his voice.

Ieronim approached him with light steps, seeking his eyes.

"I reproach you for this too, for doing what everyone else does. But what do we have in common with those others? Why have we survived—only we *two*—out of a family of 39?"

Antim tried to interrupt again, raising both arms as if he were endeavouring to fend off a restive colt which was galloping toward him.

"Now, please, at this advanced hour, *je t'en supplie*, don't start revealing family secrets!"

"I beg your pardon," Ieronim said, going to Maria, putting his right hand over his heart and bowing from the waist. "From time to time I suffer from attacks of indiscretion; the most vulgar species of indiscretion. But just now I only meant that we two, the Maestro and I, the only two survivors of the Calomfir, Antim, and Thanase families are—and surely not by chance—the only artists to have arisen from our lineage."

He turned toward Antim suddenly, trying to smile.

"But this noble vocation obliges us, Oncle Manolache. Leave it to others such as Caimata and Zamfir to play chess in desperation. We must face up to our destiny, accept tragedy as the only mode of existence worthy of an artist endowed with so many dead relatives: dead ones whom we carry, like it or not, on our backs. Too long has Fate held us in her embrace, too long has misfortune pursued us!"

Maria reddened suddenly and, frightened, sought Antim's eyes.

"Please, don't talk about misfortune," Antim tried to interrupt again. "I know it all too well, and so does Maria."

"Yet another reason for admiring her!" Ieronim exclaimed, going to her suddenly and kissing her hand. "But it isn't enough to know misfortune, Oncle Vania," he continued fervently. "We know it for nothing if we don't know what to do with it, if we don't dare to take it upon ourselves."

Approaching Maria even more closely, he scrutinized her gravely.

"Princess, if you're the genius the Maestro says you are, then you'll have to admit I'm right. We must not be afraid of a tragic destiny and misfortune. These are the preconditions of our creative genius. At least *we*, those of us present here, have no other preconditions put at our disposal. So, what can we do?—Be glad we have what we have; it might have been worse: we might have been predestined to nothingness, to death. So let's enjoy what we have—and let's assume our destiny and misfortune!"

"Ieronim, you're frightening my girl" Antim exclaimed, frowning in pretended anger. Ieronim looked at both of them, baffled.

"A genius, a Princess of the Spirit, frightened by nothing more than that?" he exclaimed with emphasis. "When ..."

"I know what misfortune is," Maria calmly interrupted him. "As long as I can remember, misfortune has followed me. As I was saying to the Maestro ..."

She stopped speaking suddenly and turned pale. In the doorway with the general's uniform hanging almost to his knees, but with the sleeves turned up so far they seemed too short, his face smeared with dust and soot, stood Iconaru, listening. In a few steps Ieronim was at his side, putting his arm around his shoulder.

"This is none other than Iconaru Vladimir, of whom I was just about to speak. I met him the day before yesterday on the street, *carrying a wounded dove in his hand.*"

"Some no-good had hurt it with a sling-shot. I was afraid the cats would eat it."

With his arm still around his shoulders, Ieronim slowly ushered him into the living room.

"Do you hear him? He doesn't realize that he was holding in his hands a whole theology, that he was carrying the faith and hope of the entire human race!"

"Don't make fun of me any more," Iconaru interrupted him, "just because you can see I'm from the country."

"Vladimir Iconaru!" Ieronim exclaimed pathetically. "How could I dare make fun of you? When I saw you with that wounded dove—even at that moment I was tempted by *doubt* and I said: maybe it's all an illusion, an hallucination of ours;

maybe it's no more than a compassionate schoolboy who gathers up wounded doves from the wastelands."

"Someone had hit it with a stone."

Antim rose from his chair and tried to adjust his glasses for a better look.

"Now, explain to me what's going on," he said. "Who is this young man?"

Iconaru took several steps toward him, stopped, clicking his heels militaristically, and presented himself.

"My name is Iconaru Vladimir, pupil in the seventh year of the Lycée Gheorghe Lazăr. I was born in the town of Adunați, district of Olt. My father was a teacher, but the war left him an invalid, and he died a year ago. I want to study the natural sciences."

Ieronim interrupted him, taking his arm.

"He believes, and he says, that he is an entomologist, but obviously he is something else and *someone* else: he's the boy who brought a wounded dove in his hand. I said that we have to reinvent Pascal's wager," he added, seeking Maria's and Antim's eyes in turn.

"But why have you dressed him in a general's uniform too?" Antim inquired.

"Because he was cold, and up there in the attic in front of the trunk, he'd started to shiver."

He turned suddenly to Iconaru.

"What a good coat—warm and heavy!" he exclaimed dreamily. "What a heavy coat, brother Vladimir, as though it were a warm body which had embraced you, to defend you from the cold!"

Unexpectedly, taking several steps resembling the gliding of a skater, Ieronim transversed a part of the salon; then he returned just as abruptly and stopped in front of Antim.

"As in 'Master and Man'—do you remember, Oncle Vania?—when Vasily Andreyevich lay himself down on top of Nikita to protect him from freezing. And he did protect him, saving his life at the cost of his own. How did Tolstoy guess what was to happen in Russia forty or fifty years after he had written 'Master and Man': that the nobility and squires would be sacrificed down to the last man, but that the peasants would be saved? How did Tolstoy guess *that*?"

"I don't understand your analogy very well," said Antim, turning to sit down again in the armchair, trying to hide his weariness.

Ieronim raised his arm straight up in the air.

"You don't have to understand, because it's a sociological interpretation, and it doesn't go with our general's uniforms ... because, Princess," he added, turning toward Maria, "this general's uniform which keeps me warm is for me art, the ludic genius, but for Iconaru Vladimir it's simply a festive costume, a costume for a masquerade. As long as we can put on our costumes and *play* we are saved!"

Maria looked in Antim's direction and smiled, perplexed.

"It's become late," she said, "and maybe the Maestro is tired."

"On the contrary, on the contrary," Antim protested. "I'm just beginning to feel good. When I listen to Ieronim, I regain my youth."

Touched, Ieronim approached him and genuflected quickly once again.

"*You* are *my* youth, Oncle Vania," he said, lowering his voice. "But what would we have done, the two of us, if destiny had not produced Iconaru Vladimir on our path; now, *when we both are so in need*? Because, no matter how well I may describe him, I still don't succeed in conveying the mystery of his manifestation ... Oncle Manolache, *he isn't afraid*! He's not afraid of big black spiders ..."

"They don't do any harm," Iconaru, smiling, interrupted him. "They have their purpose too!"

"And he wasn't afraid when Moș* Vasile Chelaru passed by us, dragging his sack of kindling," Ieronim continued, becoming animated, "nor when he heard Veronica moaning in fright and then running toward the door, murmuring between sighs, 'I don't want to die; Mama, tell them I don't want to die!' But maybe he didn't hear the words because Veronica fled too quickly, hurrying, poor thing, to reach the attic door. And as for seeing, I'm sure he didn't catch sight of them, although they were wheeling all around us."

"That's not true!" shouted Vladimir. "You made them up, just to scare me. There weren't any spooks. It was just the wind blowing!"

Ieronim stared at him absently, dreamily.

"There *were*, brother Iconaru; but because you won't believe in the existence of those poor souls, cursed to haunt the attic of the Calomfir house, they have ceased to be; they have simply returned to nothingness."

Antim removed his glasses, irritated, and holding them between his fingers he raised his hand threateningly.

"Ieronim!" he whispered sharply, "Stop that now! *Ça suffit!*"

Ieronim hurried to the elder man's chair and before Antim realized what was happening, knelt, took his hand, and kissed it.

"Forgive me, Moș Manolache!" he exclaimed, deeply moved. "But what can I do if the Fates have cursed me to *see*, to *imagine*, to *create*? I realize no one was there. There's no one in the attic of our house any longer. We heard nothing except the

---

* Literally forebear or ancestor, a term of polite address to an elder of the family [ed.].

wind through the skylight. But I ask you, Maestro, wouldn't it have been beautiful to have believed that we heard Moș Vasile Chelaru and Veronica? To have been frozen by fright, to have known, so young—and Vladimir is still a child—for both of us to have known the nameless terror and that moment without beginning or end, when we humans discover that we are never alone?"

"What a morbid imagination!" Maria suddenly burst out, hardly controlling the exasperation in her voice. "A young, cultured artist like you, inventing obsessions of terror for yourself!"

Ieronim rose to his feet and looked at her, troubled.

"Unfortunately," he said, "I haven't invented anything. I myself am the product of terror. So I defend myself as best as I can: I defend myself by play-acting, by transforming obsession and misfortune into *spectacle*."

Maria halted a step in front of him and looked at him wildly, breathing hard, trembling.

"With your family name, with your talent, boldness, and beauty, you have no right to speak of misfortune! If they abused your intelligence and talent when you were a child prodigy, you've succeeded in recovering from it by yourself, as you admitted a little while ago. But even then, when you were a prodigy, no one tried to disfigure you so you could never play again in a theatre. *Never*!"

She stopped then, looking very pale. Breathing deeply, she tried to stifle a sigh.

"The way they tried to do to me at school, when they beat me with the stick and struck my fingers, to break at least one if possible ... The way it happened to me at the threshing machine, although I begged them to let me do something else. I said that I loved the cello, that the cello was my life; I implored them on bended knees to spare my fingers. And ever since, I wake up almost every night, screaming in terror, and I touch my fingers, I turn on the light and look at them one by one. And on account of fear, I don't dare go back to bed, and I sit there with my head in my hands, crying, and I kiss my fingers! For years I've had no other taste in my mouth but the taste of the tears that come from kissing my fingers."

* * *

Iconaru sat with the box in his lap, clutching it tightly with both hands. He had memorized now the position of every one of those fabulous coleoptera from Central Africa: *Augosoma centaurus*, with its eccentric horn, was right in the middle of the box; while to its left was a *Macrorrhinia*, green, with horns like a stag's; and on its right a *Sternotomis virescens*, white with green stripes, like the one in the Soșea Museum in front of which he always lingered ("But my specimen is better preserved," Antim had said). In the second row was a *Cetonia scarabaeidae*, then a *Taurrhina longiceps* with green elytrons sparkling like precious gems; next *Phryneta leprosa*, which he had seen before only in photographs. Although he had learned their locations by heart, he still could not believe that this treasure was his. "I haven't been interested in coleoptera for a long time," Antim had said, leading him to the rear of the living room. "Look," he exclaimed, stopping to indicate the place, "here there was once a large mirror, almost as high as the ceiling. But on the day General Calomfir died his widow covered it with a velvet drape ... My passion was butterflies," he continued, opening the half-stuck door with an effort and taking the boy's hand to lead him slowly and carefully through the darkness. "The dining room was here at first, but after they sold the furniture, they turned it into a study. Now it's almost bare and the lights are defective too. I don't know what's wrong, but almost every time someone touches the switch, there's a short circuit. So, now that we've arrived, don't be surprised, if I can't give you your wish to look at the glass cases."

In the next moment the room was flooded with a blinding light, streaming from the ceiling and also from large, tall lamps situated in the four corners of the room. He found himself in the middle of a spacious room, its walls covered with glass-topped boxes inside of which were the largest, most gorgeous, most extravagantly coloured butterflies he had ever seen. Not even at the Museum was there such a collection. "Don't go near them, because if you did, you couldn't bear to leave, and Maria Da Maria is waiting for us … And now, what shall I give you?" he asked, running his eyes over the tables and stands laden with cases of insects. "Let's begin with Central Africa. Central Africa is renowned for its coleoptera."

He clutched the box with both hands, but he could not take his eyes off Maria's fingers. He seemed to be seeing them for the first time now as they moved nimbly over the strings, stroking them or pressing them threateningly, as though trying to snap them. The sounds no longer reached him. He saw only her fingers and he began to be afraid; at any moment she might break one of the strings, or make a single wrong movement of the bow—that bow which she held squeezed in her fist like a whip—and then one of the fingers, especially the smallest finger …

* * *

Ieronim was unable to listen to her, and after a few moments he did not even dare to look at her fingers. He saw her running, her face distorted by terror, pursued by that dense crowd of people, evil and faceless. He heard their shouts, and from time to time someone stopped beside him, grabbed his arm, and asked him threateningly, "Which way did she go? Speak quickly, which way did she go? Where's she hiding?"

Swallowing with difficulty, blinking fast to banish the vision, Ieronim begged the Chorus: "This is absurd! It has nothing to do with *her*! Tell them they're mistaken!"

In vain. He saw and heard them all the more clearly, all the more loudly—that throng which surrounded him, still running as though driven by a tempest, and carrying him along with it. He was jostled on all sides, shoved continually from behind. They were talking among themselves and yet he heard them addressing him: "We're looking for someone, what the devil's his name? He's well-known, everybody knows him. Much has been said about him. Don't you remember his name? He fled just when they'd begun beating him with rods, and they broke his fingers—one after another, finger by finger—and he fled with bloody hands and vanished."—"They'd just begun to crucify her," someone else said, "but when they crushed her hands she screamed so loudly they came to their senses and then they couldn't see her, and so she was able to descend from the cross, but it was hard, because her hands were crushed. She descended and fled and since then we've been looking for her, but we haven't found her yet." "It's absurd! It's a mistake," Ieronim exclaimed. "You've confused her with someone else!"—"There's no confusion!" he heard someone cry. "Everyone knows him, much has been said about him. What the devil's his name?" "She's not to blame," Ieronim persisted. "She's a great artist. Spare her hands; she plays the cello." In exasperation he threatened the

Chorus: "What's come over you? Have you lost your minds? It's just a mistake, all an error. Come to your senses! She's not at fault. Look at her; she's here before you; look at her closely. At first she was unwilling, she was too excited, her hands were trembling, she couldn't control her tears, but the Maestro begged her, he insisted. 'It's a great day,' he said, 'you must not leave this house angry.'"

* * *

The wind seemed to intensify and he was sorry, above all for Maria, because the purity of certain notes was lost. But when was there no sound of the autumn wind at that time of night, in that deserted house, with all its windows broken, stuffed with newspapers or covered with cardboard, with scarcely a door that would close tightly? Perhaps he had never felt more overwhelming sadness than on the night when they had come to the coffee house to look for him. They went to the table where he was playing chess (he was in the semi-finals with Zamfir), and bending close to his ear so the others would not hear him, Gherghel had whispered that Generăleasa was at death's door, and that he would have to come immediately if he wanted to find her still alive. A half an hour before she had summoned the priest, she had confessed and received the Sacrament, and this had alarmed everyone. But Antim could not believe it. She had been dying for many weeks, ever since she had lost her sight. And every time he approached her bed and asked her how she felt, the old lady would listen intently, with her hands folded, as usual, on top of the blanket, and then suddenly she would whisper: "But what is that I hear, Manolache? Where is that melody coming from? I don't believe you ever played it for me before. It is well you've brought your cello"—"No, *mon Général*, I didn't bring it. But if you wish ..."—"Better you stay beside me and listen!"

This time, upon entering the room in which, as always, a single candle was burning, and seeing how she was clutching lighted candles in both hands as though with a great effort and without hope, he had known the end was near. He knelt beside her and whispered, "I have come, *mon Général*. It is I, Manolache."

Without moving her head on the pillow, in a weak but surprisingly clear voice, she asked him, "How many of us are left, Manolache?"

"Five, *mon Général*."

She was silent for a long interval, as if she were labouring to count them in her mind.

"Take good care of yourself," she said suddenly. "Take care! Don't let our line be extinguished."

Then, to the amazement of everyone, she asked to be left alone with Ieronim. They left the room one after the other— the relatives, the neighbours, the doctor, and the priest— walking on tiptoe. Half an hour later the door opened and Ieronim appeared on the threshold. He stood still as a statue. "It's over," he said, looking straight ahead without seeing them. "She had started to tell me what she had to say, and she gave up the ghost."—"God have mercy on her!" everyone exclaimed at once, crossing themselves, and then they crowded into the room and began to light the candles.

Several times that very night during the wake Antim had been tempted to ask him what she had said to him, but he had not dared. For the first time Ieronim, who was then not yet seventeen, intimidated him. It was as though he had suddenly become another man. He knelt beside the bed, with his eyes open, but he seemed to see no one. From time to time he got up and went into the salon.

There he would pace from one end of the room to the other, silent, pale, his face as rigid as stone.

When, a few days after the burial, he had gone to him in his room and had asked him, Ieronim had become suddenly pale. "Forgive me, Oncle Vania, I've sworn to do as she requested. She asked me to swear not to tell anyone, not even to tell my son until he is as old as I am now. I ventured to ask her, 'What if I never have a son?'—'Then, this secret will die with you,' she replied. Forgive me, Oncle Vania," he added, smiling sadly. "I've sworn!"

But Antim had not given up, and in those two years that Ieronim had continued living in this house with them (Luchian had not yet died), several times in the evenings he had tried to draw it out of him. "I know very well that you took an oath and you have to keep your word. But I'm not asking you to tell me everything, not even the essence. I just want to know if what she told you had anything to do with the story I read when I was fourteen or fifteen."—"I know the story," Ieronim interrupted. "You've told it to me. That story about the juggler from the Middle Ages."—"Precisely. I'm asking you this because Generăleasa had her notions. She believed that the fault was mine—I mean, the hero's in the story. Generăleasa believed that he had deserted his fiancée, and whenever we talked about this question, she tried to convince me."—"No, Moş Manolache, I give you my word of honour that the secret she asked me to keep has nothing to do with your story."

Antim could not keep from looking at him a long time, searchingly, and then he added in a whisper, mostly to himself, "Strange, very strange!"

* * *

He had scarcely arrived in Bucharest when Generăleasa had asked to see him.

"Are you Ieronim, the son of Thanase and Marina?"

"*Oui, grand-mère*! Pardon, *grand-tante*!"

"With me you will speak Romanian," she interrupted him. "And don't say either *grand-mère* or *grand-tante*. You will call me, as does everyone else, *mon Général*. Not *ma Générale*, but *mon Général*, as I have been called ever since the death of Calomfir. Do you understand?"

"*Oui, m-mon Général*!" But he corrected himself immediately: "I understand, *mon Général*."

Then she took him by the hand and led him close to the largest mirror in the living room, hidden behind some draperies.

"Marina has told me that you like to make up all sorts of games and dances, and that you understand how to disguise yourself and know how to sing and recite poetry. Is that true?"

"It is true, *mon Général*."

"How old are you?"

"This fall I'll be six."

"So, you're a big boy, and I can speak seriously with you. Do you understand what I'm saying to you? Do you understand all the words?"

"I understand, *mon Général*."

She reached out and took the edge of the drapery between two fingers.

"I imagine that you have heard why I covered the mirror. But now and then, on holidays and solemn occasions such as tomorrow, my name-day, I like to draw the draperies aside. Only, as you see, after being kept in the dark for so many years, the lustre of the mirror is not what it used to be. Little by little it has lost its transparency, and all sorts of queer shapes in different colours are beginning to appear in its depths. Some of these forms possess a rare beauty, as though they were not of this world. Do you understand what I mean?"

"I understand, *mon Général*."

"And when I part the draperies you will suddenly find yourself face to face with many unfamiliar forms, and you will see yourself moving among them; but very likely in the beginning you won't recognize yourself, because, as I told you, the mirror is no longer what it once was, and sometimes it magnifies, elongates, widens, or even distorts. When this happens, won't you be frightened?"

She looked at him with an unusual intensity as if some tremendously important decision might hinge on his response. He smiled sweetly, almost ironically.

"I wouldn't be frightened, *mon Général*."

Generăleasa breathed deeply and caressed his hair.

"Good. And now, listen! This is the surprise I wanted you to give them. Of course, it's a secret. Don't tell anyone in the house! Tomorrow evening, after the champagne is served and we are all gathered here in the living room ..."

He could never forget the frigid silence which followed the whispering, the suppressed laughter, the discreet clinking of crystal glasses, when Vasile Chelaru and Anuta slowly drew back the draperies and the mirror stood looking at them all pressed together, crowded close in front of it at the rear of the salon, as Generăleasa had asked them. It seemed that no one dared to breathe.

And then, out of a fold in the draperies, he appeared, in a disguise of his own choosing, with his blond hair and sun-burnt face, wind-blown, wearing a torn, faded shirt through which his shoulders and chest could be seen, barefoot, with short pants which he had rolled up even farther, as if he were going wading. It appeared as though he had emerged from the green cavern of the looking-glass. Suddenly, without any advance warning, he leaned back his head, clasped his hands together behind his neck, and began to laugh. It was a laugh he himself had never known before, a continuous laughter, clear as crystal, irresistible, which, even if he had tried, he could not have stopped. He began to walk back and forth in front of the mirror, constantly discovering other caves and precipices, and tropical vines with flowers of incomparable beauty. Among these forms he spied the improbable silhouettes of the guests, with glasses of champagne as tall as a boot or as wide as a bucket in their hands; and in the midst of them, sitting like a priestess in her armchair, was Generăleasa. And now they were laughing too. At first it was a timid laughing, a little fearful, but quickly it became contagious and grew, and then they all were laughing. He could see in the mirror how they were looking at one another, fascinated and yet also troubled, because they did not exactly understand what was happening. And then, again quite spontaneously, Ieronim raised both his arms in the air, making a sign for them to be quiet, and he began to dance, singing in a low voice a melody he had just discovered. After that he began to recite poetry, but he never knew if he had recited some of the numerous poems he had committed to memory or if he had improvised without being aware of it verse after verse, just as he was calling up melodies and improvising more and more dance movements now slow, majestic, almost liturgical; now disjointed, wild, irreverent.

Why he had stopped at a certain moment, taking a step away from the mirror, and had bowed, bending low from the waist with his locks tumbling over his face, he did not understand, because he was not tired. He would have liked to have continued the dance and to have gone on inventing other melodies and verses.

"Encore, encore!" everyone began to shout, clapping their hands, some with considerable difficulty because they were still holding empty glasses. "Bravo, Ieronim!" Generăleasa cried. "Encore!" she added, carried away by the general enthusiasm.

He could never find out from anyone exactly what had happened next. He remembered only that he withdrew slowly toward the corner on the left and took hold of the drapery. Then, with difficulty, dragging it after him, he began waving it. The trembling folds reflected in the mirror alternately shadowed and lit other submarine caverns. At the same time he was speaking, talking as in a dream, with a voice, as they told him later, from another world, because it did not resemble any human voice. And although it was incomparably sweet, it paralysed everyone—not only the voice itself, of course, but also the words he spoke, because the people could not always understand what he meant. They gathered only that he, Ieronim, whenever he could, would steal away to the innermost chambers of the cave, to the depths of the sea, to where his many friends were awaiting his return: all sorts of creatures, from dolphins and seahorses with whom he played every morning to the invisible beings whom, fortunately, only he could see. Because, what if they should take a liking for Eglantina, with eyes of glass and cheeks of porcelain, or even Mironclai, who walks on stilts as high as a house, but otherwise is friendly and laughs constantly, and whoever has not heard him laughing twenty or twenty-five yards overhead does not know the joy of laughter? ... Yes, perhaps they *would* like some of these, but when they would set eyes on Maremore, who is neither lizard nor bird but sings more beautifully than a nightingale, or Paralene, who climbs with eleven legs at one time, like a spider, although she has the big blue eyes of a young lady and eyelashes so long that ...

"You gave us a fright!" they told him later. "Everyone was speechless, dumbfounded, as though you had bewitched them, and no one dared call out to you, to stop you."

"Not even Generăleasa," Antim once specified much later. "She too was petrified, spellbound."

"But what did I say, Oncle Vania? What did I say to you all?" he had asked then with that same exasperation in his voice, because he believed that they had all conspired never to tell him precisely.

"Who could remember?" Antim had replied. "Because, I repeat, they were not the words and sentences of a child, however precocious, but it was as though someone else were speaking through you, some demi-god or mythological hero, or one of those fabulous characters whom you pretended were your friends, whom you met whenever and wherever you wished, and not just in the looking glass ... And now I can tell you," Antim had added once, many years later, "I was afraid, and not only I—we all were afraid that something would happen to you, that you would lose your mind, because such precocity—so profound and so extravagant at the same time—exacts its price."

"And you were right," Ieronim interrupted him, smiling bitterly. "I paid in full measure and overflowing. Because that night the family decreed that I was the child prodigy of the century, and right then it was decided to present me without delay to the director of the Municipal Theater. And to my misfortune, Theodorini was a good friend of the director. I paid, Oncle Vania, for the fright I brought you on that night of St. John*; I paid more than it was right to ask a child to pay, even a prodigy."

* * *

<hr>

* The night of St. John the Baptist, June 24th, Midsummer night, known as *Noaptea de Sânziene*, is the Romanian title of Eliade's major novel, *The Forbidden Forest* (University of Notre Dame Press, 1978; also *Forêt interdite*, *La foresta proibita*, *Der verbotene Wald*, etc.) In Romanian folklore the *Sânzienele* are good fairies who traditionally appear on the night of St. John [ed.].

He suddenly recalled that Melania had liked this aria very much, and unconsciously a smile came to his face …

When he had come to announce his engagement, Generăleasa was resting, as usual, in her favourite armchair in the middle of the salon.

"Her name is Melania," he began after kissing her hand. "She is, of course, a foreigner. Needless to say, she's beautiful and intelligent, and so far as I can judge, although I'm not well versed in literature, she has read enormously!"

"Manolache," Generăleasa interrupted, "I know what you're thinking. You imagine or even hope that this time it is she."

He managed to laugh, but his joviality seemed so jarring that he stopped and shrugged, pretending to be surprised.

"How could I imagine that, *mon Général*?" he exclaimed. "How would I confuse a character out of a tale, or if you will a novella, with a living being of our own time? True, she is a foreigner but she's a creature of flesh and blood!"

Generăleasa gazed at him steadily, smiling kindly yet distantly, as only she could smile.

"And of course you have given her a résumé of the novella also, in the unconfessed hope that perhaps, who knows, among the thousands of books she has read, she has come across the story of your life."

He did not try to laugh again. Embarrassed, he removed his glasses and reached for his handkerchief to wipe them.

"I don't know that I'd call it the story of my life," he began after a while. But I have to acknowledge that …"

"Your mistake, Manolache," Generăleasa interrupted him, "is that you don't want to acknowledge your great virtue, which, at the same time is your great weakness: your modesty. You're too modest. You discovered one day that it would be a sin to spend your life studying insects when you have so much interest in music, and you discovered at the same time that you can't perfect yourself in any art, but especially in music, if you don't look up—up to heaven—instead of looking around you, to see what people are doing and what your neighbours are saying. You made this great discovery, of which we all are proud, the whole family, when you were scarcely more than a child. But being modest you gave the credit to another, to a character in a novella, who lived I don't know how many years ago."

"Mon Général ..."

"Listen! I'm not finished. Modesty is a rare quality, especially in our day, and more particularly in our family. It is very good that you want at all costs to justify your conception of art and the life you decided to live by a literary model. But what I don't understand is the connection between your artistic ideal and *Her*, that woman who left you several hundred years ago."

"This happened *in the novella*," Antim tried to interrupt.

"It's all the same. It's a question of an unknown and inaccessible fiancée, for whom you are waiting, but whom you have never tried to seek. This I don't understand," she added pensively. "I don't understand why you haven't gone in search of your predestined wife, if you know she exists somewhere in the world and is waiting for you. You don't have to seek very far. Perhaps she is here, close by, and if you haven't seen her yet it's because the sun hides her, or the shade, or people. But if you would decide to seek her ..."

He knew all these things, or had suspected them long ago. She had told him, sometimes, as now, directly, at other times very indirectly, about the five almost legendary brothers, her ancestors, who had set out from a town in Pind, each going in a different direction, each seeking a bride. What seemed so strange to him this time, and even offensive, was the fact that Generǎleasa was reproving him for not going in search of his predestined one *now*, less than quarter of an hour after he had announced that he was engaged.

"In my way," he said with an unexpected firmness, "I am searching for her. Although, possibly, I'm searching with excessive discretion. But every time I meet a foreigner, I open my eyes wide, I have a long conversation with her, I sound her out, I weigh everything she says to me and even what she doesn't say. This is what happened in the case of Melania, once I discovered she was a foreigner."

"A foreigner," Generăleasa repeated with a trace of sadness in her voice.

"Manolache, for a *man*, no woman is a foreigner. Men meet a 'foreigner' but a single time in life, and then, in any event, it is too late. And about such meetings it is not well that we speak further."

Antim kept wiping his glasses without looking at her.

"This is why I came," he said presently. "I came to tell you that next Sunday I shall become engaged to Melania."

* * *

It had happened that way once before also, when he had left the door open and was listening to Antim practicing in the living room here ...

After a few minutes he realized he was listening to the Chorus telling him what would occur in the next scene, or how things ought to happen in the play which he had read that same day. "On the seashore. A deserted beach on the coast of the Black Sea," the Chorus announced. "On a November evening."

And yet, Ieronim protested, the author clearly wrote that the scene represents a courtyard of a country house on a June morning, and that as the curtain rises a man's voice can be heard in the distance. "It is a deserted beach on the shore of the Black Sea on a November evening," The Chorus repeated. "And for a long time after the curtain has risen nothing is heard but the wind."

"So this is where you are!" Luchian's voice awakened him. Are you still listening to him, listening to him continually? Don't you ever get tired of listening to the same melody all the time?"

He stopped on the threshold. Very seldom did he enter the room. He had the habit of saying what he had to say quickly, from the doorway, and then disappearing to continue his leisurely, melancholy stroll from room to room throughout the house.

"I dreamed of Veronica again," he said that day. "Listen to me: I won't last much longer. My turn is coming. Soon, soon only the two of you will be left, all alone in the world. And then, I wonder, what will you do without me?"

He disappeared before Ieronim had time to say anything. And, as he expected, the Chorus answered in his stead. "Why are you afraid of death, Luchian? Remember what Generăleasa said: 'It pleases me that you two are not afraid of anything—neither of death nor of love. One can see that you are nephews of the Hero!'" She said it another time, after she had become blind. "It pleases me, Ieronim, that you are not afraid of anything!" She repeated it also to Antim. He came into the room once with a mysterious smile lighting his face. "Ieronim, do you know what Generăleasa said about you on her death bed? She told me, 'How well one can see that Ieronim is the nephew of the Hero!'"

"I know. She said it to me too. I didn't want to contradict her because I knew that this made her happy. But the truth is otherwise, Oncle Vania. I'm not afraid of anything, and above all not of love nor of death, but it's because after all that's happened to us, and to *me*, I have rediscovered the meaning and function of drama, the way I knew it as a child."

He wanted to continue, but he heard the Chorus suddenly: "These are matters of everyday information, the kind you ask for and get at any post office window, bank, or railway station. This is the *truth*, Ieronim, the *truth*!"

And yet, very soon afterward, he had tried to explain. Barging into the salon he had found Antim with his cello resting on his left knee, absently staring into space. He had been sitting that way for a long while, probably, because Ieronim, noticing a prolonged silence, had supposed that Antim had already left for the city. But he found him in his accustomed place, with his cello beside him, gazing vacantly.

"I'm beginning to grow old," he said, trying to smile. "I have too many memories."

"An artist never grows old, Oncle Vania," Ieronim interrupted, suddenly moved. "If God has punished us with anything, he has punished us by giving us youth without old age. I realize the punishment is heavy, but what can we do? This was predestined for us."

"Youth without old age," Antim repeated, smiling. "Easily said at your age."

"We're the same age, Oncle Vania," Ieronim continued, kneeling in front of him. "Only you have memories while I imagine things. And if I were to say that my memories surpass yours *by several hundreds of times*, simply because I've imagined them, you wouldn't believe me."

Antim set his cello on the floor beside him and suddenly began to laugh.

"Tell me how you do it," he insisted. "Tell me, how you do imagine memories?"

"First I imagine them, and then I remember them! Probably you've imagined many things in your lifetime, but you've forgotten them. You don't remember anything except what has happened to you, so to speak, *personally*. But these things, Maestro, for us who are artists, do not have the value which they have for others."

Suddenly he rose to his feet and, as was his habit when he sensed he was about to say things which he had avoided saying up to then, he began to pace across the living room, taking big steps.

"I once confessed to you that if I'm not afraid of anything it's not because I'm a nephew of the Hero, but because I've rediscovered the meaning and function of drama. But I didn't explain what this means for me. To be unafraid of anything means to regard everything that happens in the world as 'spectacle': This means that we can intervene at any time, by using imagination, and we can modify the 'spectacle' in any way we wish."

"By using imagination," Antim repeated in high spirits. "That is, through our minds. But that doesn't change reality, what is happening to us actually, what is going on around us."

Ieronim stopped directly in front of him and looked at him with surprise, as though he were not sure he had heard him rightly.

"It depends upon what you mean by 'reality'," he said. "For me, reality is *total truth*, that is, what we shall be given to know only after death. But art, and in particular theatre, spectacle, reveals this truth in all that happens around us, and especially in all that we can imagine to be happening. Actually, theatre, like philosophy, is a preparation for death—with this difference, which for me is all-important, that 'spectacle' anticipates death's revelation because it shows all these things *here*, on earth, in everyday life."

"Ieronim, I still don't understand you!"

And it seemed that the smile which had lighted his face began to fade, and his gaze looked ready to depart again, ready to lose itself in vacant staring.

"It's because you, Oncle Vania," Ieronim continued in a different tone, more gently and yet more solemn, "you persist in reducing *understanding* to an exercise of reason as in chess. But you know very well that neither art nor life can be understood through reason *only*. Anything that happens around us might camouflage a mystery and thus a decisive revelation, an awful truth. For instance, any dove could camouflage ..."

"In other words, you've started philosophizing again," they heard Luchian saying from the doorway. "I congratulate you," he added, sauntering toward Generăleasa's armchair. Sighing deeply, he sat down in it.

"I don't know what's wrong with me," he said. "I don't feel well ... But keep on with your business, continue your discussion."

From then on, all they heard was, "I don't know what's wrong with me. I don't have any pains, but I feel tired. Very tired."

Since he no longer took his walks around the house, going from room to room, he liked to leave his door open and listen to Antim. Then, one evening when Ieronim was coming to his bedside with an open book to continue the reading interrupted a half hour before, Luchian motioned to him, moving his right hand slowly and wearily.

"Ieronim," he murmured, "I don't have much time left. I say this to you very simply because, as you know, I was never afraid of love and I'm not afraid of death, but I want to give you a piece of advice. And I want, in addition, to ask you something. The advice is this: when I shall be no more, go and live in Thanase's house where you spent your childhood. I have an agreement with the tenants. They will be happy to give over the two second floor rooms to you, to avoid the risk of someone else occupying them, since of course they prefer you who are, in a sense, still the owner."

"And Oncle Vania? ..."

"He won't be able to live here much longer because the matter has been decided: the house is to be demolished. It will be done this spring or in the fall, or in the following spring—I don't know just when—but it's sure to be torn down. And then Manolache will come to your place, and you will give him a room. Otherwise, he'll be out on the streets ... Do you promise? Can I count on you?"

The Chorus was calling to him, but he was no longer listening: "Ieronim, be strong, be hard as flint! No tears. And your voice, Ieronim, don't let it tremble—because nothing is going to happen except what you have learned about already. Death; death and love."

"Can I count on you?" Luchian asked once again.

Ieronim smiled and taking his hand he patted it.

"I promise, Luchian. You can count on me."

"And now I shall make a request. My last request."

He was silent a long time, staring at the ceiling.

"What did Generăleasa say to you just before she died, when the two of you were alone?"

Ieronim took a step backward, as though he were trying to see him better.

"Luchian!" he exclaimed. "You know what I promised; that I'd keep the secret, that I'd tell it only to my son when he should reach the age of seventeen."

"I know," Luchian interrupted him calmly. "But you can already subtract me from the number of the living."

Ieronim approached his bed again.

"But Luchian," he began, trying to contain his emotion, "ever since that night when Generăleasa called me to her bedside I have done nothing else except talk about those things she confided in me! But because I swore, I could not say them in the way they were told me in the language of death—rather I reveal them in parables and myths, in anecdotes and images. Ever since Generăleasa died I have done nothing else. *I can do nothing else* except tell you, but obscurely, as in an old mirror, like our old mirror, I can do nothing else but speak, in images and parables, about the secret entrusted to me. And not only to you, my family and friends, but also to people I meet by chance. Sometimes I'm tempted to stop people on the street—naturally not just anyone, but certain people in whom I seem to discern a certain sign. Of course, that's another story. But Luchian, this is all I talk about! If I didn't speak of it, I'd lose my mind!"

"Then I shall have to pay closer attention to what you say," he murmured, still smiling, "and try to decipher the enigmas. But I don't know if I'll have enough time. I feel so tired."

* * *

"Youth! Youth without old age!" Antim repeated.

He had scarcely begun to kiss her on the cheeks when Iconaru, with the box under his arm, came hurrying toward him. He thanked him, shaking his hand and bowing his head respectfully. But as he neared the door, Ieronim caught up with him and stopped him.

"What, are you going to leave?"

"Perhaps if I go now I'll find Borban working late, and he'll open up for me in back."

"Do you want to leave," Ieronim interrupted, "when we still haven't gotten to the heart of the problem, when we haven't even discussed the existence of God?"

"It's late and the landlord raises Cain if I wake him up."

"In any event, you can't go walking around the streets at night dressed up in that general's uniform. If some police officer sees you, he'll arrest you. We'll have to find you another coat."

They heard him ascending the attic stairs on the run, then came the sounds of his footsteps overhead, this time hasty and careless, and a few minutes later he returned with his arms laden. Heaving a sigh of relief he dropped the burden on the sofa. He had brought the peasant's skirts, silk hand-kerchiefs, and scarves which he had examined at leisure two hours earlier. On top of everything was the bridal gown.

"This is for you, Princess," he said to Maria, spreading out the dress at her feet like a rug. "It's almost a museum piece, so you can ignore the symbolism. It was tailored once upon a time to adorn a bride, but on this night, fitted with some imagination around your shoulders, it will keep you warm."

"Ieronim, you'll make her angry again!" Antim teased.

Maria wiped away the last of her tears with the back of her hand, and smiled.

"I'm not angry, Maestro," she murmured. "On a night like this, I couldn't be angry."

Meanwhile, Iconaru was searching without enthusiasm through the pile of garments.

"I recognize these things," he said in discouragement. "They're all for women."

"But they'll keep you warm," Ieronim interrupted, selecting one of the skirts and throwing it over his shoulders. "And over the top, so it won't be seen ..."

He went out to the hall again and returned shortly with an overcoat. "It is true, it's rather old and probably dusty, if not perhaps moth-eaten."

He began to shake it, examining it closely.

"It's late," Iconaru protested, taking the box under his arm again.

"I don't live far from here, and if I walk fast, I won't get cold."

As if he had not heard him, Ieronim deftly draped the over-coat over the skirt which covered his shoulders.

"We'll escort him home first," he said to Maria, "to see if he can get in."

"If Borban hasn't put out the light," Iconaru broke in, "he'll open up for me in back."

"... and then," Ieronim continued, "you and I shall go for a walk on the streets. We have so much to discuss!"

With a flourish he gathered up the bridal gown and wrapped it, like a shawl, around Maria's shoulders. Everyone burst into laughter.

"Youth!" Antim exclaimed once more, accompanying them to the hall.

As he was locking the door, he heard Ieronim saying, "Princess, if you truly believe in God ..."

Only after he had seated himself, exhausted, in Generăleasa's chair did he remember that he had forgotten to offer them some of the famous *Grand Armagnac*, 1908, from the last remaining bottle. They might have used the miniscule glasses which were reserved only for such occasions.

"Youth without old age!" he repeated to himself ironically, shaking his head. "Without old age ..."

He started to get up and go to the cupboard to fill at least a glass and drink by himself to their health, but his feet felt heavy, as if they were made of lead, and he decided to rest a little, just for a few moments. Smiling, he leaned back his head in Generăleasa's chair and let his eyelids close.

He must proceed as on great and solemn occasions; "to perform the ceremonial," as he liked to say; that is, hold the crystal glass for a few seconds directly in front of his eyes, looking through the liquor of gold and copper, then elevate it, wishing them luck, and finally bring it to his lips and sip it as slowly as possible.

* * *

A little while later when he opened his eyes the light from the salon surprised him. "Thank God, they've repaired the switch!" he said, but at the same moment he saw Maria Daria Maria coming toward him slowly and he arose from his chair, alarmed.

"What's the matter?" he asked. "Have you forgotten something? Or have you quarrelled again with Ieronim on the street?"

She halted a step in front of him and gazed at him, smiling sadly. Only then did he see how beautiful she was, and what an extraordinary light animated her face.

"Maria Daria," he began, deeply moved, "you've made yourself suddenly very beautiful. What's happened?"

The girl continued to gaze deeply into his eyes with the same sad, forgotten smile lingering on her lips.

"You don't recognize me any longer, Maestro," she said very slowly.

"True, a great deal of time has passed," she added.

She was silent a moment. Then she began to recite:

"*Manole, Manole,*

Meștre Manole ..."

"Melania!" Antim exclaimed. "What is this? Why have you come?"

The girl squeezed his hand.

"Manole, Manole, Meştre Manole, you've not only forgotten your fiancée; you've also forgotten your engagement!"

She drew him slowly to her.

"We have to hurry: they're waiting for us."

He let himself be led like a child, wondering what he could say to her now after so many years. Just then they reached the far end of the salon and his eyes fell suddenly upon the mirror, sparkling, bathed in light, as it appeared only when all the candelabra were burning. He stopped, frightened and happy at the same time. But the girl kept drawing him after her.

"Where do you want us to go?" he exclaimed cheerfully. "Do you want us to pass through the looking glass?"

The girl began to laugh and turned her head.

"The mirror is behind us, Manole. Don't you see it?" and she pointed, extending her arm slightly.

He turned his head too. Indeed, the mirror was there, far away, at the other end of the salon. When the girl tugged on his arm again, he offered no more resistance, and they entered into something like a frame of light.

"Let's hurry," he heard her say again. "They're waiting for us."

He permitted himself to be led and soon he realized that they were crossing a large, brightly lit hall. Now the girl drew him along even faster in the direction of a marble staircase which he saw far off, rising in a spiral.

"Melania," he whispered in embarrassment. "I can't go in with this overcoat of mine!"

He did not understand her reply, because just then some late arrivals crowded around the principal entrance, several couples quickly ascended the stairs, and they began to hear the rustling of the hall and the musicians tuning their instruments.

"Melania!" he whispered when they had passed what must have been the highest balconies and galleries, and the girl continued to pull him along with her up that marble staircase which rose in an endless spiral.

But she seemed not to hear him. The doors had been closed, the noise of the hall began to die away, and there was no other sound but the sharp notes of a trumpet.

"Melania!" he exclaimed, and tried to stop.

Smiling, the girl turned and faced him.

"*Non sono Melania*, Maestro," she whispered.

At that moment he recognized her and remembered everything, from their meeting in front of the station when he had helped her lift her valise onto the vaporetto, until in the evening when, pressing her hand in his own hands, he had said, "*Ti voglio bene, Laetitia. E adesso, je te dirai le reste en roumain*: will you become my fiancée? Now? Right now, in this garden?" That very evening was her nineteenth birthday.

She looked at him with that same sad smile which both Maria Daria Maria and Melania had worn.

"We have to hurry," she said. "They're waiting for us."

Then the sound of applause began to be heard, and after a few moments the entire hall became hushed, attentive. Thrilled, Antim heard the baton beat out three short taps on the music stand.

"It's late," the girl insisted, trying to draw him along. "The others are waiting for us."

"Only a moment," Antim begged her in a whisper. "Only a moment, to see what they're going to play."

"They're waiting for us," the girl repeated with an undertone of despair in her voice.

She tried again to pull him after her, but with a sudden jerk Antim managed to free his hand. Once again there came the sound of the three short taps of the baton on the stand,

and then the same stony silence in the hall, unnaturally prolonged.

"Why don't they begin? What are they waiting for?" he asked.

But there was no one beside him now and, frightened, Antim looked around in all directions. Then, as though she had appeared from behind a marble column, Generăleasa stood before him.

"Manolache, who was that? Your fiancée? The 'foreigner'? ... Was it she?"

He seemed to detect a trace of irony in her voice, and embarrassed he looked down.

"It was she, *mon Général!*"

Incognito
in Buchenwald

THEY WERE ALL GATHERED in front of the window, silent, as though trying to appear indifferent, watching the snow falling. All at once, giving a start, Maria da Maria began to wipe the pane with the palm of her left hand, leaning nearer to it and blinking repeatedly in order to see better. Someone, a woman, was endeavouring to open the gate. Then Făgădău saw her too. Stepping with difficulty but without hesitation between the drifts, the woman was approaching the house. She was wearing a rain cape and boots almost as high as her knees. A shawl of faded hue covered almost her entire face. Soon they heard her on the porch, knocking her old army boots together to dislodge the snow from them. Ieronim opened the door wide and, because the stranger stood hesitating on the threshold, he took her arm and drew her inside, closing the door with his foot. The woman smiled at him with a sudden light in her eyes.

"Are you Ieronim Thanase?" she asked.

"I am."

"Is it true that you have a trained dog?"

Ieronim began to laugh.

"Not one," he said, "I have two!"

"Then I know who you are," the woman continued, and she began removing her gloves, carefully and unhurriedly. "This past summer you came to the Colentina Hospital, to the children's pavilion, to entertain the patients."

"That's right. Why once I even ..."

"Ieronim!" Maria interrupted him, grabbing his arm. "You don't need to go into details!"

"*Purgare, non est necesse!*" someone added.

The stranger tossed her head several times, with quick motions, shaking her locks, and smiled again.

"I know you well," she said. "That's why I dared to come looking for you at a time like this, even though you don't know who I am. I am Marina Davari."

"No, I don't believe we've met."

"It's not for myself I've come, but for a little girl, a sort of niece of mine. A sick girl, in a dark, dank, room. Neither doll nor teddy bear, nor any game of all the many that relatives and neighbours have brought her will make her laugh."

> "*Numai rouă dacă-ar bea,*
> *Cu cenuşă, scrum de stea …*"*

a young man with a broad, high forehead recited in a melancholic voice. Then, bowing, he added, "My name is Petru Lorinţ. Student in the third year at the Conservatory and Faculty of Letters."

Marina looked at him deeply, gravely, as if carefully weighing his response. Then she bowed her head.

"It's true," she acknowledged. "Perhaps you don't realize how true it is! … But not even the snow at her window makes any impression on her. She lies there day and night, just lies there, her eyes open and dry, staring at the ceiling. No tears … In a few days she'll be eight years old," Marina added after a moment's silence.

In a single, questioning glance Ieronim interrogated everyone. Then he made his decision.

"It will be hard," he said. "I don't keep the dogs here. It's too cold and I have nothing to feed them. So I'll have to go and get them, and then find a sleigh or some kind of car, or maybe a truck from the Theater. In this snow I'd kill them for sure, and all for nothing."

Marina began, absently, to undo the top buttons on her cape. She looked at each member of the group in turn, rather casually, then asked:

---

*   "Only if she'll drink the dew // With the star's white ashes too," from "It sits in the woods without glory," a famous poem by Lucian Blaga from *La cumpăna apelor* (1930) [ed.]

"But what do you think? Not even the doctors know what's wrong with her. But you? Do you think she'll recover?"

They pressed closer to one another and everyone burst out in one voice, loud, strange, and oracular:

"*She will live! She will live! She will live!*"

Maria turned toward Ieronim.

"The Chorus!" Ieronim exclaimed solemnly. "They constitute the Chorus. The only authentic chorus we have today in Bucharest. The only one comparable to the chorus of Greek tragedies."

For a moment it seemed Marina was struggling to stifle a sigh, but he quickly realized it was nothing more than her curious, irregular respiration, interspersed by long pauses in which she appeared to be holding her breath. She started toward the armchair with the high back which was pushed against the wall.

"I believe you," she said as she took a seat. "You're all young, and youth is never wrong when it's a matter of life."

Maria caught hold of Ieronim's arm again.

"Did you hear what she said? She said, 'When it's a matter of life!' We could begin it that way, Ieronim, just the way it happened ..."

Ieronim shrugged.

"It would be too good," he said. "That is, it would *look* too good."

The others crowded around him again, troubled and at the same time animated.

"She may be right," Făgădău ventured ... "At any rate, let's give it a try."

"I'm sure I'm right!" exclaimed Maria. "And the spectators will discover gradually that it's not a matter of a sick girl, but something else, infinitely more serious, a matter of ..."

She broke off abruptly, blushing guiltily. The next moment she was at Marina's side.

"*Doamna*," she began, taking her hand. "Will you do us a favour? A very great favour? I'll explain presently what it's all about. Just a moment."

She drew her after her gently in the direction of the door. There she stopped and helped her button the top buttons on her cape and wrap the shawl around her head.

"Don't catch a chill," she warned, "although it won't take more than a minute. Go out onto the porch, knock your boots together as though you were shaking off the snow, and then be ready to come back inside. When Ieronim opens the door, *ask him the same questions*."

"What questions?"

"Those you asked him a little while ago: 'Are you Ieronim Thanase? Is it true you have a trained dog?' and so forth. There weren't many."

She opened the door and pushed Marina onto the porch, obviously quite excited.

"Silence!" she whispered without turning her head. Then, to Ieronim: "Now, get set! The door!"

When he opened it, a snowy blast burst into the room. Irritated because Marina kept standing in the doorway, Ieronim took hold of her arm and pulled her inside. Absently taking off her scarf, Marina smiled at him with sudden warmth, almost lovingly, and yet she seemed to be forcing herself to maintain a certain gravity.

"Are you Ieronim Thanase?"

"I am."

"Is it true that you have two trained dogs?—Oh, pardon me!—Is it true …"

"That doesn't matter," Maria encouraged. "Continue!"

"It is true," Ieronim replied.

"Then I know who you are ... Last summer you came to the Colentina Hospital, to the children's pavilion ..."

"This is absurd!" Ieronim exploded. "It makes no sense!"

The Chorus recited slowly, almost in a whisper, but reprovingly: "*The meaning we create, Ieronim. The meaning we reveal, through* spectacle. *Through* spectacle, *Ieronim, without beginning and without end!*"

Turning to Marina, Ieronim began to laugh.

"You've guessed this has to do with the *beginning* of a play, an experimental play. But ..."

"That's where it *also* begins," Făgădău interrupted. "Or, more precisely, it *might* begin there and that way also, if we know ..."

"And even more precisely, if we succeed in understanding *what happened* there," Maria continued.

"I, personally, know what happened there," Făgădău resumed. "I was there myself."

"Brat," Maria threatened him, "*purgare non est necesse*! Say what you have to say, and make it short and concise. *Show* us!"

Făgădău took several steps, then turned around abruptly, frowning, with a fierce expression on his face, his fists thrust against his hips. He looked like a different person.

"Are you another one of those people from over there?!" he shouted in a wild voice which seemed to burst from a throat thickened by tobacco and alcohol.

"I am," Lorinț replied.

"Is it true that you have here, at Number 18, the one who claims to be a miracle worker?"

"He's never said he's a miracle worker."

"But what then does he claim to be? A fakir? A snake-charmer?"

"He says he's a Bodhisattva."

Ieronim threw up his hands in exasperation.

"No, no, no! It simply can't begin that way! For the time being, let's forget the whole thing, and then later we'll try something else."

Maria helped Marina undo the buttons at the top of the cape, then made her sit down in the armchair.

"My name is Maria Daria Maria, but they call me Maria da Maria. I don't belong to Ieronim's troupe—I'm a musician, a cellist. But his ideas fascinate me. Just imagine ..."

"I believe I've understood some of it," Marina interrupted. "The scene takes place in a concentration camp, an extermination camp—let's say, Buchenwald."

Maria da Maria jerked her head around and looked at the others in alarm.

"But how did you guess? Did someone tell you?"

Marina tossed her head again, then stroked her face for some moments with the palm of her right hand before answering.

"No. No one has told me anything. But it seemed obvious to me: your gestures, tone of voice, vocabulary."

"You heard it? You heard it?" cried Făgădău.

"But I don't understand what a Bodhisattva has to do with Buchenwald," Marina added.

Several members of the troupe began to laugh, youthfully, happily, exchanging meaningful glances.

"If *doamna* assures us she'll be discreet, shall we tell her?" Ieronim asked.

"We've told her the essential thing already," the eldest member of the group spoke up.

Blond, pale, with small reddish blotches on his cheeks, he was clad in an old overcoat, much too long for his height.

"I'm Valerian, and they say I'm the wisest," he continued. "Ieronim thought of the Bodhisattva because he wanted to divorce the problem of freedom from the contexts in which it has been debated up to now—Judeo-Christian, Existentialist, and Marxist—and place it in another perspective, a *new* perspective. To avoid stating at the outset that it's new, he's camouflaged it under the exotic term Bodhisattva. Isn't that right, Ieronim?"

"Approximately," Ieronim replied, smiling wistfully. "Because, *doamna*," he continued, turning to Marina, "we, this little band, came to the conclusion long ago that only by means of the theatre, that is, 'spectacle'—including, of course, mime, choreography, and the chorus—only by means of drama could we succeed in *showing* that, although conditioned and hemmed in on all sides, we as well as our contemporaries in other countries and continents are not like mice trapped in a cage ..."

"Even if someone is ready to drench us with gasoline and set us on fire," Valerian added.

"And I ask you to keep this image in your mind," Făgădău interposed, "because this is what Buchenwald means: the place where people were caught like mice in a cage, doused with gasoline—and reduced to carbon ... Pardon me, Ieronim. Go on now with what you were saying."

"There's a lot to say," Ieronim resumed. "But if, as we believe, only drama can *show* that people of our day are not in the situation of caged mice, then we must specify the modality of freedom which they have available. It is evident, for instance, that in a situation such as Buchenwald freedom can only be *interior*, and thus almost impossible for others around us to verify. On the other hand, interior, absolute freedom is not easily obtained. Actually, its conquest is just as difficult as that of exterior freedom—for instance, escaping from a modern prison."

A girl approached and tapped him on the shoulder.

"Being the youngest," she said, addressing Marina, I'm considered the most ignorant—although I do have a beautiful name, Sofia Speranța … But Ieronim," she added quickly, "because we speak of freedom and we affirm that we're not like caged mice, what do we do *now*, in this case? It's a matter of a sick little girl whom your dogs may be able to make laugh and perhaps hasten her recovery. And yet, look, just because it's snowing one evening, *we can't do anything*! And if it should snow all night, even if you get the truck from the Theater, you still won't be able to get to where she is … Is she very far away, *doamna*?" she asked, turning her head.

"Rather far," Marina replied. "But think no more about it," she added, rising from the chair. "You've calmed me. I *know* now that nothing's going to happen. And once the snow lets up …"

She stopped speaking abruptly and fixed her gaze on the far end of the drawing room where she could barely distinguish a wall repaired in a strange fashion: it looked like a door blocked with boards nailed one atop the other without plan or design.

* * *

"If your meeting's not *really* important," said Manole, emphasizing the word "really," then I pray you be patient a little while longer. You won't meet with anything like this back in Charlottenburg where you come from!"

"The fact of the matter is, I live in Zurich now," Condurachi revealed.

"She'll be arriving at any minute now," Manole continued. "She said she'd come *exactly one year later*, and from all I know about her—which is actually very little—I have no doubt she'll come … If you're too warm," he added, "take off your jacket."

Condurachi walked over to the painting.

                                   INCOGNITO IN BUCHENWALD

"No, I'm not too warm," he said. "But I don't see what she could change or add to it. It's simply perfect. Of course, I'm no expert on paintings."

"Nor am I," Manole interrupted, "but it captivated me the moment I set eyes on it."

"It's the most beautiful female form I've ever seen—in painting, in sculpture, or in reality."

He turned to Manole and smiled.

"But what did Generăleasa say? How did she take it?"

Manole began to laugh.

"That was something we hadn't planned on! And of course, here in the drawing room is the only place for it. What would be the use of hanging it in one of the other rooms where no one ever goes? Ah, me! When Generăleasa came home and laid eyes on the painting she was dumbfounded. We didn't know what to think. Did she like it or didn't she? All at once she exclaimed, 'It's beautiful, wonderful!—But we can't keep it here.' 'Why not?' I asked her. 'Because it's a female nude?' She looked at me curiously, the way she does, and said, 'Manolache, a woman's ass doesn't upset me any more than a man's ass did when I was young. But as you know, a lot of children wander through here.'

"In a way she was right," Manole added. "So we made an agreement that on holidays when relatives and children should come, we would cover the painting with a drape, just as we cover the mirror."

"Actually," Condurachi interrupted, "you could almost say it's not a woman's body. It's really more like that of a goddess."

"That's just what Zamfira said herself when she showed it to me. 'I'm bringing a goddess into your house,' she said."

He remained thoughtful for a moment, then began laughing again.

"And that's the way we met. I was here with Luchian when we heard the doorbell ring. I answered it. A stranger, a woman of about fifty, dressed almost shabbily and yet, I don't know how to describe it, with good taste. She seemed to be in distress and very tired; it was all she could do to smile. And yet there was something noble and so to speak 'enigmatic' about her face.

"'*Maestro* Manole Antim?' she inquired. 'I have heard that you are people of means and that you like beautiful things. How would you like to have a goddess? I don't mean a goddess from antiquity, but one from our own times. Ten years ago I attended her wedding.'

"She signalled to a young man who had remained outside, whom I had not seen when I had opened the door. The youth entered, greeted us timidly, and propping the painting against his knee he began to untie the cords. Then he removed the wrappings which covered it and leaned it against Generăleasa's armchair. Luchian and I both were astonished.

"'It's a few centimeters shorter than the original,' she told us. 'When I saw her the last time, the goddess was eighteen years old and stood 2.45 meters tall.'"*

"Really?" Condurachi exclaimed.

"No, this was just part of her 'mystery', as we like to call it. She invented all sorts of strange tales, just as she had invented for herself I don't know how many pseudonyms. Her real name was Zamfira, but her friends called her Marina. She even claimed she wasn't a painter, but that her true vocation was sculpture."

"Zamfira what?" Condurachi interrupted.

"I suspect that it is, or was, Darvari."

Condurachi shook his head dubiously.

---

* Approximately eight feet [tr.].

"I've never heard of a sculptor or a painter by that name."

"No, of course not. Because, as I found out later, and quite by accident at that, she signs her works at exhibits with all sorts of pseudonyms. And since she doesn't especially want to sell—she sells only abroad or in provincial towns—she remains unknown."

"Very strange!" exclaimed Condurachi, stepping to the picture again. "Then why did she offer you the goddess?"

Manole began pacing the floor, his hands behind his back, as though trying to hide his nervousness.

"If she was telling the truth, what had happened was this: her cousin, Dragomir, was in urgent need—that is, in two or three days—of a certain sum. She assured him—of course she admitted in our presence that she had lied—she assured him that she could raise I don't know how many thousands of lei by demanding payment on some old accounts, and that she would only have to ask her clients to draft and remit checks in his name. I don't know what he believed, or how much, this Dragomir. I repeat what she told me: that she had gotten into the carriage with some four or five items. This one, she assured me, was the only painting. The rest were sculptures. And she took them to several addresses, to men of wealth but not professional collectors. And of course the prices were so ridiculous that she had not experienced any difficulty. She claimed that she knew about us, that someone from her family knew someone or other from our family; in brief, she offered us the goddess. The price was about as much as the value of the frame."

"It's incredible!" Condurachi exclaimed.

"But, of course, she imposed this condition, that she would come back a year later ..."

He stepped quickly to the painting and from the back of the frame carefully detached a slip of paper.

"Look, written in her own hand: '12 July 1930.' And today is July 12, 1931." Seeing Condurachi glance nervously at his watch, Manole added, "Make an effort to stay another five or ten minutes. You won't regret it!"

Condurachi sat down resignedly in the easy chair and reached for his cigarette case.

"If only she keeps her word and comes," he said.

* * *

"... Once the snow lets up," Marina repeated absently, "I'll come with a heated car. The car of a friend in the diplomatic corps."

Apparently only now did she become aware of how large the drawing room was, and in what a state of ruin. She walked slowly to the fireplace and gazed at it intently. Beneath the ashes could be seen the remains of the embers which pulsed from time to time when stirred by a gust of wind from the snowstorm blown under the door. At the front of the hearth there remained a half-burnt piece of wood, surprisingly thick, that had belonged to a piece of furniture. When she turned her head, surprised, Ieronim smiled.

"Do you think that's a table leg?" he asked. "No. The table legs we burned last week. This is the trunk of the hall tree. The heaviest hall tree in the whole neighbourhood. The pride of Generăleasa!"

Marina shuddered as though she had taken a sudden chill and buttoned her cape at the top. Then she ventured farther into the room, walking alongside the bare walls, their paint having peeled and fallen off, was mended here and there with cardboard and newspapers clumsily pasted to them.

"But what will you do in a day or two? You have nothing left to burn. You can't use these last few chairs for fuel!"

Ieronim began laughing. All at once he seemed to be in a very good humor.

"There are plenty of things in the other rooms," he indicated the directions vaguely with his arm— "and in the attic lots of things are left: bundles of books and newspapers, old trunks, and other junk. You know," he added, lowering his voice, "this house was to have been torn down last fall, but certain complications arose. At any rate, in the spring it will not escape any longer. They have in mind to erect a twelve-story building here."

Marina listened, fascinated, unable to take her eyes off his lips.

"But until then?" she insisted. "Until then, what will you do? Winter's scarcely begun!"

Ieronim shrugged.

"No one lives here any more. We just come for rehearsals. Each of us, thanks to Providence, has at least a warm bed of our own."

"And yet you have to gather here for your rehearsals," Maria continued, looking around forlornly.

"As I told you, we still have many different combustible objects. And even here, look, you see we have a wardrobe left. There hasn't been one like it made in a hundred years. An uncle of mine brought it from Bavaria. It weighs four or five hundred kilograms. It'll warm us for a week at least!"

But Marina was no longer listening. Increasing her pace slightly, she went to the corner on the left, near the door. There the wall seemed better preserved: just a few deep cracks rising toward the ceiling. In the middle, between the cracks, the surface seemed less faded and the edges were almost straight. Only upon closer inspection did she realize she had been mistaken. The wall here was just as deteriorated as in the rest of the room.

"But why at *Buchenwald*?" she asked suddenly in a surprisingly loud voice. "What do you know about Buchenwald?"

"No, no, *doamna*!" Marcian interjected. "Please forgive my tone, but that's the way I am, argumentative by nature. Anyone today understands the essence and message of Buchenwald. But that's not the problem. Ieronim had begun to explain it a little while ago when unfortunately someone interfered who oughtn't to have interfered ..."

"Brat, watch what you say!" Maria da Maria scolded. "We aren't alone!"

"I beg the pardon of those who deserve it," Marcian continued, suddenly removing his glasses and placing them in the upper pocket of his overcoat. "But if the lady has been admitted into the secrets of our play, then let her know the essential thing. Namely, what Ieronim said, that interior freedom is almost always unrecognizable. Let us imagine that there are there, among those condemned to incineration, a number of saints, martyrs, Bodhisattvas—call them what you wish. Once they've refused, out of charity or love for their fellows, the 'magical' solution of the *miracle*—opening doors by magic, collapsing walls, etc.—and have accepted, apparently, the condition of others, since they *might have shown* in another way the freedom which ..."

"Watch!" Maria da Maria interrupted him, raising her arm.

Făgădău strode heavily, solemnly, as though wearing military boots, with his hands on his hips. He came to a halt in front of a tall, thin youth with deep-set eyes.

"Do you claim to be one of those people from 'over there'; who says he's a fakir?" he demanded.

"I could be a fakir if I wanted to be, but this doesn't interest me any longer. In India, China, and Japan they'd call me a Bodhisattva."

"At any rate, a miracle worker. All right then, do a miracle so I can see you!"

"I *have*, already, several times in fact. The last time there were two doctors present, especially sent from Headquarters. Even they were convinced. I didn't feel the red-hot iron, not even on my tongue, and when they carved out one of my ribs with a scalpel I told them to be careful because I'm ticklish."

Făgădău struck him with an invisible horsewhip and the young man began calmly to wipe the blood from his cheek.

"The miracle is," Făgădău resumed, "that you don't know what's waiting for you!"

"Oh, but I do know, very well: the crematorium. But what use will it be if you won't be there too to see me—how I shiver and shake with the cold and blow on my hands to keep warm?"

Ieronim went to them and interrupted them gently.

"Enough for today. *Doamna* will see the rest at the premier. And, let us hope, she will understand."

"I've understood more than you imagine," Marina declared gravely. "I've understood that the one you call the Bodhisattva will die by fire, but he will die free. And it is probable that if he had not been a Bodhisattva he would have evidenced his freedom in another way, in a public manner: for instance, by spitting in the face of the Camp Commandant."

"You're incredible!" Ieronim exclaimed. "How did you guess? Until quite recently this was a part of the scene you were watching: after he says that it will be cold to him in the crematorium since for him, of course, they've chosen the ultimate punishment, burning alive—after he says this, he was to spit in the guard's face. But we realized that such a *heroic* act was not suitable for a Bodhisattva, just as it would be unbecoming for Jesus or a Christian martyr."

Marina had listened with rising excitement, looking deeply into his eyes.

"I'm glad you're struggling to respect historic truth," she commented. "But when I asked you, why Buchenwald? I was thinking of something else. As I understand it, for Ieronim and for all of you, the Play proposes to reveal to the spectators not only the supreme goal, the conquest of interior freedom, but also the means by which this freedom can be attained."

"Exactly!" said Ieronim.

"But in that case you've chosen the most difficult episode to illustrate," Marina continued. "We all know what happened at Buchenwald, even if we don't know, and never shall know, how heroic and holy certain victims were. But how will you show the means by which interior freedom was won?"

Everyone began applauding enthusiastically. Pleased and excited, with his cheeks flushed, Ieronim turned to the group.

"Shall we tell her?" he asked. "No, we can't tell her!"

"It wouldn't be right," declared a tall, thin young man in a calmly serene voice. "My name is Petru Petrovan," he added, addressing Marina. "I'm a poet, but out of desperation, because I'm also tubercular, I became an actor. Of course in the way Ieronim understands that one must act to be a true actor!"

* * *

"It must be her!" Manole whispered when he heard the doorbell. "Didn't I tell you she'd come?"

On opening the door he was unable to conceal his surprise. On the threshold stood Marina, smiling at him and looking as she might have looked fifteen or twenty years before. She was dressed in a youthful but sober style. In her hand she held a bouquet of red roses.

"For the mistress of the house, whom I have not yet had the pleasure of meeting," she announced.

Embarrassed, he placed the bouquet on one of the stands, leaning it awkwardly against an enormous seashell. Only then did he realize he had not made introductions.

"The engineer Ştefan Condurachi," he pronounced slowly, self-consciously, trying to appear solemn. "He has lived abroad a great deal. Doamna Zamfira Darvari."

Marina smiled absently, her eyes on the painting. She started toward it slowly, stopping at intervals to contemplate it.

"She is truly a goddess," Condurachi began. "And, according to what Manole's told me, she exists in flesh and blood."

Marina turned around and looked at him in surprise, as though she were seeing him then for the first time.

"I hope she's still living. But I no longer hear from her. She left the country eleven years ago, and since then we've received no news from her. It's true that she doesn't know how to write very well; but her husband was an accomplished linguist, speaking and writing Romanian perfectly."

Manole took a few steps toward her and asked timidly, "What of your husband? Have you found him yet?"

Marina tried to hide her smile—a melancholic one, yet betraying amusement.

"Not yet. He's been waiting for me ten years. And I'll wait just as long for him."

Manole blushed and began rubbing his hands together.

"Then may I offer you something? Coffee? Sweets? I'm so sorry that Generăleasa isn't home at the moment."

"No, thank you. I came just to exchange the paintings. I've brought for your selection a nude by Bonnard, another by Pătraşcu, and several seascapes by Iser, almost the only ones he painted."

When she turned her head around again and saw Manole, she burst out laughing.

"But I won't take it away *forever*!" she exclaimed. "I'll bring it back after a year."

"And yet, *doamna*," Condurachi intervened, "I don't see what you could add or change. It's simply perfect—a masterpiece!"

"Thank you," said Marina, "thank you very sincerely. But I don't think I want to change anything. I have need of the goddess—a personal need," she added, slightly lowering her voice.

Embarrassed, Manole stared at her, not knowing what to do with his hands.

"We've become accustomed to the goddess," he said finally. "We'll miss her …"

"A year passes quickly," Marina interrupted. "And when you see what I've brought to take her place —!"

She crossed the room quickly, opened the door, and after a few minutes returned accompanied by a very young couple.

"Freshly engaged," she said, introducing them.

Then the three of them, with great care, began untying the cords and removing the paintings one after another from the wrappings which had covered them.

* * *

As usual, as they did whenever they felt there was nothing more to *say*, nothing more to try, they crowded together around the window, watching the snow falling. It was impossible to distinguish anything now except the pillars of the porch and, a few meters beyond, near the street, the pine tree. But no one dared to leave. Gradually, as the drawing room became warm again, one by one they turned away from the window and went to the fireplace. Valerian, the first to remove his overcoat, even tried to start a poem.

"A wardrobe, just a wardrobe!" he whispered. "An ancient, venerable, worn out—or maybe, wise?—wardrobe ..."

Ieronim had broken it into pieces with great skill, in a scientific manner, wielding the axe gently, capably, intently, almost lovingly. When the fireplace began to radiate heat, Maria da Maria held her hands as closely as possible to the flames, rubbing and stroking them.

"I know what you're thinking about," she said suddenly without turning her head. "And that's why nothing succeeds for us, neither what we *say* nor what we *show*. Your mind's not on the Play. You're still asking, why did she ask us to look at those stains."

"She didn't ask us," Ieronim corrected her. "She just said that if we knew how to look at those stains ..."

"How to look at them and *understand* them," Făgădău added.

"Those stains, discoloured by the sun and deepened by dampness ..."

"Actually, what she said was, 'sensitized' by the damp."

"At any rate, she didn't *ask* anything," Ieronim continued. "Nor did I allow her, moreover, to ask anything ... But at a certain moment I had the impression she was looking at me ironically, perhaps with some pity, perhaps even sarcastically, as if to say: 'You've wasted your youth chasing chimeras, you've squandered your talent trying all sorts of experiments, when you have here, before your very eyes, these stains faded by the sun and dampness.'"

He approached the wall, gazing at it intently, concentrating, blinking his eyes, turning his head slowly, now to the left, now to the right, in order to catch every possible nuance. They were stains without precise forms whose contours were modified according to the angle from which they were viewed. Only the crack which rose almost diagonally toward the ceiling kept the same direction and depth no matter how one looked at it.

"Faded by the sun and dampness," Lorinț repeated dreamily. "Then I understand. This is what she wanted to tell us: you have here an exemplary model of the union of opposites: humidity and sunshine, that is, water and Fire …"

Ieronim shook his head.

"That would be too commonplace. It has to be something else."

"I read once about a rabbi from Cracow who dreamed continually about a treasure," Făgădău began.

"Everyone knows that one," Ieronim interrupted. "He had gone in search of it, I don't know where, maybe to Warsaw, and in the end he discovered the treasure in his own house, hidden under the ashes of his hearth. Everyone knows the story of the Rabbi of Cracow," Ieronim repeated. "This woman, Marina Darvari, wanted to tell us something else. But perhaps in order to get even with us for not introducing her to certain secrets of the Play, she tried to appear very enigmatic and mysterious, like an oracle. 'If you *knew*, if only *you* knew *how* to look at them, how to *look at these stains*,' etcetera, etcetera, etcetera."

"But don't you see, she's succeeded," Maria da Maria interrupted. "We won't admit it, but every one of us can think of only one thing. Enigmatic and mysterious like an oracle, as you so aptly put it, but *what did she mean*?"

"I admit very frankly," Ieronim resumed, "that however absurd it may be, this enigma obsesses me. If she was alluding to the more or less mysterious history of this house or my family, *I'm not interested in that*. I know everything that happened, but although I retain the memory of it, it doesn't interest me. I'm the sole—or the last, if you prefer—survivor of the Antim, Calomfir, and Thanase families, but this fact doesn't move me in any way. I consider myself the first of a new dynasty, a second 'founder' of the Antim-Calomfir-Thanase line. With me begins a new history, on another plane, more elevated and more creative. Little do I care for enigmas or nostalgias connected with the past of this house, or the past of my families. Nothing interests me but the future, as I believe I can fulfil it by living *freely* any epiphany of the *present*, no matter how tragic it may prove to be, how born of misfortune and destined to despair."

With upturned faces, everyone had listened, deeply moved.

"This is something we've learned too," said Petru Petrovan, "in learning to imagine ourselves imprisoned at Buchenwald. No other way of salvation exists."

"I avoid using the term 'salvation'," Ieronim interrupted in a melancholic voice, "because it might give rise to confusion. Any type of salvation presupposes faith in a Savior. I respect and envy those who believe in a Savior, but I haven't been gifted with such a faith. So, then, I have to seek elsewhere, because without freedom I should be unable to exist."

"But Ieronim," exclaimed Marina, "did I speak to you about the past as anything other than a means, and the one most readily available, for living *exclusively in the present?*"

Surprised, bewildered, everyone turned to look at her. Marina was coming toward them slowly, like a character from a silent film of the early part of the century, dressed in an astrakhan fur coat, with a bouquet of violets in her hand. If they had not recognized her voice, they would not have believed it was she—Marina—so young did she appear. And instead of her military boots she was wearing a pair of fur-lined galoshes such as they had never before seen.

"But how did you get in?" Ieronim asked her, managing not to betray his feelings.

"I spoke to you exclusively about the present," Marina continued. "And when I told you to learn to look at those stains, I meant only that you should learn to look at them as they are *now*, purely and simply *as they are* in the present moment, and then you will understand."

She went to Maria da Maria and, with a smile, offered her the bouquet of violets.

"Actually," Marina added, "what I proposed was another variant for your play about the freedom which can be won even in Buchenwald. True, it's a less spectacular variant."

She fixed her eyes for a moment on Maria who was still standing with the violets in her hand, not even daring to smell them.

"I'll come to see you again," Marina promised, "and we'll have a good talk. But now I must go, because someone's expecting me. I just stopped to say that our little girl is laughing and playing, and she wants me to make a snowman for her right in front of her window. And I've promised to do it."

* * *

"When did you get back?" Manole inquired.

"A few days ago," Condurachi replied absently, obviously preoccupied.

"Have you heard? France has declared war too!"

"It was expected," said Manole. "But what's wrong with you? You seem tired."

"I've got too much on my mind. But never mind that. How have things been going with you?"

"The same as with everyone else. Troubles, sicknesses, hardships."

"By the way," Condurachi interrupted, trying to smile. "Hasn't she brought the goddess back yet?"

Manole shook his head, and suddenly, involuntarily, he became sad.

"She hasn't returned it, and I've given up hope she ever will. We must content ourselves with Bonnard," he added mournfully. "If we don't sell it, that is. We've been offered three million."

"But what of the painter?"

"Zamfira Davari, or whatever. She claims she's a sculptor primarily."

"Have you had another meeting with her?"

Manole shook his head once more.

"I've seen her a few times, but she didn't see me, or else she pretended not to see me. Once she was with a group."

"Still as young and beautiful?" Condurachi interrupted.

Manole laid his hand on his friend's shoulder.

"*Mon cher*, you won't believe me, but she's aged frightfully. She's unrecognizable! The fact of the matter is when I saw her the last time, this past spring, she was an old crone!"

* * *

Eleazar halted abruptly in the middle of the room.

"Are you listening to me, or would you rather look out the window?"

"I'm listening to you," said Lorinţ, but I can't keep from looking out of the window. 'Never was the autumn more glorious ...'"*

---

*   From a poem by Tudor Arghezi:
Never was the autumn more glorious
to a soul rejoicing at death.
The meadow is pale and spun with silk.
Against the clouds the trees weave brocade ... (Tr. MacGregor-Hastie) [tr.].

"Then let's go out to the garden and talk about something else!"

Lorinț sat down again in the easy chair.

"No, no, I was sincere when I said I was interested. But, either I don't understand anything any more, or else you've become confused somewhere."

"I'm not confused. I read you excerpts from Adrian's letter. It all began with that party, when two of the girls got drunk, and when they started to go somewhere they slipped and fell in the middle of the drawing room. Trying in vain to get to their feet, with their short, thin dresses, you can imagine what it was like and what was seen. Especially since all the rest of us, with the exceptions of Adrian and Leana, were more or less intoxicated. Viki started to help them, but dizzy-headed as she was, and trying to lift them both at the same time, she stumbled and they fell in a heap, all three of them! Now no one dared to help them, because they were laughing deliriously, tumbling over and over on the floor. Who knows what would have happened if Elefterescu had not suddenly risen to his feet, pale, trembling slightly with excitement, and exclaimed: 'The same thing happened to Prince Siddhartha!'"

"What had gotten into him?" asked Lorinț, amused.

"He'd read a life of the Buddha and since then, every time he had an opportunity, at the office or at parties, that was all he'd talk about: how one day Prince Siddhartha saw for the first time a sick man, then on the next day for the first time a dead man … you know the story. All of us were very familiar with the tale because he'd told it to us repeatedly, and the girls knew it too. And probably they also recalled the gravity with which Elefterescu had told it. Oh! how many times, and almost with the same words—they recalled the gravity with which he had told us the story of the 'Great Going-Forth', of course with capital letters, the night when Prince Siddhartha had left his family, his palace, and his harem. How he had seen as he crossed the women's quarters all his concubines sleeping nude, in all sorts of grotesque and immodest postures, and how this last supreme vision of the Eternal Feminine was of great use to Siddhartha when the Prince had become the ascetic Gautama."

"I see the life of the Buddha has remained well imprinted on your mind too!" Lorinț interrupted him.

"What friend or acquaintance of his wouldn't remember it? He repeated it so often we were sick of hearing it!"

"And what about the girls on the floor?"

"I was just coming to that," Eleazar resumed. "Very likely they too remembered about the 'Great Going-Forth' and the scene in the women's quarters.

"They began to laugh all the more hysterically, rolling over and over on the carpet, playing their roles, trying to appear very sensual, while Vera cried, 'Siddhartha! The scriptures have been fulfilled. Now is the moment to leave everything and depart for the Himalayas!'

"Elefterescu, looking quite pale, remained standing, still as a statue except that his lips were trembling. Then Elvira, who had been beside him at the table and was rather tipsy also, began to cry and called out, 'Siddhartha! I'm your wife, your dearly beloved Yaśodhara; don't leave me!' — 'Oh, but he must leave, he must leave, to fulfil his destiny!' shouted the girls on the carpet, rolling about provocatively. Someone at the end of the table, I don't know who, wanted to heighten the drama, and he went quickly and switched off the lights. Everyone began to shout, yell, sing, and laugh. It seemed like an 'orgy' such as our parents read about in novels. Some cried, 'Lights! Turn on the lights!' Others repeated the refrain, '*À poil! À poil!*'* All this couldn't have lasted more than two or

---

*   Fr. "Naked. Naked" [ed.].

three minutes. But when the lights came on again, Elefterescu had disappeared. And that's how it began."

Lorinț turned to look out the window again, he shrugged.

"I don't see the connection with what we're going to do, or more precisely, with Ieronim's Play."

"Then you weren't listening carefully when I was reading excerpts from Adrian's letter. Because, I forgot to add, when they turned on the lights again and we realized Elefterescu had disappeared, Adrian stood up, he also looked very pale, and made a signal with his arms for silence, but in vain because the uproar did not diminish. But I heard him clearly, since I was quite near him at the table, and I felt sorry for Leana because she seemed frightened and despondent. You know his story, don't you—that is, their story, the Orpheus and Euridice myth?"

"I know it, of course."

"Adrian at the moment was in one of his periods of lucidity, and everyone was delighted to hear he was writing again … But I don't intend to tell you that story now. I want to tell you what I heard Adrian say. He tried to convince us of the gravity of the event. 'I remain an occidental,' he said. 'I have a mythology which was predestined for me, and I know what it means to have the message of a myth revealed to you. If Elefterescu has had revealed to him the secret of a myth which obsesses him, he can't escape it any longer. Either he follows the model with the risks which are entailed in it, or else he resists it and is crushed!'"

"Yes, but we all know Adrian," Lorinț interrupted. "He's a poet and he translates everything that happens around him in terms of his personal myth."

"But there's more to it than that," Eleazar insisted. "It's not just a matter of how much he was impressed by Elefterescu's disappearance. There's also the matter of what Adrian says in his letter of last summer from which I read you some excerpts. I don't know how he heard, where he was at the time, about your play, but when he heard, Adrian recognized immediately the connection: it all started from that point, from that party. Because, the next day at the office when we saw Elefterescu we began teasing him: 'Still here, Siddhartha, among the courtesans and Bucharestians?' Of course, he tried to laugh, but I sensed that something about him had *changed*."

"Changed?" asked Lorinț in surprise. "In what sense?"

"I felt that what had happened the night before might have had a certain significance. I told you; he had read the life of the Buddha."

"Yes, yes," Lorinț interrupted him impatiently, "but I don't see the connection with what we're doing."

Eleazar began to pace the floor with long strides, as if trying to control his exasperation. Suddenly he came to a halt in front of Lorinț.

"Doesn't your play have to do with a Bodhisattva and Buchenwald?"

The other shrugged.

"In a way, yes. But Ieronim presents things quite differently. In the first place there's nothing, not even an allusion, having to do with Siddhartha, who became the Buddha, and all the rest. The one who calls himself a Bodhisattva, because he has no other name to use—I repeat, we don't want to make him a saint or martyr in the Christian sense of the term—the one who calls himself a Bodhisattva is a former engineer, a pacifist, and hence an anti-Nazi, imprisoned like so many others at Buchenwald."

Eleazar listened to him, impassive, with a sarcastic smile in the corner of his mouth.

"I'll try to summarize," he began when the other had turned to look out of the window again. "At the time all these things took place, no one knew anything about Buchenwald. It was the fall of 1939. The war had begun. In time we became convinced that Elefterescu had taken Buddhism quite seriously. He read every book on the subject that fell into his hands, and he'd begun to drive us to distraction with his theories."

"What sort of theories?"

"His Buddhistic theories that he'd read in his books. But this one especially: 'Let's suppose,' he said, 'even if just for fun, that a new Buddha, a Bodhisattva, should appear among us. How would we recognize him?'"

"Now it's beginning to get interesting!" exclaimed Lorinț. "Let's hear some more!"

"I was sure that if you'd listen closely to me, you'd see immediately the connection. So, how would we recognize him? Because, he wouldn't be reincarnated in a princely family, and he wouldn't appear at first to be a genius or a saint. He'd just be an ordinary man. He'd serve in the army, have a trade, or even if he weren't married, he'd live like everybody else. But of course, since he would have been reincarnated in order to bring the message of salvation—or of liberation, whichever you prefer—he would be forced at a certain moment to *preach*, to proclaim his message in a public manner."

He fell suddenly silent, took a few steps toward the open window, then returned and halted in front of Lorinț.

"Now, here's where we confused him with our questions. 'You see,' I said to him, 'no matter how closely he may resemble the rest of us, when he begins to preach he'll reveal his identity! Hence, he'll be recognized as a Bodhisattva.'"

"And how did he respond?"

"He didn't know quite how to respond. His thesis was that *perhaps*—I realize that he always said *perhaps*—*perhaps* one of the philosophies, gnoses, or religious sects, or one of the contemporary artistic creations camouflages the new version of salvation, formulated for our era and in terms accessible to our culture—formulated and proclaimed, he said, by a Bodhisattva!"

"Very interesting," said Lorinț, becoming pensive. "But are you sure he mentioned, along with philosophies and religious gnoses, *contemporary artistic creations*?"

Eleazar shrugged with embarrassment.

"After all these years I can't repeat his words or expressions exactly. Of course," he added, "he had read a lot of philosophy and history of religions."

"Tell me more! What happened to him?"

"To Elefterescu? He died at the front, in the first days of the war, in July, 1941."

"A shame!" exclaimed Lorinț, getting up suddenly from the chair. "He was an interesting man. Ieronim would have liked him ... But I want to assure you that, although he might have heard of Elefterescu, Ieronim wasn't inspired by his case. The Play is constructed within a totally different perspective."

"But what about the idea that a new Bodhisattva will inevitably be camouflaged and therefore anonymous? Where did he get that? I read you excerpts from Adrian's letter a little while ago."

"I know, I know!" Lorinț continued. "But I repeat, even if he had heard of Elefterescu's idea about the impossibility of recognizing a contemporary Bodhisattva, the Play is constructed in a different way and proceeds in a different manner."

"Namely, how?" Eleazar demanded irritably.

"I'm not at liberty to tell you. I can add only one thing: the chorus, the dance, the music, and the lights are all just as important as the dialogues. What is *said* to you is also *shown* to you, and this kind of drama is completely new. Actually," he resumed after a pause, thoughtfully, "I don't know if we can still call it 'drama' in the current sense of the word."

He was ready to leave, but seemingly he could not bear to separate himself from the garden which he could see through the window.

"'Never was the autumn …'" he murmured softly.

"All right, I understand," Eleazar said calmly. "You want it to be the great surprise of the season. But you can at least tell me how it begins."

Lorinț looked at him in surprise, smiling enigmatically.

"I'll tell you, and yet you won't believe I'm telling you the truth. But the truth is, *there is no beginning*!"

Eleazar broke into a laugh.

"You're making fun of me!"

"Or, perhaps there is one, but we haven't found it yet. Don't think we haven't searched for it! We're still searching for it now. But how do you recognize the *true beginning* when the whole play is founded on the most banal mystery—banal in the sense that we bump into traces of it at every turn, every day … But, after all, it would be too much to tell!"

* * *

When she saw her coming, treading heavily and yet with elegance in her army boots through the drifts, amidst the falling snow now in its third successive day, Maria da Maria wrapped her scarf around her head like a turban and went out to greet her.

"*Doamna*," Maria whispered, "please don't go inside now. The rehearsal's just begun and Ieronim's so insanely happy he's unrecognizable. He says that this time …"

   INCOGNITO IN BUCHENWALD

Unhurriedly Marina wiped away the flakes that had settled gently on her cheeks, and smiled.

"That was the reason I came—just to tell him this: that he doesn't need to search for the beginning, because it will find itself, without any effort."

Only then did Maria da Maria realize the woman was crying.

"Why do you look at me so?" Marina asked. "Because I'm crying, or because I seem to have become old overnight?"

But she did not allow Maria time to reply.

"Ah, if only I knew how to answer that question, how many other answers would we no longer have to seek, to ask for them again—over and over again!"

* * *

For several days a fine, dismal rain had been falling, and the air was like fog. Ieronim stopped on the pavement in front of the house and took his beret from the pocket of his rain cape. He stood for a few moments holding the hat in his hand, watching the three workmen on the roof who were preparing to throw some large, almost square pieces of rusty sheet metal into the yard below. He adjusted the beret on his head, pulling it slightly down on his forehead. Then his eyes sought a place where he could cross the street between the puddles of mud and slush mixed with black oil left by the trucks. He had met the last truck, loaded with a hodgepodge of wood, scraps of metal, and blocks of stone, at the street corner a few minutes earlier. He had started hurrying then, fearing he would arrive too late. But while still at a distance he became calm. The house seemed to be intact, although the steps at the principal entrance and the doors were gone, and the windows looked like great empty sockets staring in fear. Not until he was directly in front of the gate on the pavement did he realize that the rooms on the far side had disappeared, allowing a view of a solitary wall with blue wallpaper, badly tattered, and above, on the second floor, the remnants of the wooden stairs leading to the attic.

He looked once again, but as far as his eye could penetrate through the fine rain there was nothing to be seen save the same street, buried under slush and here and there drowned under puddles. He almost did not hear the noise of the pieces of sheet-iron when they fell onto the rubbish heap in the courtyard. The next moment he realized that the pine tree had been cut down and that there had even been an unsuccessful effort made to uproot the stump. Two other empty trucks stopped, smoking, in front of the house, and Ieronim sought another vantage point from which to see better. Several workmen with metal helmets appeared from behind the house. The rain intensified and the mist began to resemble a choking fog with a taste of smoke in it.

"I was sure I'd find you here," he heard Marina say close behind him.

He jerked his head around suddenly in surprise, but coming to his senses he smiled involuntarily. Marina looked into his eyes, laughing, her face illumined by a childish grin, as though she had played a trick on him.

"How did you know?" he asked her.

Marina decided to open her umbrella, but she tilted it sharply to the left, in order to be able to see him better.

"I passed by here this morning when they were cutting down the tree," she said. "I don't believe you have any regrets, do you?" she asked quickly, with a guilty look in her eyes.

Ieronim shrugged his shoulders and pushed his beret down on his forehead.

"Why should I have any regrets?" he said, turning toward the house. "It was a ruin long ago. Even the mice had abandoned it."

"I asked you that because I learned at school about regretting the past, and also from certain novels," Marina began after a long silence. "The past. Holy relics of the past …"

"A part of the life I've lived," Ieronim interrupted, "my childhood and adolescence buried forever, without a trace, etcetera, etcetera."

And because she saw his pensive look as he watched the arm of the crane about to strike the wall with the blue wallpaper, Marina added, "Etcetera, etcetera! You're right. Any life, no matter how noble or how unique it may be, can be summed up at any moment in that formula, etcetera, etcetera!"

"We are in perfect accord," said Ieronim, continuing to follow the manoeuvres of the crane.

"Yes, but I'm afraid that although you understand, you *still* don't realize where this understanding has to lead."

Just then an entire wall collapsed, taking with it half the rooms that had been left standing. Marina paused to allow time for the echo to die away.

"Don't be afraid," Ieronim said. "I know where that kind of understanding leads. I knew that long ago. What I didn't understand, however, was the connection …"

Despite the fact that the rain was falling harder now, the dust penetrated through it to where they were standing. Ieronim started coughing. Smiling, as though in cheerful spirits, he reached for his handkerchief.

"The connection?" Marina asked later.

"Yes, the connection among things, events, everything that happens around us."

A truck became stuck in the mud right in front of them. The driver flung away the butt of a cigarette he had been keeping in the corner of his mouth, swore, and gestured to one of the workmen in the courtyard.

"Actually," Ieronim continued in a different, warmer tone of voice, "we're looking this time at those stains on the wall, the stains you pointed out to us last winter. For a long while I hadn't understood what you meant. But now I believe I'm beginning to understand."

"Is that all?" Marina interrupted, suddenly deciding to close her umbrella.

"Is that all you understand?"

"Wait," Ieronim continued, smiling, "I'm just giving the history of my discoveries!"

The truck's wheels caught hold suddenly, and a moment later Ieronim began wiping drops of mud from his chin with childlike fascination.

"The lesson was too simple, and that's why it's taken me two months to understand it ... Don't interrupt me, please," he added hastily, with a sudden note of exaltation in his voice. "You wanted to tell us something which, as far as I'm concerned, I knew long ago, but yet I didn't see its connection with the damp patches on the wall. You wanted to say to us that *anywhere* and *at any time* we can be happy, that is, free, spontaneous, and creative. There's no need for a paradisal landscape, nor for noble and exalted presences, angelic music, and so on. *Here*, as well as in any other place, *at any time*, in any circumstance—if we know how to look, how to understand, then ..."

"Ieronim!" Marina whispered. "Ieronim!"

He had not noticed when the rain had stopped falling and the fog had lifted, when the sky had become clear, rising and at the same time seemingly becoming wider. Trembling, he gazed at the light growing stronger and more dazzling, which was diffusing itself over the city, transforming the buildings into immense crystals resembling the infinite fire of gold and precious stones. The crystals rose and came together, imperceptibly blending their flames into one.

"It's true!" Ieronim murmured, not realizing he was talking to himself.

"I know it's true! And they saw it like this too!"

It blinded him now, and yet he did not blink. The light blinded him, as if the city were aflame with an unnatural icy incandescence.

" ... I know they saw it like this too, there, at Buchenwald ... But how can I show it to others?" he exclaimed suddenly, his voice abruptly rising. "How can I show them that this same light is hidden everywhere, in all things, however ugly they may be? In any spot of dampness on any wall, in any spattering of mud?"

Hearing the sound of his own voice, he became silent, smiling in embarrassment. His heart began to beat faster and faster, then all of a sudden it stopped, and in that moment he heard an endless thunderclap which seemed to erupt from all sides at once; and he realized, without sensing it, that he was sinking, dissolving in a white, supernatural incandescence ...

* * *

"Those fools!" he heard someone say. "What's got into them?"

Some strangers passing by, huddled under umbrellas, had caught sight of them standing in the rain. Bewildered, Ieronim turned his head to follow them with his eyes.

Marina put her arms around him and kissed him on both cheeks. It seemed to him he was meeting her now for the first

time—this young woman, indescribably beautiful, like none
he had ever met in life, in books, or in dreams. He gazed at
her mutely.

"Ieronim," she whispered. "I knew that one day I'd find you
again!"

In the Shadow of a Lily

HE HAD BARELY TAKEN HIS FINGER off the button when the door opened suddenly, with a creak. He realized he was holding up the bottle of wine threateningly, as if to defend himself, and he blushed.

"Don't you know me any more?" he asked, somehow managing to smile. The other man stared at him suspiciously, frowning, not trying to hide his irritation.

"I'm Postăvaru, Ionel Postăvaru. We were classmates at Lycée Sfântul Sava."

And because the other man only shrugged, he asked him: "Aren't you the lawyer Enache Mărgărit, from Bucharest?"

"Yes, I am ..."

"Well, then, we were classmates in the first four years at the lycée. At Lycée Sfântul Sava!"

Mărgărit smiled melancholically and shrugged his shoulders again. "That was a long time ago," he said. "A very long time! Forty-eight years ..." "But we met once since then, in Bucharest, on the eve of the War. I can even tell you the date: March, 1939. We met on the Boulevard, in front of the Cartea Românească Bookstore."

"I'm awfully sorry," Mărgărit interrupted him. "I don't remember now ..." He pronounced the words slowly, as though it were an effort for him to speak.

"Forgive me for insisting," Postăvaru began again after a few moments' hesitation. "I realize you're busy ..."

"I'm expecting a friend," Mărgărit interrupted again. "When I heard the doorbell, I thought it was him. And that surprised me, because ordinarily he's late."

Postăvaru took out his handkerchief timidly and wiped his forehead.

"Again, I beg your pardon. But it's about something very important. Very important for me, I mean. Only yesterday did I learn your new address. And tomorrow morning I have to leave, and I don't know when I'll have occasion to stop in Paris again … It's something very important. And it won't take more than five or six minutes—ten at the most … I've brought you some wine," he added, thrusting the bottle toward him awkwardly. "They assured me it was the very best they had. I didn't like the paper they wrapped it in, so I wadded it up and left it in the taxi."

"Thanks, but you shouldn't have gone to so much trouble. Come in, please. As you can see, things are in rather a mess. I've just moved in."

He set the bottle down on a shelf, absently, but catching sight of the label he picked it up again with both hands and examined it in amazement.

"But this is too much!" he exclaimed in a whisper. "This bottle cost you a fortune!"

"Think nothing of it," Postăvaru interrupted him. "I said to myself, we must celebrate our reunion in Paris. We've known each other for 48 years. And, I repeat, for me it's very important. There's something I want to ask you."

He sat down on the couch and pulled out his handkerchief again.

"Ask," Mărgărit encouraged him, drawing up a chair. "But I warn you, I don't have much news. I fled the country nine years ago. Things have changed a great deal since then. I'm sorry …"

"I know, I know," sighed Postăvaru. But I want to ask you something, something having to do with the last time we met, in March of 1939. When I recognized you then, you were in a very heated discussion with a friend in front of the Cartea Românească Bookstore, and I approached you and shook your hand. I saw you another time too, but I didn't dare speak to you then, either because you were surrounded by people who intimidated me, or else because I was in too much of a hurry ...”

He broke off abruptly and folding his handkerchief he replaced it unhurriedly in his pocket.

“Don't smile,” he began again after a pause, but I assure you that those few words, that phrase your friend said then—I never knew his name, but I know he was your friend, and maybe he still is, if he's yet living ... Although, it's been almost thirty-five years since then. There was the War, and then all that came afterward ...”

“I don't exactly understand,” said Mărgărit. “I don't see what you're driving at.”

Postăvaru looked at him directly again, shyly, and tried to smile.

“I'm sorry; it's my fault. I've been walking all morning and now I'm rather tired. And I confess, expecting your friend to arrive at any minute, I don't know how to begin in order to be able to say it all, and say it quickly.”

Mărgărit smiled. “Don't be alarmed; he's a good friend. A Romanian refugee, also. If he comes and you want to talk with me in private, I'll ask him to wait in the other room.”

“No! He can stay. You'll see; there's nothing secret about it. But now that you've reassured me, may I ask you something else? Perhaps you have a bottle of beer handy, cold. I'm awfully thirsty. My mouth's dry.”

Mărgărit got up and headed silently for the kitchen. He returned promptly with a bottle of beer and a glass, both of which he placed with exaggerated, ironic politeness on the little table in front of the couch.

“Nothing simpler!” he said, about to fill the glass.

But Postăvaru caught hold of his arm, smiling awkwardly.

“I heard you! You just now took it out of the refrigerator. It's too cold; it won't make a head. We must let it stand a little, to make it come to life! As our chemistry professor used to say—Vasile Safirim: you remember him don't you?—as Safirim used to say, 'Everything around us can freeze, even beer.'"

Mărgărit took a step backward, surprised, even startled, and stared at him curiously, as though he had just then realized who his guest was.

"Ah, yes, Vasile Safirim! I was walking through the Belu Cemetery once. It was a beautiful fall day. I remember it very well. I stopped to light a cigarette—in those days I smoked a lot—and when I flipped the match away I caught sight of a fresh grave, covered with flowers. And I read, 'Professor Vasile Safirim, 1880–1943.' Poor man! That was the first and last time I saw his grave. A little while later there were the American air raids, and that part of the cemetery was blown up. You remember ..."

"Poor Safirim! He was a great savant. He said to us, 'Everything around us can freeze ...' He was thinking, of course, of the cold of the ground. But to keep from frightening us he added, in jest, 'even beer.'"

He picked up the bottle and held it in his hands for a few moments.

"Now, yes, I can pour. You'll see how the foam rises. Watch!"

Mărgărit shifted his position noisily in the chair.

"Well, and who was this friend of mine? I mean, what did he look like? Blond, brunette, tall, well-dressed?"

"I can't remember," Postăvaru admitted, "because, I repeat, that was the last time we ever met, in March, 1939. It was on the Boulevard, in front of the Cartea Românească Bookstore. You were both talking at the same time, heatedly, as though you were about to quarrel. Your friend ..."

"But what did he look like? Was he young, like us, or old?"

"He seemed about our age. He was wearing a hat with a narrow brim, pushed a little to the back of his head, and when he spoke, he gesticulated in a strange way."

"How do you mean?"

"I don't know how to explain it. He kept raising his arms as if he wanted to run his fingers through his hair, but he couldn't, because he had a hat on, you see. And then he didn't know what to do with his hands, so he stuck them quickly into his overcoat pockets. But it was obvious he was upset. He kept raising his voice higher and higher ... Don't you remember now who he was?"

"No. A hat with a narrow brim ..."

"But what he said was interesting," Postăvaru continued. "I repeat, you were both irritated, ready to quarrel. From what I could gather, you were trying to persuade him to make up with some mutual friend of yours. I never understood what the quarrel between *them* was about, because neither of you made any direct allusion to it. But I was profoundly impressed by what he said. I'd never heard anything like it. Those words, I mean, or more precisely the philosophical concept—or perhaps it was even a mystical one—which he expressed suddenly, without any preliminaries ..."

"But what did he say?!" Mărgărit broke in, scarcely controlling his impatience.

Postăvaru picked up the bottle of beer, then changed his mind abruptly and set it down again on the tray.

"He said—but wait, I have to add one detail. In exasperation, you asked him whether or not he'd decided to make up with your mutual friend, the one with whom he had quarrelled. He looked at you very intensely, with sadness—and yet he smiled. It seemed to me a sarcastic smile. 'Oh, yes,' he said. 'I'll make up with him in the shadow of a lily in paradise!' Notice: *in the shadow of a lily.*"

"Strange, I don't remember the conversation at all. You say he was blond and had a hat with a narrow brim ..."

"And he gesticulated constantly," Postăvaru added, talking faster and faster. "And he stuck his hands in his coat pockets, apparently in exasperation because he couldn't run them through his hair ... Please, try to remember! March, 1939. In front of the Cartea Românească Bookstore. After he left, we walked a few steps together, but not many, because you were angry and had no desire to talk. You never suspected how much those words impressed me: that he would be reconciled with that friend *in the shadow of a lily in paradise*! And later they began to obsess me. Yes, to obsess me! After I was wounded at the Dniester Crossing. More precisely, shortly after I'd fallen, riddled with machine gun bullets, and I came to for just a moment or so with my face in the mud on the side of the road. Since then, I haven't been able to forget them. And every time I've passed through a dangerous situation—and, like everyone else, I've been through many—there has come into my mind again your friend, with the narrow-brimmed hat, and I've heard him say again: 'Oh, yes, in the shadow of a lily in paradise.'"

Mărgărit turned his chair around and drew it closer to the couch.

"It's exasperating!" he exclaimed. "It's exasperating that I could forget."

"Please, I beg of you!" insisted Postăvaru. "Try to remember! You have no idea what this means to me. Maybe it will come to you later, after I go. I'll leave you my telephone number at the hotel, and my address in Zurich. Call me any time, any time at all. It's very important!"

Mărgărit listened to him absently, passing his right hand over first one knee, then the other.

"But actually," he burst out suddenly, "I don't really see in what sense I could help you."

"If you can remember who it was, you'll remember this detail also: if he and the friend ever made up, if they're still alive, and anything else you know about them. It's very important for me!" he repeated emotionally.

Just then Mărgărit heard footsteps approaching the door, and he rose to open it.

"Thank God you've come!" he said under his breath.

Postăvaru rose timidly from the couch and stepped to the middle of the room.

"Domnul Eftimie, the friend I was expecting," Mărgărit presented him.

"And this is Domnul Ionel Postăvaru, a classmate of mine from Lycée Sfântul Sava," he added, smiling.

Eftimie shook his hand, looking him in the eyes almost severely.

"I'm glad to meet you," he said, taking a seat in the armchair to which Mărgărit had pointed him. "I see you like the sofa," he continued, again looking him in the eyes enigmatically.

"This is where our friend, the host, seated me," Postăvaru started to explain, smiling. "In fact ..."

"From Lycée Sfântul Sava, you say," Eftimie interrupted. "What a school!" he exclaimed, settling himself more comfortably in the chair. "It all started there, at Sfântul Sava. I was just talking with Dr. Tăuşan. 'Really,' I said to him, 'what possessed him to tell those boys—mere children, fourteen to fifteen—to tell them about that business of the shadow of the lily in paradise?' Because it all started there ..."

Postăvaru realized suddenly that he was blushing, and he reached for his handkerchief. He heard Mărgărit trying in vain to laugh sarcastically, but he didn't dare look at him.

"I didn't know," Mărgărit began, emphasizing each word, "I didn't know that you were in the habit of listening at the keyhole before ringing the doorbell!"

"What do you mean?" Eftimie replied calmly. "Who's been listening at the keyhole?"

"The matter of the shadow of a lily in paradise."

"That's something I said to Dr. Tăușan, waiting for the metro. And we agreed: it was a foolish thing for him to say."

Postăvaru directed his gaze toward Mărgărit, then stood up suddenly.

"Pardon me!" he began. "Pardon me for interrupting. But I confess that I, like Mărgărit, can hardly believe you. Because, as Mărgărit will confirm, I came to see him—and I hadn't seen him since March of 1939—I came to see him precisely on account of that phrase, 'In the shadow of a lily in paradise'."

"Yes, yes," Eftimie interjected, "the phrase the professor spoke to the boys in Lycée Sfântul Sava."

"No, no," Mărgărit said, becoming irritated. "Don't mix things up. We, Postăvaru and I, were classmates at Sfântul Sava ..."

"Forty-eight years ago," Postăvaru specified.

"But the story with the shadow of a lily in paradise took place later."

"In March, 1939."

"The story with the shadow of the lily has nothing to do with Lycée Sfântul Sava—at least, the Sfântul Sava of our adolescence."

He stopped, exhausted, and sat down again in his chair.

"I'll tell you what I said to Dr. Tăușan," Eftimie began again calmly. "This happened after our meeting—the meeting of our group—at the Cafe Excelsior. I'm sorry you weren't there too, Enache, because things have become complicated." He lowered his voice. "And there could be consequences for us all—us Romanians in exile, I mean."

Mărgărit sprang to his feet. "I feel as though I'm going to lose my mind and start screaming! ... What's going on?"

Eftimie regarded him a few moments in bewilderment; then his face brightened. "I'm sorry," he said. "I thought you knew. I'd forgotten you weren't at church last Sunday."

"I was in the country. On account of them again. The same old thing. Always, the same old thing!"

"Now I remember ... Well, in brief, we met according to agreement at the Excelsior, to see what we could do to help Iliescu."

"What's happened to him?" Mărgărit interrupted.

"You'll find out directly. But tell me first if you know Iliescu, the engineer."

"Not personally, but I know who he is, of course. I read about him in the papers, how he managed to make it to Vienna hidden for *five days* in a trunk."

"It was even more extraordinary than that! I'll tell you the whole story someday."

"But what's happened to him?" Mărgărit insisted.

"I'll tell you what Iliescu told me. Imagine—he's been transferred from Briançon and still he hasn't been told what department he'll be sent to. For the time being, he is, as he says, on vacation. More seriously, he's become suspect. He feels—or, rather, he *knows*—that he's being followed. And all this just because he told some of his colleagues what he found out from Valentin!"

"Hold on," Mărgărit interrupted, leaning on the back of the chair. "I don't exactly understand what this is all about."

"But I haven't finished!"

"I know, I know you have more to say. But before you go on, I want to ask what you'd like to drink: coffee, orangeade, wine ..."

"At this time of day, I'd say wine."

Mărgărit started toward the kitchen somewhat gravely. "And I'll bring you another bottle of beer," he said over his shoulder to Postăvaru, smiling.

The longer the silence lasted, the more Postăvaru felt the severe looks of the other man.

"The same phrase!" he murmured. "There are tens, perhaps hundreds of thousands of Romanians in exile, scattered over the face of the earth, and it happens that today, of all days, while I'm passing through Paris to seek out Mărgărit, to ask him about a phrase I heard in 1939, you come in, and no sooner have you entered than you utter *the same phrase*. What a coincidence!"

"If you meet Iliescu, don't talk to him about coincidences. For him, a mathematician and specialist in statistics, the most extraordinary coincidences are as natural as the simple rule of three."

"Mathematically he might be right, but ..." He interrupted himself in order to help Mărgărit to set the tray of refreshments on the little table.

"I see you're spoiling me," said Eftimie, lifting his glass and holding it ceremoniously in his right hand.

"Mathematically, I say," Postăvaru resumed, "he might be right; and yet—*the same phrase*!"

"But it wasn't *his* phrase," Eftimie pointed out, smiling mysteriously. Then, after taking a swallow of the wine, he added, "Excellent! I repeat, you're spoiling me!"

Mărgărit drew up the chair again and sat down. Then, with a sudden gesture, he took a pack of Gauloises out of his pocket.

"It's my first cigarette today," he explained, a little chagrined. "In fact, I don't smoke any more. But I always keep a pack handy. When I feel too nervous, I light up. Last Sunday," he said, addressing Eftimie, "I smoked almost a whole pack!"

"That was a bad thing to do," Eftimie replied. "You'd have done better to stay in Paris and meet Iliescu ... So you'd know what to expect!"

"But why? Why?" asked Mărgărit, exasperated.

"We'll talk about this later. But please, don't interrupt me. I'll start from the beginning ... That is, from two years ago when Iliescu took Valentin Iconaru under his wing. You know, Iliescu works at the Center for the Supervision of Motor Vehicles, and for several years he lived in Briançon. He had a big house, even though he's a bachelor, so when he met Valentin he invited him to come live with him, as a kind of secretary. I don't know him, but according to Iliescu's description and those of other Romanians who have visited him at Briançon, this Valentin was twenty-five or -six and didn't seem too bright. He didn't try to learn to speak French very well, although he knew how to read it, and he read constantly. But he read only about animals and insects—especially insects. And when he spoke, which was seldom, he would talk about nothing but animals and insects. Iliescu couldn't depend on him, because he would disappear from the shop or the office, and when he reappeared—sometimes after two or three days—he always had the same excuse: that he had been chasing a butterfly, or a beetle, or whatever, and had gotten lost in the mountains."

"He ought to give him a lecture, and then send him back to Paris, to let him see what exile means!" Mărgărit exploded.

"Iliescu has a heart of gold," Eftimie went on, after filling his glass. "And he admitted to us that, crazy as the young man was, he had interested him from the first, from the evening when he had spoken to him about how Fabre's *Souvenirs entomologiques* ought to be rewritten today ... But, as I told you, everything started with a seemingly banal event. About two months ago, the two of them were resting on a large rock in the full sunlight and he, Valentin, caught a blue lizard and held it in his palm, staring at it as if he couldn't get enough of it. And all at once he heard him say, talking mostly to himself: 'When we all get to paradise, in the shadow of a lily,

I'll understand what this lizard is saying to me now.' Iliescu looked at him curiously and asked him, as a joke: 'But how do you know that lilies grow tall in paradise?' The young man smiled, without looking up. 'This was something a professor at Sfântul Sava told us. Actually, he wasn't a teacher by profession, but he had changed his name and had obtained false papers. He was discovered by the Securitate and arrested.'"

Mărgărit jumped up from his chair and put his hand to his forehead.

"Of course!" he exclaimed. "It was he! Flondor. Emanoil Flondor, the architect. How could I have failed to remember? With the narrow-brimmed hat. At that time, that spring, he wore a hat. Soon after that he gave it up and from then on he went bareheaded."

Postăvaru crossed himself and, very moved, he rose to his feet. "Thank God you've remembered! And did they make up? This is what I came for," he added, taking a step toward Eftimie. "To find out if he ever made up with his friend."

"With Sandy Valaori, the newspaperman. They were good friends, and they had quarrelled over some trifle. But eventually they were reconciled. They even decided to have a party, just the two of them, at their favourite tavern, as soon as the war would end. But they never did it. Sandy was implicated in the Maniu trial and was given twenty-five years at hard labour. Then Flondor disappeared, changed his name, somehow obtained a diploma and false papers, and became a professor of history, first at a gymnasium in the provinces and then in Bucharest, to replace a faculty member at Sfântul Sava who had been killed in an auto accident. But after five or six months he was arrested—apparently someone informed on him—and he was sentenced to fifteen years."

"But do you know anything else about them? Are they still alive?"

Mărgărit sat down absently on the chair and sought his pack of cigarettes again.

"I heard that Sandy Valaori had died after a few years in prison. At any rate, I never saw him again. As for Flondor, I know nothing precise. Some say he too died, without specifying when or in what circumstances."

Eftimie did not try to hide his irritation at having been interrupted, on hearing Mărgărit's last words, he turned his head quickly.

" ... Others say he escaped and crossed the border, but again, it isn't known when or how."

"This is something Iliescu can tell you about," Eftimie intervened. "That is, not he, but Valentin, the young man we were speaking of a little while ago. Valentin claims that your man is alive, that he has seen him several times, that they've even spoken with each other."

"Extraordinary!" exclaimed Mărgărit in a whisper.

"But he," continued Eftimie, "Valentin, won't tell anyone how they met or what they talked about, because he says no one would believe him."

"What does he mean by that?" asked Mărgărit, rubbing his forehead. "I don't understand."

"I'm not sure I understand what he means myself, because I was told all this by Iliescu, and since there was so much to tell, he didn't have time to go into details. In any event, Iliescu is an engineer, a man with both feet on the ground, and he doesn't let himself be taken in by illusions, visions, or whatever. And when Valentin confided to him one day that after midnight *certain trucks disappear* as soon as they pass a curve at a certain kilometre on the highway, Iliescu smiled. 'Very interesting,' he said to him. 'I want to see them disappearing at the curve for myself. But how will I know if they disappear or not? I'll have to take Marc along too' (Marc is his co-worker, a man he trusts), and we'll keep watch, ten or fifteen meters apart, on either side of the curve.' And so they did. A little before midnight they 'camouflaged' themselves (as he put it) behind the trees, and whenever a truck would approach, Iliescu would whistle, imitating the call of some nocturnal bird."

Eftimie reached out, picked up the glass, and before lifting it to his lips added: "All three of them had learned long before this how to imitate the short, shrill whistle of that nocturnal bird." Then he sipped his drink slowly and sought a more comfortable position in the armchair.

"For the first two hours everything went normally. But suddenly there appeared a truck, heavily loaded yet travelling exceptionally fast, and ten or fifteen seconds after he had signalled, Iliescu heard Marc's whistle, indicating that the truck had *not* passed him. Iliescu ran to check. Indeed, on the highway that made a gradual ascent through the forest immediately beyond the turn, no trace of the vehicle could be seen. Only, far away, much higher up, they could distinguish through the trees the lights of the truck that had preceded the other by five or six minutes."

"Extraordinary!" whispered Mărgărit.

"We said the same thing when we heard it," continued Eftimie. "But Iliescu is a man of science. When Valentin asked him, 'Do you agree that I was right?' he answered him calmly, 'For the time being it's impossible to draw any conclusions. Let's see what will happen.' And the two men switched positions: Iliescu 'camouflaged' himself in a thicket directly opposite the turn, and Valentin gave the same signal to announce the approach of each truck. And that night, Iliescu told us, *three more* trucks disappeared. 'Now you've been convinced!' Valentin insisted. 'You've been convinced I wasn't lying!' 'But I still haven't seen your professor from the Lycée Sfântul Sava,' Iliescu countered. 'And until I do see him, I won't believe it!' Marc, who is younger and less experienced, became panic-stricken. 'We must inform the authorities immediately!' he whispered. 'On the contrary,' Iliescu cut him short. 'We're not saying a word to anyone. This *could* create complications.'"

"I wonder why," Mărgărit interjected.

Eftimie coughed several times, emptied his glass, and lowered his voice.

"Because Iliescu suspected what it might be about from the beginning. He didn't say so in front of Valentin, but to Marc he confided the next day that, very probably, it was some sort of military secret: probably a new system of camouflage by means of … (here he mentioned a technical term I didn't understand). In any case, Iliescu repeated, the authorities, their colleagues, and above all the newspapers must not find out about their discovery. Because it was, indeed, a discovery. They kept watch on the following three nights and confirmed that they were not mistaken: they *saw* how the trucks were disappearing. Once two, another time five, and the third night one. It was true, Iliescu admitted, that on the third night—the fourth actually of their vigil—they were so tired they went home early."

"And yet, it was found out," Mărgărit interrupted, "if you say that Iliescu and all of us Romanians in France are under suspicion!"

"A piece of bad luck!" Eftimie exclaimed. "About two weeks ago, one evening, at a bar in Briançon, a discussion got started about flying saucers, what are called today 'unidentified flying objects' or UFOs. Marc said—probably he had drunk too much—he said that he had seen some similarly mysterious means of transport … and on the National Highway! He quickly realized his indiscretion and didn't go into details. Nevertheless, he had made a blunder, and a reporter who had been in the bar published the information that a new type of 'flying saucer' had been sighted near Briançon, and in a few days everybody in the whole region was talking about it. Imagine, therefore …"

Mărgărit got up from his chair suddenly, and signalling the others to be quiet, he went to the door. The moment the bell rang, he opened the door slowly, with great caution. Then, turning toward the others, he announced: "It's Dr. Tăușan!"

"Pardon me, dear friend," the doctor apologized, entering. "I'm being followed! Probably you were followed here too," he said, addressing Eftimie. "We're all being followed! I came to warn you. If they ask us what we were discussing in the Excelsior, let's be sure we're in agreement, so we don't contradict one another."

"That is—?" interjected Eftimie. "In what sense?"

"So we all say the same thing: that Iliescu was discreet and didn't divulge any details; that he told us that as a result of a *malentendu*, an article appeared in a midi-gazette and that …"

Again Mărgărit put his finger to his lips and started toward the door, treading lightly. Dr. Tăușan sat down on the couch. After a few minutes, not hearing the doorbell, Mărgărit called out, "*Qui est là?*"

And because there was no answer, he repeated the question in a sterner voice: "*Qui est là?*"

"*Nous venons de la part de monsieur Iliescu.*"

"*Mais, j'ai des invités*" Mărgărit began. "*Quelques amis.*"

"*Monsieur Iliescu nous a prié de vous consulter.*"

Squaring his shoulders like a soldier, Mărgărit opened the door wide. When he saw them entering—a tall young man, thin, blond, accompanied by a robust older man, past fifty, with a jolly face, dressed very smartly—Dr. Tăușan leaned toward Eftimie and whispered, "They aren't the ones who were following me!"

With some solemnity, Mărgărit made the introductions: "Monsieur Jean Boissier"—and the young man bowed his head politely—"and Monsieur Gerald Lascaze." Then he brought two more chairs from the dining room.

"*Mais de quoi s'agit-il?*" asked Tăuşan.

"Let's speak Romanian," Gerald Lascaze began, smiling very cordially, "because I don't have very many chances to, and I like the Romanian language very much."

"If I didn't detect a very slight accent," exclaimed Eftimie, "I'd swear you were a Romanian yourself!"

Lascaze looked at his companion, amused, and laughed in a surprisingly spontaneous and friendly way.

"I spent my childhood in Romania, and my wife's Romanian ... I'm sorry to disturb you," he continued, addressing the doctor and Eftimie, "but, as you've guessed, things are getting complicated. That's why the engineer Iliescu suggested we consult you. We know what you discussed last Sunday at the Excelsior, and this compounds the confusion."

"But why?" asked Eftimie and Tăuşan together.

Lascaze laughed again, much amused, turning his head toward Boissier.

"Because you weren't alone in the cafe. There were others present who knew Romanian. And we're in danger of the story about what happened at Briançon being repeated—the article from *La Dépêche* about the UFO, and so forth."

"But Iliescu says that the flying saucers and all the rest are nonsense!" Eftimie exclaimed.

"This is precisely what's so serious," continued Lascaze in a rather official tone. "Domnul Iliescu has told you that according to his impression, it must have to do with a military secret, and this is more serious than unidentified flying objects. That's why we had to resort to certain precautionary measures. You found out, certainly, that traffic was prohibited in the area for twenty-four hours and since then has been rigorously supervised. We can speak about this … it's no secret. I'm informing you confidentially that we probably will be forced to invite—oh, just for a few days!—invite all of you to a hotel on Corsica: everyone, that is, who found out directly or through a third party about Valentin Iconaru's statement that he saw his former professor of history in an automobile, and that he even spoke with him …"

"But that Valentin is an imbecile!" Eftimie interjected, starting to rise from the armchair. "How can you give any credence to what a young fellow says who barely speaks French?!"

Smiling ironically, Lascaze exchanged looks with his associate again.

"*Mais Valentin parle assez bien le français,*" said Boissier, "*et il est très apprécié au Musée. Il a fait des observations sensationnelles sur les coléoptères de la zone alpine. On lui a publié plusieurs articles. Bien entendu, sous un pseudonyme,*" he added with meaning, casting his eyes in Lascaze's direction.

"*En tout cas …,*" began Dr. Tăuşan.

"Let's continue in Romanian," Lascaze broke in. "I feel more 'at home' in it, if you'll pardon the expression."

"In any case," Tăuşan began again, "it seems to me insulting, if you'll excuse the expression, or at least exaggerated, to be suspected and possibly invited to Corsica just because Valentin claims that he's seen his former history teacher who supposedly said …"

"'When we shall meet,'" Lascaze broke in, "'in the shadow of a lily in paradise.'"

Postăvaru flushed and reached for his handkerchief. He didn't dare lift his eyes to look at Mărgărit.

"In other words, you know about that too," whispered Eftimie. "You know about Lycée Sfântul Sava."

"Domnul Iliescu told us," explained Lascaze.

"It all started there," Eftimie continued, "with their professor. What purpose did he have in speaking to them, mere lycée boys, about the shadow of lilies in paradise?"

"I've wondered the same thing myself," Lascaze interjected. "But, for the time being, it isn't this problem that interests me."

He stole a glance at his watch, and continued. "I'd like for us to dwell a little on this phrase. My associate, who reads and understands Romanian but doesn't speak it, wishes me to ask you if this expression, 'in the shadow of a lily', doesn't have for you Romanians some special meaning, if it isn't perhaps a metaphor."

"A metaphor?" repeated the doctor. "You mean, that it refers to something else in Romanian? But what?"

Lascaze gave him a long, scrutinizing look, then cast his eyes around the room at the others.

"For instance, the return from Exile," he suggested finally. "Because Jean Boissier has had many talks with Valentin (his 'secret' passion is entomology) and in their talks he has gotten the impression that for Valentin, the 'Exile' means more than the condition of being a refugee, as we understand it. He was struck, once, by something Valentin said: that the 'whole world lives in Exile, but only a few know it.'"

"*Une infime minorité*," Boissier specified.

"And my associate wonders if the meeting in the shadow of a lily in paradise might not refer to a blissful, triumphant return from Exile, as the Israelites returned from the Babylonian Captivity ... Obviously," he added after a pause, "in this case it would not be a matter of East European exiles only, but of the great majority of Europeans ..."

"I'd never thought of such a thing," confessed the doctor.

"Nor I," Eftimie avowed.

Lascaze waited a few moments before resuming.

"You know what Valentin answers every time Domnul Iliescu asks him to tell him in what circumstances he met his former history professor and spoke with him. He replies that he doesn't dare say, because no one would take him seriously!"

"But how can a man of science like Iliescu ...," Dr. Tăuşan began.

"That's another problem," Lascaze interrupted, "and it's an even more serious one. Iliescu met Valentin for the last time exactly one week ago, after Valentin telephoned him from the Museum. (In parentheses, be it said that when he disappears, he never informs Iliescu where he goes; Iliescu found out, through that telephone call a week ago, that Valentin had been coming to Paris to work at the Museum.) Well, when he met him then, Valentin answered, perhaps joking, that he would consent to tell everything that has happened ... to either a leading religious personality or a great scientific figure."

"What impertinence!" Eftimie exclaimed.

Lascaze looked at him and smiled.

"This, obviously, has put us in a bind," he continued. "We consulted with the necessary persons, and we found a major religious personality whom Valentin will trust. But we wasted several days' time. When we informed Domnul Iliescu of the news, we both took a plane to Briançon to bring Valentin back (he stayed in Paris only two days), but he had disappeared. That is, we haven't found him yet."

"Although," Dr. Tăuşan intervened, smiling, "I imagine he too was being followed."

"Naturally he was being followed, as was Domnul Iliescu, from immediately after the article in *La Dépêche*, and as you gentlemen have been, and still are."

"We know," murmured Eftimie.

"And yet," said Mărgărit, "it's impossible for you not to find him. An individual, a young foreigner, can't stay hidden very long."

"Of course we'll locate him," Lascaze agreed. "But we're losing valuable time. Already we've lost a great deal. I don't suppose that any of you gentlemen has run into this Valentin in the past few days ..."

"No!" Eftimie declared emphatically, and the others shook their heads vigorously.

When the telephone rang, Boissier glanced at his watch and, standing up suddenly, he said to Mărgărit, "*Je m'excuse. C'est pour nous!*"

He lifted the receiver and listened for several moments without saying a word. Then he looked at Lascaze and shook his head. Lascaze drew up his chair, sat down, and took the receiver. At first he didn't attempt to hide his surprise, but as the conversation continued, his face became increasingly bright.

"*Perfect!*" he exclaimed at length, and gave Boissier a meaningful look. As he continued to listen, he consulted his watch from time to time. Finally he said softly, "*Tant mieux!*" and replaced the receiver quietly in its cradle.

For a few moments he hesitated as though trying to decide what to do next. He looked about the room, fixing his gaze in turn on each of the four, who appeared somewhat cowed; then he drew the chair close to the couch and sat down again.

"*Et alors?*" asked Dr. Tăușan.

"The latest news is good, but at the same time things are more complicated.

"What I can tell you is that Valentin has been received in audience with His Eminence, the Archbishop of Paris. How Valentin knew that an audience had been set for today at three o'clock, and that it was with the Archbishop, we will find out later. For the time being, His Eminence has telephoned to responsible persons and has related the contents of his interview with Valentin. I can't go into detail, but I believe that I commit no indiscretion in saying that His Eminence was very impressed by the—shall we say—'revelations' of the young naturalist. Moreover," he added, smiling, "Valentin will spend the night tonight at the Archepiscopacy, and His Eminence has asked permission for Valentin to accompany him tomorrow when he flies to Rome."

"*Alors, le vieux a compris!*" murmured Boissier.

"*Hélas, les autres aussi!*" Lascaze replied between his teeth. "*Le pauvre pilote!* It seems that the audience with the Holy Father was arranged long ago," he added, turning to the others.

"But what did Valentin say?" the doctor made bold to interrupt. "What sort of 'revelations' did he communicate?"

Lascaze shrugged, no longer trying to smile. "I hope I'll find out myself later on. His Eminence assured us, however, that the expression, 'in the shadow of a lily in paradise', doesn't contain any heretical element. He invited us to read the Gospels and the Church Fathers."

"But what about the ex-professor of history whom Valentin is supposed to have met?" Eftimie spoke up.

"His Eminence didn't say exactly, but he stated only that he has no reason to doubt his reality."

"So he's alive!" Mărgărit exclaimed. "But where? In what country?"

"This we shall find out later also. For the present, what interests us—both us and you Romanians in France—is the fact that you will no longer be obliged to spend the next five or six days at a hotel on Corsica."

"Finally, a piece of good news!" exclaimed the doctor.

"Very good news, from all points of view," Lascaze agreed.

Eftimie shifted his position noisily in the armchair, preparing to speak.

"But what about the trucks?" Mărgărit inquired suddenly.

"Just what I was going to ask," Eftimie broke in. "Really, those trucks that disappear—do they or don't they *exist*?" And seeing that Lascaze had turned his eyes toward Boissier, he continued: "Or, as Iliescu believes, is it a matter of a military secret?"

"That's why I said the news was good, but at the same time it complicates things," Lascaze began. "It complicates things because we won't be able to observe them any more. From now on, the enigma of the motor vehicles which become invisible at a precise point in space and a given moment in time ... will be the concern of others."

"What do you mean?" asked Eftimie.

"Valentin assured His Eminence that these mysterious trucks have changed their itinerary. From now on, their route will pass through a neutral country."

"*Un pays neutre?*" Boissier asked, frowning.

Lascaze turned and gazed at him long and calmly. "*C'est ce qu'il a dit, et il l'a répété: un pays neutre.*"

Boissier jumped up from his chair. "*Mais, il s'agit d'une métaphore!*" he exclaimed. "*Je connais bien Valentin; il nous faut le rejoindre. Et assez vite!*"

Lascaze stood up too, somewhat troubled. Then the telephone rang again, and, after hesitating a moment, Mărgărit picked up the receiver.

"Who? Ah, yes. Right. He's here. I'll put him on."

He motioned to Eftimie. "It's Domnul Iliescu. He wants to speak with you."

Everyone stood up and waited anxiously. Eftimie listened with a rather solemn expression, shaking his head as usual.

From time to time he shrugged his shoulders, irritated, but he did not venture to utter a word. Only after some minutes did he speak, and then in a whisper.

"Yes, they're here too … I'll tell them. In fact, several men are here. I'll tell them all … Good!"

He turned around looking triumphant, yet pensive. He started back to his chair, then stopped, changing his mind, and remained standing like all the others.

"It was Iliescu," he began. "Valentin called him by phone fifteen minutes ago, told him where we were, and asked him to give us a message for him. But I'll be damned if I understood what Valentin meant by his message! I understood only that *for the time being* we are in no danger. But we must not forget that the Exile is nearing its end, and we must prepare for the end of it now. 'How shall we prepare?' Iliescu asked him. 'That depends on the individual,' Valentin replied. And he went on: 'The one who has never loved flowers must learn to love them. Only thus will he understand the secret that children know, but which they soon forget.' … And Iliescu told me something else," Eftimie added, embarrassed, "but I didn't understand, and I've forgotten it already."

"Something about the shadow of the lilies in paradise?" suggested Postăvaru.

"No!" replied Eftimie sharply. "About *that* I'd have remembered. But, please, don't interrupt, because I'm afraid I'll get Valentin's recommendations mixed up … So, after the matter of the flowers, Valentin said: 'The one who has never spoken to any animal but his cat or dog should try to talk with other animals too—for instance, with birds in parks, or snakes in the *Jardin des Plantes*. He mustn't be discouraged if at first he doesn't understand their replies. With love and patience he *will* understand them—and then he'll begin to wake up and marvel at the splendor of his own existence' (or something like that: I can't remember his exact expression) ... And he told me something else," Eftimie added after a short pause, "but I didn't understand. 'For example'—and Iliescu repeated this sentence twice—'for example, we should look at the sky *without* stars and at empty train coaches with the lights turned out, we should smile—*especially* at the old men and old women we meet on the street ...' and other things I didn't understand and haven't retained."

"But what about Iliescu?" Dr. Tăuşan interjected. "What was Iliescu's reaction?"

Eftimie hesitated and laid his hands on the back of the armchair as if he wanted to rest them.

"Iliescu seemed very much impressed," he continued, fixing his gaze momentarily on Lascaze's face. "He said: 'Valentin was right, not I. He understood.'"

"What did he understand?" Mărgărit insisted.

"That's all he said: that *Valentin understood.*"

"But what about the trucks that disappear after midnight?" Tăuşan asked.

Eftimie removed his hands from the chair back, took out his handkerchief, and wiped his forehead.

"Iliescu only alluded to them. But he told me that all Valentin had said to him on the phone—the message he asked him to transmit to us—all these things have allowed him (and *will* allow us) to understand why only *certain* trucks disappear and what happens to them. Then we shall understand also what awaits us ... that is, what will happen to *some* of us."

"So far, I don't understand any of this!" Lascaze exclaimed, starting for the door. But stopping abruptly, he addressed Eftimie: "Where did Iliescu call from?"

"From a telephone booth. He said there were two or three people waiting in line, and that was why he was in such a hurry."

"And we're in a hurry too!" said Lascaze, shaking hands with Eftimie.

At the door, he turned his head toward Boissier who had taken out his pocket appointment book and was leafing through it perplexedly.

"*Il faut nous presser, mon vieux!*"

"But he said something else," Eftimie murmured. "He said he was leaving this very evening."

Lascaze began to laugh. "It doesn't matter. We'll be going with him. And he won't be surprised when he sees us. The engineer Iliescu has known for a long time that he was being followed step by step."

Eftimie shook his head, then added timidly: "I didn't want to repeat what he said just before he hung up …"

Lascaze looked at him quizzically. "What did he say?"

"He said for you not to bother following him any more—that he has done his duty and has conveyed the message to you."

"That's what *he* thinks!" Lascaze rejoined. "But there are other problems we have to discuss."

Eftimie wiped his hands, one after the other, with his handkerchief.

"He also said, 'If Inspector Lascaze insists, at all costs, on meeting me, ask him to wait for me tomorrow morning, between 2:00 and 3:00, at kilometre 109 on the Basle-Schaffhausen Highway. But we won't be able to talk. I'll be in the third truck, along with Valentin's former history professor.'"

"*Sans blague?*" exclaimed Lascaze, much amused. "And did he not say something else?"

"He said, 'Thank Domnul Inspector Gerald Lascaze for being so amiable, and remind him of our first discussion. If, that evening, when we were separating—if he hadn't said to me, "*Heureux les pacifiques*," who knows what my soul might have chosen?'"

* * *

They could hear the two men hurrying down the stairs, because the host had remained standing in the doorway, holding open the door. When they were gone, Mărgărit dropped exhausted into a chair.

Eftimie spoke in a very weak voice: "I don't know if I did the right thing or not, not to tell them everything."

Mărgărit turned his head in surprise.

"I repeated only Valentin's message," continued Eftimie. "But I didn't tell them the conclusion at which Iliescu has arrived with regard to the trucks that disappear ... Iliescu said: 'Valentin was right: a new Noah's Ark is being made ready.'"

"In what sense?" Mărgărit inquired, much troubled.

"Those mysterious vehicles are transporting many people selected from all countries. The trucks don't vanish, but they pass into a space with other dimensions than those of our space."

"Speak more clearly, man!" Mărgărit demanded, interrupting again.

Eftimie smiled melancholically. "I don't understand very well myself what happens, but Iliescu told me that actually it's a matter of a camouflage, serving the same functions as any other camouflage: that is, to hide, but at the same time to attract the attention of those who have been informed in advance. Iliescu specified—and this I can repeat verbatim—that 'the passage to the new Noah's Ark can be effected instantaneously and in an invisible way, but, for our own good, it is sometimes camouflaged by means of a truck.'"

"Why, *for our own good*?" the doctor inquired.

"He didn't have time to explain that to me. But from all he did say, I understand that it has to do with certain signs that are made to us, and which some of us discern. Because he repeated: 'Dear Eftimie, signs of all sorts are being made to us continually. Open your eyes and try your best to decipher them!'"

"That means," Mărgărit exclaimed sadly, "that the end of the world is near. The Flood! The Apocalypse!"

"No, no!" Eftimie interrupted. "Iliescu assured me that signs have been made to us for a long time, for centuries. Only the camouflage changes—according to the age in which we live. Today, in our era dominated by technology ..."

Mărgărit stood up suddenly and placed himself directly in front of Eftimie, staring at him quizzically. "But Iliescu didn't tell you that—the matter about this being an era dominated by technology ..."

Eftimie blushed, smiling sheepishly. "No, he didn't actually say that. He didn't have time, anyway. But I guessed it myself, a little while ago. Really, Valentin and Iliescu are right: signs are being made to us, but we pass them by without seeing them."

And because Mărgărit kept staring at him in disbelief, he continued.

"Take, for instance, our meeting today: four Romanians, two Frenchmen, and two telephone calls; and all of these—the meeting, the conversations, the calls—having something to do with the same expression: 'in the shadow of a lily in paradise'. Doesn't that strike you as strange?"

For some moments the other three men stared at him, troubled and hesitant.

"So, in conclusion," the doctor said, venturing to break the silence, "what do you think will happen to us?"

Eftimie sat down calmly in the armchair.

"Let's wait a little while," he said with a smile. "Maybe the telephone will ring again, or the doorbell ..."

"Even if one of them were to ring," began Mărgărit, "even if ..."

But he broke off his sentence and, turning pale, he hurried to the telephone and lifted the receiver.

"Hello! Hello!"

He waited a few moments, then repeated, almost shouting:

"Hello! Hello!"

The doctor approached, frowning at him.

"He doesn't answer," Mărgărit murmured.

After a while he replaced the receiver and added, "No one's there!"

* * *

MIRCEA ELIADE (1907–1986) was a Romanian-born historian of religion, fiction writer, philosopher, professor at the University of Chicago, and one of the pre-eminent interpreters of world religion of the 20th century. Eliade was an intensely prolific author of fiction and non-fiction alike, publishing over 1,300 pieces over a span of sixty years; including his essays *Yoga: Essai sur les origines de la mystique indienne* (1936) *Images and Symbols: Studies in Religious Symbolism* (Princeton University Press1991). On the basis of his academic work, Eliade is considered one of the most renowned expositors of the psychology of religion, mythology, and magic, and his work sought to show that myth and symbol constitute a mode of thought that not only came before that of discursive and logical reasoning, but was an essential function of human consciousness. His novels *Maitreyi* (or *Bengal Nights, 1933*), *Noaptea de Sânziene (The Forbidden Forest, 1955)* went some way to secure his reputation as a fiction writer through their translations outside Romania, and in 2007, his novella *Youth Without Youth,* was made into a feature film by Frances Ford Coppola starring Tim Roth, followed by *The Bengali Night,* a 1988 film directed by Nicolas Klotz starring Hugh Grant, which was based upon the French translation of his novel *Maitreyi (1933),* inspired by his years of study in India as a young man. In an effort to bring his unknown fiction writing to the English-speaking world, Istros Books presents these stories to accompany the previously published early novels, *Diary of a Short-Sighted Adolescent* (2016) and *Gaudeamus* (2018)

MAC LINSCOTT RICKETTS (1930-2022) devoted a significant part of his life to translating Mircea Eliade's Romanian oeuvre into English. This is the first new volume of his translations since his death. Although all but two of the present five tales have previously appeared in English, this volume represents a significant collection.